## Praise for Anna B[ennett's]
### Wallflow[er...]

### *The Rogue Is Back in Town*

"Fans of Regency romance authors Eloisa James, Tessa Dare, and Mary Jo Putney will go wild for the final installment of Bennett's Wayward Wallflowers trilogy."
                                        —*Booklist* (starred review)

"Smart and sassy romance . . . simply a joy!"
                                        —*RT Book Reviews* (A Top Pick)

"A standout historical romance novel . . . truly delightful."                        —*Romancing the Bookworm*

"Bennett's gift for writing a page-turner of a plot is on full display . . . a solid Regency story of true love."
                                        —*Kirkus Reviews*

"Entertaining . . . [offers] plenty to satisfy Regency fans."
                                        —*Publishers Weekly*

### *I Dared the Duke*

"Sharply drawn characters, clever dialogue, simmering sensuality, and a dash of mystery make this well-crafted Regency thoroughly delightful."        —*Library Journal*

"Readers will enjoy this sassy Regency take on the classic *Beauty and the Beast* tale."                —*Booklist*

"A captivating page-turner that will become a new favorite among romance enthusiasts!"        —*BookPage*

"Will truly win readers' hearts."
                                    —*RT Book Reviews* (A Top Pick)

"Bennett brings new life to traditional Regency stories and characters."                            —*Kirkus Reviews*

"Scrumptious . . . I devoured every word! A hot and wounded hero, a heroine you wish could be your friend in real life, and witty scenes that sparkle with life . . . The Wayward Wallflowers just keep getting better!"
                                    —Laura Lee Guhrke,
                                    *New York Times* bestselling author

### *My Brown-Eyed Earl*

"Heart, humor, and a hot hero. Everything I look for in a great romance novel!"              —Valerie Bowman

"One bliss-giving read . . . witty and whimsical."
                                    —*USA Today*

"Delightful historical romance."
                                    —*Night Owl Reviews* (A Top Pick)

"Heartwarming and joyous . . . a delightful read."
                                    —*RT Book Reviews*

# The Duke Is
# But A Dream

## ANNA BENNETT

St. Martin's Paperbacks

This is a work of fiction. All of the characters, organizations, and events portrayed in this novel are either products of the author's imagination or are used fictitiously.

THE DUKE IS BUT A DREAM

Copyright © 2019 by Anna Bennett.

For information address St. Martin's Press, 120 Broadway, New York, NY 10271.

ISBN: 978-1-250-19948-5

Our books may be purchased in bulk for promotional, educational, or business use. Please contact your local bookseller or the Macmillan Corporate and Premium Sales Department at 1-800-221-7945, extension 5442, or by email at MacmillanSpecialMarkets@macmillan.com.

Printed in the United States of America

St. Martin's Paperbacks edition / July 2019

St. Martin's Paperbacks are published by St. Martin's Press, 120 Broadway, New York, NY 10271.

10  9  8  7  6  5  4  3  2  1

*For Emma,*
*Who's always had big dreams*
*and an even bigger heart.*

*The Debutante's Revenge*
*(Inaugural Edition)*

*Dear Debutantes,*
*Be forewarned: This column is not intended for the meek or retiring. It shall contain information of a direct and, sometimes, shocking nature. If you are likely to take offense at its provocative prose and intimate illustrations, pray, avert your eyes now.*

*For this space is hereby dedicated to the edification of the so-called gentler, fairer sex. It is reserved for the subjects you shan't hear discussed in genteel drawing rooms, the lessons that your very proper headmistress failed to teach, and the frank conversations that would have your dear, sweet mama calling for her smelling salts.*

*This column is about the joys and perils of courting, which include flirtation, desire, intimacy, and, most of all . . . love.*

*If you would prefer to avoid such scandalous topics, you are advised to turn at once to the fashion pages, where the most controversial debate is likely whether the color of the season shall be jonquil or lavender. But if you are curious about matters of the heart, read on . . .*

# Chapter 1

*"Read the forbidden books—the ones hidden at the back of the top shelf that will surely make you blush—for they are, undoubtedly, the most edifying."*

—The Debutante's Revenge

Miss Lily Hartley plucked a silk pillow off the settee in her sister's drawing room and hugged it to her chest, carefully observing Fiona's expression as she read the paragraphs Lily had drafted that morning for their wildly popular column in the *London Hearsay*. She wanted her sister's opinion on this week's installment before delivering it to the newspaper's offices.

Noting Fiona's widened eyes and arched brow, Lily braced herself.

"'If she so wishes, every young woman on the marriage mart should experience a real kiss—the sort that starts with a brush of the lips but progresses to knee-melting pleasure,'" Fiona read, nodding as though she was impressed. She lifted her gaze from the paper and swept an auburn curl behind her ear. "*Have* you kissed someone?" she asked, a conspiratorial grin lighting her face. "Like that?"

Lily sighed, deflating. "Much to my chagrin, no." She found it ironic—tragic, really—that the authoress of The Debutante's Revenge, the column that had scandalized proper matrons and dutiful chaperones throughout London with its salacious advice and provocative drawings, had never been properly ravished.

"It's only a matter of time," Fiona sympathized. "You'll find someone who makes your heart beat faster *and* who admires your generous, adventurous spirit."

Lily had heard Fiona's reassurances before. But if the dance floor were a metaphor for life, she was still lingering on the perimeter, squished between the potted palms and a wall of matchmaking mamas.

Over the last few months, Lily had watched wistfully as her older sister fell in love and married a handsome earl who adored her. Lily couldn't have been happier for Fiona, but she missed having her at home. Everyone said Lily's turn was coming, but so far, no prince had appeared. She'd had her share of suitors, but each one had been looking for a reserved, genteel wife. Someone to decorate his arm and nod in awe while he waxed on about horses or hunting. She wasn't about to give up her spot among the potted palms for a man who thought women were mere ornaments.

Happily, however, she and her sister would be together for the next fortnight. Fiona's husband, Gray, was traveling to Scotland to conduct some business, and Fi had invited Lily to stay with her while he was gone.

Lily walked to her sister's desk and shuffled through the array of Fiona's sketches strewn across the polished surface, each one dreamier than the next. A vignette of a broad-shouldered soldier bowing over a young woman's gracefully extended hand. A man and woman seated on a park bench beneath a parasol, their heads intimately inclined toward one another. The silhouettes of a couple facing each other, their bodies only a breath apart—as though they were on the very brink of a kiss.

But the drawing that made Lily's breath hitch was a rough, unfinished sketch on a scrap of paper no larger than her palm. It showed a man gazing at a woman with blatant admiration and awe. His expression said he was head over heels in love—and that the woman, shown only from the back, held his whole world in her hands.

If a gentleman ever looked at Lily in just that way, she'd probably swoon on the spot. And she'd know he was the love she'd been looking for.

Lily brought the little drawing to the settee where Fiona sat and showed it to her. "I didn't think it possible, but you grow more talented with every sketch. This is so . . . poignant and lovely. May I keep it?"

"It's just a rough drawing, but if you like it, it's all yours," Fiona said kindly.

Lily carefully folded the paper and tucked it into her bodice. "Thank you."

Fiona frowned slightly. "May I ask you something—about the column?"

"Of course."

"Do you ever worry that one of our readers will find herself in trouble because of our advice?"

Lily considered the question. "I suppose that if a reader was caught doing something improper, her reputation could suffer a bit. There are worse fates."

Fiona nodded, thoughtful. "She could be forced to marry a man she doesn't love."

"You have a point," Lily conceded. "But our readers know the column isn't meant to be taken as gospel. The advice is on the daring side and a bit tongue-in-cheek. Still, truth lies at the heart of all we say. We should not shy away from that truth."

Fiona pulled Lily into an unexpectedly fierce hug. "You're absolutely right. Someone needs to champion all the shy debutantes and meek wallflowers out there, and I can think of no one better than you." She pressed a kiss to Lily's temple.

Lily wriggled away from her sister's embrace. "I'm eager to deliver the column and sketch to the *Hearsay*'s offices." She peered at the elegant clock on the mantel. "It's only an hour until they close—I must leave soon. When I return, I'll arrange to have some clothes sent from home. Just think, we'll have two whole weeks together. We shall stay up late chatting, raid the kitchen for midnight snacks, and then lounge about all day."

"It will be lovely," Fiona agreed. "Like old times."

Lily nodded. "Just like it used to be." Except that now Fi had a doting husband and a home of her own. For all Lily knew, Fi was expecting a babe already. The gulf between them seemed to widen daily. "I'm going to change. Is my disguise still in the trunk?"

"Yes." Fiona smirked. "Unless one of the maids mistook the items for dust rags."

"Heaven forfend," Lily said, grinning. The outfit was one of her favorite parts of the job.

She, Fiona, and their dear friend Sophie had agreed that no one must discover they were the creative forces behind The Debutante's Revenge. Though the column was all the rage, it also had plenty of detractors—aristocrats who found the advice too scandalous, too shocking, and too *true*. Which was why no one could know about the three friends' involvement.

One whisper of their connection to the column would destroy their reputations. They had no wish to be cast out of polite society or to bring shame upon their families—not before Lily and Sophie had made matches. And especially not before they'd had sufficient opportunity to convey all they wished to say to the young, female population of London.

So, each week, Lily took the precaution of donning her disguise prior to delivering the latest column to the newspaper's offices. The editor assumed she was merely a scrawny messenger boy rather than the controversial column's author.

Lily hurried to the guest bedchamber where she slept whenever she visited her sister and brother-in-law's house, closed the door, and opened the trunk at the foot of the bed. Buried deep in a corner were an old pair of boy's breeches, a dingy white shirt, and a jacket with patched elbows, along with socks, shoes, and a cap.

She unlaced her gown and let the deep green silk slide off her shoulders before removing all of her undergarments and tightly binding her breasts with a long swath of linen. She wriggled her hips into the breeches, which were vexingly snug across her bottom—but that couldn't be helped. She remembered to slip the little sketch Fiona had given her into her pocket—for good luck. And a few minutes later, she stood before the full-length mirror, carefully tucking the last long strand of dark hair under her cap.

Her transformation was complete. A lad of fourteen or so stared back at her, smooth-faced and slight of build. As long as she kept her head down and her stride sure, no one would suspect she was a woman, much less the authoress of The Debutante's Revenge.

And they *definitely* would not suspect she was Miss Lily Hartley, sister of the Countess of Ravenport and an heiress in her own right.

Enjoying the familiar ease and freedom of her breeches, Lily slung the strap of her leather bag across her body and hurried downstairs into the drawing room. "I'm ready to go," she announced, expecting only Fiona.

But it was Gray who greeted her, albeit cautiously, as she entered. "Lily?" Her brother-in-law backed away slowly and tilted his head to see her face beneath the brim of her cap.

"It is I." She pointed her toe, made a theatrical bow, then grinned up at him. "Nice to see you, Gray."

The earl chuckled and dragged a hand through his hair. "Good to know the Hartley sisters are up to their usual tricks. Though I didn't realize you were planning on staying here till Fiona mentioned it just now."

"Oh, is it a problem?" Fiona and Gray had never treated her as a guest in the past, making it clear she was welcome to drop in whenever she chose.

"Not at all," he assured her, but Lily sensed something was amiss.

Fiona wrung her hands. "Gray just informed me that he'd hoped to surprise me with a little trip. He wants me to accompany him to Scotland . . . but I've already told him it's out of the question. You and I intended to have a couple of weeks of sisterly bonding, and so we shall."

Lily pasted on a smile so bright that no one would dream she felt a twinge of disappointment. "A romantic holiday in Scotland! Fi, what's this nonsense about not going? You absolutely must. I insist that you march upstairs and pack this instant. I *know* you want to go, and I want you to go as well."

"But we were so looking forward to our time together, and there was a particular matter I wished to discuss."

Lily waved a dismissive hand. "We shall schedule a visit for another time." She paused and searched her sister's face. "Unless the matter is urgent?"

"No." Fiona worried her lip. "You're certain you don't mind?"

"Of course not," Lily said. She had The Debutante's Revenge to occupy her, after all. In the months since she'd started the column, it had become much more than a pet project. It was a way to explore who she was and what she believed, as intertwined with her identity as her name or her family or her home. She was never truly alone when she was writing.

Besides, Lily intended to take advantage of her sister's trip to surprise her with a new studio. She'd been conspiring with Gray, who loved the idea and had given Lily free rein to renovate the library whenever she was able. Now she'd have the perfect opportunity.

"What about The Debutante's Revenge?" Fiona asked, her brow furrowed. "We'll need columns for the next two weeks, and Sophie is staying in Brighton with her aunt. She won't be able to help with the editing."

"Leave it all to me." Lily strode to the desk, collected a couple of Fiona's sketches, and carefully placed them in her bag. "You've already drawn beautiful illustrations, and I have two columns ready to go. I'll simply deliver columns for this week's and next week's editions at the same time tonight. It shan't be a problem."

"You see," Gray said, pressing his lips to the back of

Fiona's hand. "Everything is settled. If we leave now, we can make it to a charming little inn before nightfall."

Fiona's gaze flicked from Gray to Lily, and she nibbled her lip, clearly torn.

Lily rolled her eyes and smiled widely. "*Go*," she said encouragingly.

"Very well." Fiona threw up her hands. "I confess, I can't resist the idea of a romantic trip to Scotland."

"No happy bride would," Lily said, waving the couple away with the back of her hand. "Off with you now."

"Will you explain to Mama and Papa where we've gone?"

Blast. Until that very moment, Lily had forgotten that her father and stepmother planned to leave for Bath the next morning. Mama insisted taking the waters would do wonders for Papa's weak heart, even though he'd never looked healthier to Lily. She was supposed to inform her sister that their parents would return in two weeks. "Actually, they've decided to—"

"Pardon the interruption." Gray's butler swept into the room and cleared his throat. "The coach is out front, my lord, whenever you and the countess are ready."

"Thank you, Burns."

"What was it you were saying about Mama and Papa?" Fiona asked.

Lily hesitated. If she told Fiona about their parents' excursion to Bath, she'd cancel her own trip in a heartbeat—just so Lily wouldn't be stuck in town alone. "I'll be sure to let them know where you two lovebirds are headed."

Fiona wrapped her in a grateful embrace. "I'll make this up to you," she vowed.

"I know you will," Lily said cheerfully.

"Can I be honest with you about something?" Fiona asked.

"Always."

Grinning, Fiona tweaked the brim of Lily's hat. "I feel like I'm hugging a chimney sweep."

"Interesting," Lily mused. "Perhaps next week's column shall be devoted to the subject of dressing as the opposite sex."

Gray groaned, but the hint of a smile played around his mouth. "I beg you to exercise restraint."

"Restraint has never been Lily's forte," Fiona said proudly. "It's one of the many reasons I adore her."

Lily laughed. But Fiona's assessment hit the mark. Ever since they'd attended Miss Haywinkle's School for Girls, Lily had been known as the pupil most likely to stretch rules. To push the limits. Fortunately, her well-meaning but ever-vigilant family kept her wilder side in check.

But the next two weeks afforded a rare opportunity. While her father and stepmother stayed in Bath and her sister and brother-in-law toured Scotland, Lily would be left to her own devices in town. Each side of the family assumed she'd be looked after by the other, and Lily would be free.

Free to venture to places where proper young misses dared not go.

Free to mingle with people from other walks of life.

And, best of all, free to experience the passion she'd only written about.

Perhaps she wouldn't rush directly home after visiting the *Hearsay*'s offices. She had the unique chance to see London through the eyes of a lad—and she'd sooner eat a toad than squander it.

* * *

Eric Nash, Duke of Stonebridge, wasn't in the habit of driving his curricle through the storm-soaked streets of London after dark, but he'd been cloistered in his town house so damned long, he was pacing his study like it was a Newgate cell. He needed the biting wind and stinging rain on his face. He needed some assurance that the world outside his house—however cruel and imperfect it might be—continued to exist.

As he strode toward the stable and harnessed the horses, a footman fretfully pointed out the late hour and the torrential rain—as if Nash were incapable of seeing lightning streak across the sky with his own bloody eyes. As if he couldn't feel the cold droplets seeping under his collar and trickling down his spine.

The problem was, if he didn't leave the house immediately, he'd go mad.

As mad as most people already assumed he was.

Nash waved the footman away. "Go to bed and tell the others to do the same. I'll be home late."

In truth, Nash had no plan at all beyond escaping the house for a while. Earlier that night, he'd fought with his younger sister, Delilah. Again. It wasn't enough for her that after spending the last five years at their country estate, he'd recently agreed to return to London. Now that they were in town, she wanted to attend endless balls, host soirees, and plunge headlong into the social whirl.

He'd known that Delilah would crave such entertainments, and, deep down, he knew she deserved to experience them.

But he needed to protect her, somehow. And it was damned hard to let go.

He didn't blame Delilah for hating him. Most days, he hated himself.

Ignoring the ever-louder rumbling of thunder, he clambered onto the seat of his vehicle and grabbed the reins. He'd find a dark pub with sloping floors and ancient walls where he could sit at a corner table and enjoy a glass of ale in complete anonymity. Or maybe he'd just drive for hours and remember what his life had been like before.

Before he'd suddenly, tragically, become a duke.

Before he'd buried Emily.

And before he'd turned into the sort of man who scorned the notion of love, earning himself the name Duke of Stoneheart.

Tonight, he was just Nash, a man in search of a pint—and a measure of peace.

# Chapter 2

*"Fans are an excellent defense against sweltering
ballrooms. But for flirtation, the weapon of choice
is invariably a sultry gaze."*
— *The Debutante's Revenge*

After delivering her columns and Fiona's sketches to the
*Hearsay*'s offices, Lily acted on her earlier impulse, elect-
ing *not* to hail a hackney cab and immediately return
home to her cozy bedchamber, the comforting pages of
her journal, and her often frustratingly sheltered life. Instead, she wandered the neighborhood on foot, seeing
the streets as she never had before—through the eyes of
a delivery boy.

As businesses along the street locked their doors,
workers gathered outside and sat on overturned crates,
telling jokes and puffing on pungent cigars. In the al-
leys, women beat rugs and emptied dirty pots. Men spit
tobacco near her boots. When a couple of rambunctious
children playing tag nearly bowled her over, she scooped
up the ball they'd been tossing and joined in their game
for a bit.

Her foray into this part of town gave her a glimpse

into another world—alive and real. As full of joy and pleasure as it was pain and sorrow.

Perhaps if she hadn't been adopted by the Hartleys as a baby, she would have grown up in a place like this. It was odd to think how being abandoned on a doorstep in Mayfair could have so drastically altered the course of her life. Not that she had an inkling as to where she came from. All she knew was that someone had named her Lily and had left her in a basket—swaddled in a blanket and wearing one bootie with her initial embroidered on it. Fiona liked to imagine that Lily was descended from royalty, but that was the stuff of fairy tales. She'd always suspected she came from hardworking folk who, for some reason, couldn't take care of a babe.

Lily tamped down an unexpected wave of sadness and resolved to take advantage of her evening. She longed to talk to some of the young women scurrying past but couldn't risk compromising her disguise. So, she contented herself with observing from a distance, allotting an hour or two—no more.

She watched as women, some younger than she, flirted with brawny men. Sometimes the women rolled their eyes and laughed off their partner's overtly appreciative glances, but just as often, they took control. Unencumbered by the ton's oppressive rules, they made their own desires known with a sultry smile or the squeeze of a muscular bicep. Impressed by the women's confidence and composure, Lily took mental notes. And she realized—not for the first time that day—that for someone who purported to be an expert on romance, she knew shockingly little of the world.

Sighing to herself, she resolved to go home and record all her new findings in her diary. But just as she began looking for a hackney, thunder rumbled and the skies opened. Torrential rain blanketed the streets.

Blast. Confident the deluge would soon pass, Lily ducked into a dingy tavern in a wholly unfamiliar part of town. It was the sort of rough establishment Miss Hay-winkle had counseled her students to avoid at all costs—which made it exponentially more fascinating to Lily. This was her first time stepping inside a tavern, and she had no doubt the interesting locale and its patrons would provide more valuable material for her journal. Still, knowing she was in forbidden territory made her heart beat fast with a mixture of excitement and trepidation.

Her palms clammy, she stole across the room and tucked herself into a dimly lit corner booth. When a tall, ruby-lipped barmaid approached, Lily ordered a shep-herd's pie and a glass of ale in as gruff a voice as she could manage—which was not nearly gruff enough. The barmaid narrowed her eyes at Lily before saunter-ing behind the bar to fetch her drink.

Gads. She would have to be especially careful now that night had fallen and the taproom nearly burst with ruddy-faced men.

With every pint the barkeep served, the conversation around her grew louder and courser. She and Fiona had been known to utter a curse on occasion—when they were alone. But eavesdropping on the lewd, unfiltered stories in the tavern was akin to translating a foreign language—one that was extremely enlightening. Equal parts sexual innuendo and graphic detail, the conversa-tions made Lily's cheeks heat, but she listened intently, committing the interesting parts to memory in case they should prove useful for future columns.

While she sipped her ale and waited for her food, she witnessed manners that would have made Miss Haywinkle faint straightaway: drunken customers pawing at a barmaid's breasts, a trio of scantily dressed women singing bawdy songs at the piano, and a skirmish that left one man with a bloody ear. For the first time that evening, a frisson of fear skittered down Lily's spine.

Perhaps she was in over her head.

At least she'd already delivered the columns. She took comfort knowing they were safely at the *Hearsay*'s offices, especially since a few of the tavern's patrons had stolen glances at her bag—as if they were curious as to the contents. She prayed they were not so desperate or depraved that they'd demand she hand over the few coins she'd brought with her. She'd thought about slipping them into one of her boots for safekeeping, but she needed the money to pay for her meal and her ride home.

By the time the barmaid plunked a pewter plate on the table in front of Lily, her appetite had evaporated. She speared a carrot chunk with her fork and moved it from one side of the dish to the other, scolding herself for her current predicament.

To make matters worse, she'd begun to suspect she was the only sober soul in the tavern.

Except, perhaps, for the man who sat in the corner opposite her. The stranger hadn't bothered to remove his black cloak, but the fine wool didn't conceal the considerable breadth of his shoulders. His light brown hair, still damp from the storm, clung to the edges of a face chiseled in stone. His slightly crooked nose, high cheeks, and strong jaw might have seemed harsh if not for the unexpected fullness of his mouth. Eyebrows a couple shades darker than his light brown hair slashed above eyes that seemed to glow like amber.

Something about him struck Lily as familiar. She couldn't imagine that she'd met him before, for she surely would have remembered him. Indeed, his dashing good looks would have taken her breath away if he weren't scowling over the rim of his glass. He'd been nursing the same pint of ale for the last half hour while his shrewd gaze lingered alternately on a high-stakes poker game, a melodramatic lovers' spat, and *her*.

Lily's heart pounded in her chest each time the stranger glanced at her, but her disguise had been good enough to fool others. The stranger couldn't know she was a woman. He probably just thought it odd that a younger lad sat alone in a tavern at this late hour.

Still, his presence discomfited her so much that she resolved to leave at once, the storm be damned. She reached into her bag, slapped a few coins on the table, and slid out of the relative safety of her booth. Pulling the brim of her hat low, she prepared to navigate her way to the exit, which suddenly seemed miles away.

She'd barely taken two steps when a trio of rough-looking men blocked her path. The tallest poked her in the shoulder, hard. She stumbled backward but caught herself just in time to keep from hitting the filthy floor.

"Where are ye headed, lad?" the towering man spat, revealing a missing top tooth.

Dear Jesus. Lily's knees wobbled, and her heart beat so loudly, she could hear it in her ears. But she schooled her features into what she hoped was a half-bored, half-annoyed expression and attempted to shoulder past the men without responding.

The middle man, a red-haired brute, grabbed her by the wrist and frowned as if he couldn't reconcile her delicate bones with her boy's clothes. Blast.

The third scoundrel twirled the end of his braided beard between his fingers and drawled, "Let's have a look at that bag, shall we?"

With her free hand, Lily clutched the pouch tighter. "No."

"Good grief, ye sound like a lass. Next you'll be pissing your breeches."

The dimwits laughed as though the quip was the most humorous of the century. Good heavens. If she could just slip past the drunken oafs, she was certain she could outrun them—especially while wearing trousers. When the girls at Miss Haywinkle's had raced to the lake and back, she had always come in first.

All she had to do was make it to the door. Before she knew it, she'd be in a hackney cab headed for the comfort and safety of her cozy bedchamber.

But she needed to keep her wits about her—and act quickly.

While the men still chuckled, she narrowed her eyes and looked over their brawny shoulders, focusing on a spot near the bar. When all three turned to follow the direction of her stare, she lifted her foot and brought the heel of her boot down on the toe of the man holding her arm. Hard.

He released her, yelped, and bent over in pain.

Lily ducked and ran, scrambling around tables, chairs, and merry patrons oblivious to her plight. But halfway across the taproom, she slipped on the rain-slicked floor and landed so forcefully on her bottom that her teeth clattered. Her hat stayed on her head, thank heaven, but the brutes were upon her in an instant, all traces of their earlier amusement gone.

The bearded one grabbed her by the collar, hauled her to her feet, and shook her, his dirt-streaked face only inches from hers. "You're a cocky little bugger, aren't you?" Spittle sprayed Lily's nose. "I'll have that bag now."

She swallowed and nodded stiffly. Let the thieves take the bloody bag and the few coins she'd stowed inside. She'd find another way home. Only two things truly mattered—maintaining her anonymity and escaping bodily harm. If she managed to do both, she'd thank her lucky stars forever.

With deliberate slowness, she reached for the bag's strap that crossed her body and began to lift it over her head, careful not to disturb her cap.

"Leave the boy alone." The command, low and lethal, turned Lily to a statue. Her head was bent with the strap halfway over it, but she knew without looking that the voice belonged to the handsome stranger. She'd been invisible to everyone else in the room for a spell—except him.

None too pleased, the petty thieves turned their attention to the man. The firm set of his jaw and the deadly look in his eyes said he'd rip them apart if he needed to.

And relish every minute of it.

The tall thug squared off against the stranger till their chests almost bumped.

For the moment, the nasty trio had forgotten all about her. She should run while she had the chance.

As if echoing her thoughts, the stranger with the molten eyes tilted his head toward the door. "Get out of here," he ordered.

She settled the bag's strap back onto her shoulder, but her feet remained rooted to the sticky floor. She knew she should flee, but she couldn't quite bring herself to abandon the stranger, leaving him to spar with the three thieves in a lopsided fight. "I'll help you," she said.

And then she smiled.

As she did, she *may* have momentarily forgotten that she was playing the part of a boy.

Dash it all, she'd smiled like a lovestruck damsel who'd been rescued by a devastatingly attractive prince.

And now, thanks to her, that prince was about to have the pulp beaten out of him.

Nash blinked, momentarily stunned. Something about the boy was off. His smile didn't fit with the rest of him. It was too soft and warm and—

*Bam.* The heathen's fist slammed into Nash's jaw, almost knocking him off his feet.

Shit. He should never have taken his eyes off his opponents—especially when he was outnumbered three to one. The thugs stood shoulder to shoulder, forming a foul-smelling wall of muscle and flesh. They shuffled toward him menacingly, their snarls revealing both yellowed and missing teeth.

Nash cracked his knuckles and grinned. He hadn't come to the tavern looking for a fight, but he was far more pleased at the prospect than he should have been. He worked hard to keep his anger caged. But some nights the rage inside him churned so violently, it rattled the locks on his soul. His fury needed someplace to go. He might as well unleash it on these three fools.

He started with the tallest—the one who'd thrown the first cheap punch. Nash grabbed him by the shirt, landed a blow to his nose, and tossed him onto the floor like last night's cravat.

The ginger-haired bloke growled and hurled himself at Nash, but he picked up a stool as if it were a cricket bat and swung it at the man's ribs. Howling, Brute Number Two clutched his midsection and landed on the floor, face-first.

The third fellow stroked his braided beard and circled Nash, his expression a chilling combination of bemused and calculating. With one slick move, the man pulled a knife out of his boot and held up the blade between them. "I never seen you here, so I'll tell you how things work. We mind our own bloody business."

Nash snorted in disgust. "When you're not stealing from defenseless lads?" The boy still stood to the side, wide-eyed and wary. He clutched the neck of an empty bottle in one hand, as though ready to smash Nash's foe over the head if necessary.

The bastard turned and spat on the floor. "Leave. Now. Before I cut you and your fine jacket into little pieces and feed you to the fish in the Thames." He twirled the knife through his dirty fingers.

Nash rubbed his jaw as if he were actually considering his options. In truth, he knew precisely how this scene would end. Could see it play out in his head with utter clarity. He *never* backed away from a fight, and he had plenty of anger left to fuel this one.

"Fuck off, Blackbeard. I'm not going anywhere."

When the idiot lunged at Nash, he was ready, whipping the man's knife-wielding hand behind his back and pulling it up till it cracked. The pirate-reject let out a wail, but Nash wasn't finished with him. He hoisted the man by his jacket collar and threw him several yards.

Just as the scrawny lad bolted in the same direction.

The boy's eyes turned to saucers, and he squealed as the force of the impact sent him flying like a rag doll. Smack into a table.

Holy hell.

Nash leaped over the pirate and dropped to his knees beside the lad.

Only, he wasn't a lad. He was a *lass*.

Shit. The young woman's cap had fallen off, revealing a tangled mass of dark, glorious curls that spilled over her shoulders and across her pale face. Delicate brows arched above eyes fringed with black lashes. Nash had launched a man twice her size at her like a cannonball, and now she was unconscious.

Swallowing the lump in his throat, he cradled her head in his hand, leaned close to her parted lips and felt a faint breath upon his cheek. By some miracle, she was alive. But she was so still.

Desperate, he looked around the crowded taproom which had grown eerily silent. "Does anybody know her?" he shouted. "Can someone send word to her family?"

A concerned barmaid weaved her way through the on-lookers and peered down at the injured woman. "She ate alone. Didn't say much. I ain't seen her before—neither in her disguise nor out of it."

Nash swore under his breath and made a split decision. "She needs a doctor. I'm taking her with me."

The barmaid turned her attention to the ailing trio of bullies who had the good grace to look ashamed for pushing around a woman.

At least *they* hadn't almost killed her.

Nash shrugged his cloak off his shoulders and wrapped her in it, taking care not to jostle her head more than necessary. He carried her out of the godforsaken tavern to his curricle and held her steady as he drove through the dark, damp streets toward his town house as fast as he dared.

# Chapter 3

*"Dreams are where we may safely train for real life—where we may exchange heated glances with earls and sneak forbidden kisses with dangerous rakes."*

—The Debutante's Revenge

Nash carefully carried the injured woman from the carriage house to the back door of his Mayfair town house, where Stodges appeared instantly—as if he'd been anticipating his return.

His faithful butler's incredulous expression, however, said he had *not* been expecting Nash to come home holding the frighteningly limp body of an unconscious woman. Dressed as a boy.

"Your Grace." Stodges frowned at the soaked, bruised, pale person in Nash's arms. "Who is that?" he asked, his voice laced with concern.

"I don't know." Nash angled past the butler and headed for the stairs. "There was a fight. She struck her head on a table." After he'd shoved an ox of a man in her direction.

Stodges leaned forward, squinting his wise old eyes in order to better examine her face. "Is she . . . alive?"

"Yes." At least Nash thought so. She had to be. "I'm taking her upstairs to the guest bedchamber."

"I'll send a footman to fetch Dr. Cupton at once," Stodges said, already striding toward the servants' hall.

Nash nodded his thanks as he headed for the stairs. When at last he reached the landing, he walked down the hall, kicked open the bedroom door, and laid the woman across the bed's pristine counterpane. He gently lifted her torso, removed the bag that was still strapped across her body, and settled her head on the pillow. She didn't so much as moan or flutter an eyelash, damn it all.

Hoping that the bag held some clue as to her identity, he lifted the flap, turned the satchel over, and gave it a good shake. A few coins and hairpins tumbled onto the mattress, but nothing more.

He pulled a chair close to the bedside and studied her. A heart-shaped face with dark, arched brows, a gently sloped nose, and sinfully full lips. It wasn't exactly gentlemanly of him to stare while she was unconscious, but damned if he could help it. She was average height for a woman and thin—although he detected curves beneath her rough trousers. He'd been an idiot to believe for one second that she was a boy.

"Nash?"

He jumped guiltily and turned to find his sister, Delilah, in the doorway, cinching the sash of her robe. Her thick blond braid draped over her shoulder and her bare feet made her look younger than her eighteen years. She stared at him with a mixture of curiosity and trepidation.

Jesus. The last thing he needed was to draw his sister into this mess. "Why are you still up?"

"I couldn't sleep." She gestured toward the patient. "Who is she?"

Nash winced. "I don't know. She was injured in the tavern where I was having a drink. No one seemed to know her name, so I brought her here. The doctor is on his way."

Delilah inched into the room and tilted her head as she stared at the young woman. "She looks as though she could be my age." Shooting a sideways glance at Nash, she added, "She's pretty."

"I suppose so," he said casually. As if her beauty hadn't robbed the breath from his body from the moment her cap fell off.

"Why is she dressed like that?"

"Good question," he said. "I don't know anything about her."

Delilah nodded thoughtfully. "Why don't you have someone send up fresh water and towels? In the meantime, I'll fetch one of my nightgowns and change her into it."

Nash found himself oddly reluctant to leave the woman. "You'll need help."

Delilah blinked.

"Not mine," he added quickly. "One of the maid's, perhaps."

"Yes." His sister reached for a dark curl that lay against the stranger's cheek and tenderly brushed it away from her face. "We'll remove these clothes, slip a gown over her head, and clean the small wound on her head. Dr. Cupton will be able to properly examine her the moment he arrives."

Nash returned the coins and hairpins to the young woman's bag and set it on the nightstand. "Very well.

But be careful." He swallowed, recalling the thug's huge body slamming into her slight one. "She could have internal injuries."

Delilah placed her hands on his shoulders and firmly guided him toward the door. "I promise to be gentle."

Dr. Cupton moved away from the patient's bedside and spoke quietly to Nash, who waited by the door. "The poor lass has obviously suffered a nasty blow to the head. She has some bruises too, but I don't think anything is broken. Hopefully, she'll stir soon." He reached for his bag and snapped it shut. "But we'll know more within a few hours."

Nash's gut twisted as he gazed at the still form resting on the bed. The young woman's lovely dark hair, fanned across the pure white bed linens, gleamed in the candlelight. Dressed in a lacy but modest nightgown, she looked nothing like the urchin he'd seen sitting alone in the tavern. More like a goddess who'd decided to spend an evening in the mortal world. "Is there nothing else to be done for her?"

"Try to make her comfortable. Give her a few sips of water if she'll drink. Keep the room dark." The doctor smiled, sympathetic. "And, if you're so inclined, prayers wouldn't be amiss."

The moment the doctor left the room, Delilah joined Nash beside the bed, slipping her hand into the crook of his arm. "I'm sorry I argued with you before you left tonight. I hate it when we're at odds. It's the reason I couldn't sleep."

"It wasn't your fault." Nash squeezed her hand as he inclined his head toward the window and the London skyline beyond, faintly illuminated by moonbeams. "I know I can't protect you from everything that's out there. I'm trying to let go. It's just going to take some time."

Delilah nodded. The push and pull between them was nothing new. But lately their arguments had become more frequent. More heated. Deep down, he knew he was on the brink of losing her to the unpredictable and often cruel world. And he was terrified that he wouldn't be able to keep her safe.

"Why don't you go get some sleep?" she suggested. "I'll sit with our patient for a while and wake you if she stirs."

"I'm not tired," he said flatly. "And it's my fault she's injured. She's my responsibility."

"You would never hurt someone," Delilah countered.

"Not intentionally." He sank into a chair next to the bed, thinking about the thugs who'd tried to rob her. "Unless they deserved it."

Delilah tilted her head, thoughtful. "I wonder why she disguised herself as a boy."

He considered this for a moment but didn't hazard a guess. "Maybe we'll find out tomorrow," he said. "I appreciate your help tonight, but you should go to bed."

Delilah nodded reluctantly. "Fetch me if she wakes?"

"I doubt she will. I'll see you in the morning." He planted a quick kiss on her forehead and closed the door, hoping that she somehow understood all he wished to say to her—but couldn't. That despite being orphaned at thirteen and left in his care, she'd grown into a clever, thoughtful young woman. And that he couldn't be prouder of her.

He pulled his armchair closer to the bed, so he'd hear the woman if she stirred. Her ghostly pallor frightened him far more than fighting a trio of brutes had. He was *not* inclined to pray, but out of sheer desperation decided to make a deal with whatever deity might be listening.

*Don't let this woman die. If she survives, I swear I'll stop acting like such an ogre where my sister is concerned and . . .* He forced himself to utter the words aloud. "I won't argue with Delilah the next time she wants to attend a ball."

To anyone listening, the offer wouldn't have seemed like a huge concession, but Nash trusted that any higher power who'd inadvertently heard his plea would know the truth. Would know what a sacrifice he was willing to make.

Oddly comforted, he leaned back in the chair and stared at the young woman's profile—the smooth sweep of her brow, the perfect line of her nose, and the plumpness of her parted lips. He imagined he could see the subtle rise and fall of her chest, and matched his breaths to hers.

Before long, his eyelids grew heavy and he nodded off.

Only to be plagued by dreams of a dark-haired woman flashing a dazzling smile.

One hundred canons exploded inside her skull, firing in rapid succession. Each blast radiated down her neck and spine. Echoed back to her head. If she were able, she'd have tucked her knees to her chest and curled into a ball. But her head was a slab of marble, her body a pile of bricks, both too heavy to command.

She tried to pierce the curtain of pain with her voice, but the only sound that escaped her lips was a low, pitiful moan.

A large, warm hand covered hers. A man's deep voice

floated above her and settled over her like a thick blanket. "You're safe," it said. "I'll stay with you."

Even in her fevered state, the voice comforted her. Grounded her. Her head still throbbed, but she didn't feel quite so alone.

Suddenly, it seemed very important to see who the voice belonged to. To lay eyes on the man who was her lifeline. Summoning all her strength, she opened her eyes and tried to bring the blurry face into focus.

She saw the shadow of a rough beard peppering a jaw chiseled from stone. A nose that bent a little to the side, giving him a rugged, dangerous look. Full, slightly parted lips that appeared capable of everything from the wickedest grin to the warmest smile. Thick, light brown hair that her fingers inexplicably itched to touch. And dark, slashing brows that framed arresting eyes . . . eyes glowing like a tiger's in the night.

She didn't know who he was, but it didn't matter. The image of his face was forever burned into her mind. Her instincts told her she could trust him. The handsome man with the golden eyes had said he was going to stay with her, and she believed him.

She held his promise close as her eyelids fluttered shut.

The next morning Delilah breezed into the guest bedchamber wearing a cheery pink morning gown that provided the perfect foil to Nash's current mood. Her forehead creased in concern as she looked at the pale figure on the bed. "Any change?"

He shook his head soberly. "No." He neglected to mention that brief moment in the wee hours in the morning when the woman had stirred and looked at him—truly looked at him, as though she saw the very essence of him.

Silly maybe, but it felt too intensely personal to share. "I was able to get her to swallow a little water, but she's been like this all night. Dr. Cupton said he'd return this afternoon to check on her."

"I wish we knew who her family was." Delilah wrung her hands. "If she had loved ones here, perhaps they'd help bring her out of this stupor. At the very least, I wish we knew her name. It feels odd that we cannot properly address her."

"I'm guessing that's the least of her worries," Nash mused. Surely, she should have woken by now. The fact that she hadn't didn't bode well.

His sister rolled her eyes. "I only meant that her chances for recovery might improve if she heard us call her by name. If she was aware that someone who knew and cared for her was by her side."

Nash rubbed the stubble on his chin. He'd promised to stay with the woman, but maybe his bedside manner left something to be desired. "You could be right."

Perhaps if he returned to the scene of last night's skirmish and made some inquiries, he could learn who she was. But he wanted to remain with her, just in case she awoke. Because he'd promised her he'd stay.

"I'm going down to breakfast," Delilah added. "Will you join me?"

He gave his sister an apologetic glance. "I don't want to leave her."

"It's just as well." She shot him a too-sweet smile. "I was reading old issues of The Debutante's Revenge last night and would have been tempted to quote it to you over coffee."

"Glad I dodged that bullet," he said dryly, shaking his head as she left the room.

He turned around and squinted at the mysterious woman lying on the bed. Perhaps his lack of sleep was to blame, but it almost seemed that her lips moved.

"Where . . ." she said in a raspy voice. Her eyes—green as a spring lawn—fluttered open and narrowed as she peered at his face. "Where am I?"

Jesus. He moved a bit closer and spoke softly. "My town house, in Mayfair. You were injured last night, and I brought you home with me so a doctor could tend to you. You're safe here. You've nothing to fear."

Her gaze flicked around the room, from the seafoam-green walls to the mahogany bureau to the pair of towering posters at the foot of the bed. "Who are you?"

"Nash," he replied without thinking. Not the Duke of Stonebridge or even Stonebridge. What the hell was wrong with him? "I . . . I happen to be a duke."

"A duke," she repeated in a tone that suggested she was either disbelieving or unimpressed.

"Yes." Gathering his wits about him, he uttered the question that had plagued him for the last twelve hours. "Who are you?"

# Chapter 4

*"Your fantasies are just for you. And every girl should be permitted a few secrets."*
                              *—The Debutante's Revenge*

The man—Nash, he'd said—sat on the edge of the bed and gazed down at her, the harsh lines of his face somewhat softened by the concern in his extraordinary eyes.

"Who are you?" he repeated in a deep, low voice that seeped beneath her skin and vibrated through her body.

She opened her mouth to reply and stopped, confused. It was a simple question. The simplest of them all, actually. Why on earth, then, was she incapable of answering?

Perhaps she was not yet completely awake. She bit her bottom lip to see if she felt the pinch and quickly ruled out dreaming.

No matter. The monstrous headache of the previous night was no doubt to blame for her current fog. Surely if she started the sentence, the rest would fall out of her mouth from pure habit. "I am . . ." she began. When the next words failed her, she cleared her throat and tried again. "I'm . . ."

The handsome man—a duke, if her ears had not failed

her—arched a brow expectantly. Encouragingly. The last thing she wished was for him to think her daft, but maybe she was. Because for the life of her, she could not recall her own name. Panic bubbled in her chest. Her fingers tingled with fear. Something was very, very wrong with her.

"I'm afraid I'm a bit confused at the moment." She lifted an arm, unusually stiff, and pressed a palm to her forehead.

"Does it hurt?"

She blinked. "Hmm?"

"Your head," he said gruffly. "Does it ache?"

"Like the devil," she admitted. To be precise, it throbbed like the worst hangover of her life, which, unsurprisingly, she could not recall. She *was* aware, however, that proper young ladies did not drink to excess or suffer from hangovers or utter mild curses in the presence of a duke.

"You received quite a blow last night."

Ah, *not* a hangover, thank goodness. "I did?"

A slight frown marred the duke's strikingly handsome face. "You don't remember what transpired? In the tavern?"

She closed her eyes, hoping that an image of the place would pop into her head. That she'd recall some familiar detail. One small clue to who she was. But her mind was frighteningly blank—a bone-chilling void.

"No. I believe I . . . I'm still rather tired, is all." Surely, that was the problem. Fatigue *must* be to blame for her fogginess. Even now, while she swam in a toxic whirlpool of pain and fear, her eyelids grew heavy and her body demanded the solace of sleep.

"Forgive me." Nash pressed his lips together then

exhaled. "This wasn't meant to be an inquisition. Rest some more. By the time the doctor returns to check on you, I'm sure you'll be feeling much more like yourself."

"I suspect you're right," she said, praying it was true, because the alternative . . . well, the alternative was downright terrifying.

Delilah swooped into Nash's study the moment Dr. Cupton took his leave. "What did he say? Will she recover?"

Nash leaned back in his chair, watching as his sister paced the length of the room, from his desk to the tall mullioned windows, and back. "She'll live—which is more than the doctor could assure me last night. But her memory loss is concerning, to say the least."

Delilah stopped in her tracks and faced him. "But she'll remember eventually, won't she?"

"Cupton's hopeful, but not entirely confident. He's only seen one other case like this—a man who washed up on the beach, presumably after a shipwreck, with no recollection of who he was."

"What happened to him?" Delilah asked.

Nash rounded his desk, sat on the edge, and folded his arms. "He made a new life for himself. Became a blacksmith, married, and is quite happy, by all accounts. But he never remembered who he was."

Delilah frowned. "There must be *something* we can do to help her remember. I imagine her family is frantic with worry. They're probably scouring the streets of London searching for her as we speak."

Nash snorted, skeptical. A young woman who frequented seedy taverns dressed as a boy was not likely under the close supervision of her family. She was probably accustomed to fending for herself. Granted, she hadn't done a smashing job of it the previous night, but she had seemed independent. And she'd shown uncommon spunk, stomping the foot of a man twice her size.

No, Nash sincerely doubted that there were an earl and countess in a drawing room somewhere wringing their hands over their missing daughter. "Cupton recommended that we refrain from asking her questions or pressing her in any way—at least for the next few days."

"Of course," Delilah agreed quickly. "We wouldn't want to distress her. How shall we respond if she asks *us* questions?"

"Answer as simply as possible, so as not to overwhelm her with information," Nash replied. "But tell her the truth."

Delilah's golden curls bounced as she nodded emphatically. "Very good. I shall entertain her by reading to her or teaching her to play chess. Perhaps she already knows how."

"Be careful. Do not grow too attached to her," he cautioned his sister. Maybe he was warning himself as well.

Delilah's blue eyes crinkled at the corners. "You make her sound like a lost puppy."

"She could regain her memory and leave this afternoon," he said.

"Or she could remain with us for weeks."

"That is highly improbable." Nash hated to dim his sister's enthusiasm, but it was the truth. Somewhere outside the walls of his house, the woman had a home, a family—maybe even a husband. Once she recalled her past life, she'd be eager to return to it. "Whether it's a day or a few weeks, her stay with us is temporary. Besides, considering I found her in a tavern, I think it's safe to assume she doesn't move in the same circles you do."

Delilah sniffed. "That's because my circles are incredibly small and the only people you permit in them are either spinsters or saints."

Her jab—admittedly well-deserved—reminded him of the deal he'd made last night. The woman had survived, and now he owed Delilah a ball. Damn it, he should have bargained his soul like any self-respecting duke—it would have been infinitely easier.

"I know you're eager to attend more social events and meet more people." It was a constant source of tension between them. He wanted her to enjoy all London had to offer, but the prospect scared him too. She seemed determined to experience the kind of romance she read about in that column she loved. The same sort of dangerous, head-over-heels passion that had led Emily to elope. But he'd made a promise, and he had to keep it. "You're right. You should."

Delilah blinked. "I beg your pardon?"

He chuckled. "It's time that we ventured out. I'll escort you to the ball of your choice. Pick an invitation from the pile you've amassed and inform the hosts we'd be delighted to attend."

A triumphant smile lit her face as she threw her arms around his neck and hugged him fiercely. "Oh, Nash, you won't regret this."

"I already do," he teased, "but you deserve a night out." He extricated himself from her embrace and retreated behind his desk. "I've neglected my work all morning. I should get back to it now."

"Very well. While you toil away down here, I shall be upstairs, trying on ball gowns," Delilah said with a smirk.

"There's one more thing I forgot to mention," he said.

His sister paused, concern furrowing her brow.

"We cannot tell anyone that the woman is staying here. Since we don't know who she is or what her circumstances are, it's best if no one knows—for now."

"You have a point." Delilah tilted her head, thoughtful. "She's not wearing a wedding band, so I assume she's unmarried."

The lack of a ring hadn't escaped Nash's notice, but it wasn't definitive proof she was single. "She might have removed a ring when she donned her disguise."

His sister nodded. "Which means the woman in our guest bedchamber could be *anyone*. Maid or duchess. Single or promised to another. Whatever the case may be, we must protect her reputation. If she is, indeed, a lady, and certain members of the ton learned she was staying here unchaperoned, she'd be ruined."

Nash frowned. "Your reputation could suffer too."

Delilah dismissed his concern with a wave of her hand. "We may not know who the woman is, but one thing is certain." She paused and wiggled her eyebrows. "She's very pretty." With that, she scurried from the room, humming a happy tune.

Nash let out a groan. The sooner the injured woman was reunited with her family, the better off they'd all be. She'd return home, Delilah wouldn't have the chance to play matchmaker, and he could go back to his blessedly predictable, ordered life.

"How is the broth?" asked a young woman as she bustled into the bedchamber. Blond-haired and fresh-faced, she plopped onto the edge of the bed and smiled as if she were a longtime acquaintance.

Perhaps she *was*. She swallowed her soup and quickly

dabbed her lips with a napkin. "I beg your pardon. Have we met?"

"Forgive me. I'm Delilah, the duke's sister."

"It's a pleasure to meet you. I have so many questions and only spoke to your brother briefly. He didn't tell me his exact title."

"Gads. You must think the entire family frighteningly lacking in manners. He's the Duke of Stonebridge." She stared expectantly—as though she half-expected his title to ring a bell.

Alas, it did not. "He said his name was Nash."

Delilah arched a knowing brow. "Did he now?"

Oh dear. Best to nip this line of questioning in the bud. "You must think me devoid of manners as well. I can't imagine how I ended up here, but I find myself already in your debt. Thank you for allowing me to stay here while I"—*figure out who in the world I am*—"convalesce."

A kindly maid scurried into the room. "Shall I remove your tray, miss?"

"Yes, I'm finished. Thank you."

Delilah scooted closer and patted her hand affectionately. "You mustn't fret. You are welcome to stay with us as long as you'd like. Indeed, I shall be exceedingly grateful for the company. I would say that even if the alternative wasn't spending hours on end pretending to embroider."

"Pretending?"

Delilah leaned forward dramatically and whispered behind a hand, "All I really do is create elaborate knots and spend a vexing amount of time untangling them. It's a vicious circle."

"Well, I am certain you have better things to do than sit with a patient who can't recall her own name." No sense in skirting around the truth.

She sighed. "Not really."

"But you are young and lovely and"—she glanced at Delilah's hand—"unmarried?"

"Yes," she said, a bit forlorn. "Not a suitor in sight."

"But your social calendar must be full of engagements." Though it was not her place to pry, it was infinitely easier to discuss this stranger's problems than to consider her own plight.

"A logical assumption, but no. My brother—that is, Nash—is rather protective of me." As if she read the question in her patient's eyes, she added, "He's my guardian now. Both our parents are gone."

"I'm sorry." How odd to feel genuine compassion for Delilah's loss and wonder about her own parents at the same time. Were they alive? If so, were they desperately worried about her?

"My mother died while giving birth to me, and my father . . . He died a few years ago, quite suddenly. Nash and I have only each other now."

"I suppose it's only natural that he'd want to keep you safe."

"Wanting to keep me safe is natural," Delilah said dryly. "Wanting to cloister me in this house is not."

"Is he very strict, then?" The handsome duke had seemed gruff but kindly. She hated to think he might be an ogre.

"I am eighteen and can count the number of balls I've attended on one hand. Two fingers actually."

"Goodness."

A wide smile split Delilah's face. "In my brother's defense, we were living at our country estate till recently. And Nash has agreed to escort me to the Delacamps' ball next week. I cannot think what came over him."

She laughed at that, and it felt good. "Thank you for cheering me up. I've been quite anxious since the doctor left." She'd slept much of the day away and now night was about to fall, but she still had no inkling as to who she was or how she'd ended up in a duke's bedchamber. Er, *guest* bedchamber.

Her mind positively spun with questions. How was it that she could recite the days of the week and the ranks of the peerage and the first several lines of Homer's *Iliad*— *in Latin*—by heart, but still not know something as simple as her name?

How could she feel relatively healthy and able-bodied while her mind seemed so broken? And most importantly, how and when would she remember who she was . . . and become whole again?

Each time she'd queried the doctor, he'd given measured yet vague responses—as though he feared saying something that would upset her. He counseled her to be patient and try to relax, which was nigh impossible. She was like a wildflower that had been plucked from a field, taken indoors, and jammed into a vase. A lovely vase, to be sure. But that didn't change the fact that she had no roots—nothing to ground her.

"I don't blame you for being anxious," Delilah said, sympathetic and sincere. "What can I do?"

She cast the kindhearted young woman a grateful smile and sat up straighter in the bed. "Dr. Cupton seemed hopeful that my memory will return in due time.

He said that something as simple as a familiar song or smell might trigger it. So, the more you talk to me, sharing glimpses of what's going on in the world, the better chance I have of remembering who I am."

"I promise to help you any way that I can," Delilah said solemnly. "Together we will figure out your identity. Just think, you could be a princess."

She raised a skeptical brow and managed a grin. "It's much more likely I'm a fishmonger's daughter."

Delilah wrinkled her nose and smiled. "We shall have to see if the smell of cod conjures any memories."

"May I be so bold as to ask another favor?" she ventured.

"Of course."

"Will you promise to be frank with me? About my condition and my identity. Even if the truth is less than flattering, I would like to know it."

"You have my word." Blue eyes twinkling, Delilah clasped her hands. "I've just had a brilliant idea."

She rubbed her hands together eagerly. "Do tell."

"I was thinking that while you are recovering and trying to recall who you are, it might be nice if we had a name for you—a temporary nickname. So that we wouldn't have to refer to you as our *patient* or the *mystery woman*. What do you say?"

"*Mystery woman* has a rather nice sound to it," she teased, "but for practical purposes, a temporary name sounds prudent. What do you suggest?"

"If it is to be your name, it seems only fair you should choose it." Delilah stood and wrapped an arm around the post at the foot of the bed, pondering the possibilities. "It's not often a person is permitted to pick his or her own name, so you mustn't squander the opportunity. Choose something classic or glamorous or royal—whatever suits you."

That was the problem—she had no idea what suited her. So she said the very first name that popped into her head. "Caroline?"

Delilah beamed. "I like it."

"What do you like?" Nash stood in the doorway, his expression curious. The dark slashes of his eyebrows slanted, and his amber eyes narrowed, making him look more feral wolf than titled peer.

"Good evening, Your Grace," she—Caroline—said smoothly. "Delilah and I were just discussing my new name."

# Chapter 5

*"Compliments are easily given and cost a gentle-
man nothing. Of greater value are his time, attention, and thoughtfulness."*

—The Debutante's Revenge

Nash growled inwardly at the cozy scene—his sister and
the young woman laughing, sharing confidences, and
plotting God knew what. In the short time since she'd
arrived, the beautiful stranger had upended his orderly
world. She'd drawn him into a tavern fight, apparently be-
friended his sister, and—worst of all—made him *feel*
things. The sooner she remembered who she was and returned to her parents—or husband—the better.

Delilah tossed her blond curls, an unconscious habit
that might have been charming if it didn't usually sig-
nal she was about to spar with him. She slipped an arm
around the dark-haired woman's slender shoulders. "I
was just saying that Caroline is a fine name. Temporary,
of course, for I'm certain we shall soon know her true
identity."

"Caroline," he said, testing out the name, trying to

reconcile it with her face. It suited her. "May I have a word with you, privately?"

His sister squared her shoulders like a mother bear preparing to defend her cub. "She needs to rest, Nash."

Caroline shot Delilah a grateful smile. "I'm not tired, and I don't mind speaking with your brother."

"Would you prefer it if I stayed?" She cast a scolding glance at Nash. "He's not nearly as ill-mannered as he'd like you to believe, but I am happy to act as a chaperone if you'd like."

Caroline patted Delilah's hand. "I appreciate your concern, but I shall be fine. Besides, one advantage of not having a reputation is that it cannot suffer." She winked at his sister like they were bosom friends, and the seed of a headache sprouted at the base of his skull.

"Very well," Delilah said reluctantly. "I shall be just down the hall if you need me."

He quirked a brow as his sister breezed out of the room, leaving the door open a crack. She was clearly already attached to the stranger he'd brought home—Caroline. If he wasn't careful, he'd be next.

As he sank into the armchair beside her bed, he grudgingly noticed the improvement in her appearance since that morning. She'd been beautiful before; now, her cheeks radiated a light pink glow and her eyes sparkled like emeralds.

"Delilah told me you are the Duke of Stonebridge," she said without preamble.

"Does the title sound familiar?" He crossed his arms, thoughtful. "Maybe you've heard the stories about me?"

"No." She arched a brow. "But I'd like to."

He thought about the rumors—that he'd gone mad after the deaths of his twin and his father. That he never smiled anymore. That he was a shell of the man he used to be. "They're only half true," he said with a shrug.

"Is that why you didn't tell me your title before?" Her mouth curled in a teasing, knowing smile. "You feared your reputation preceded you?"

"You were fighting for your life when I introduced myself," he replied earnestly. "I thought it best to dispense with formalities."

"Well, I'm feeling much better now." She gazed at him, her expression suddenly serious. "Thank you for allowing me to stay here."

"It was the least I could do." Given that he'd shoved the brute who in turn sent her flying across the tavern and into a table. "How did you decide on the name Caroline?"

"Delilah suggested I choose something I liked," she said, absently tucking a dark curl behind her ear. "It was the first that came to mind."

"And you don't know why?" he probed.

"No." She stared at her lap, her expression wistful and serious at the same time. "Earlier, I asked Delilah's maid, Molly, to bring me a looking glass. I thought that if I studied my reflection, I would know my own face. That I'd remember. Do you know how odd it is to look at a mirror and see a stranger staring back at you?"

He shook his head, sober. "I imagine it is unsettling."

"I believe you mentioned earlier that you found me in a tavern." She looked up at him, her green eyes imploring. "Would you tell me more about what happened that night?"

"For one thing, you were dressed as a lad."

Her eyebrows slid up her forehead. "I beg your pardon?"

"When I met you last night at the tavern, you were wearing trousers, a boy's shirt and jacket, and a cap."

One corner of her mouth curled in an intoxicating combination of disbelief and amusement. "I was disguised as a boy?"

"From head to toe," he confirmed.

She glanced around the room, clearly curious. "May I see the clothes I was wearing?"

"I believe a maid whisked them away, probably to wash. But I'll see that they're returned to you."

The disappointment that flashed across her face quickly gave way to wonder. "Twenty-four hours ago I was in a tavern pretending to be a lad," she mused, more to herself than to him.

He nodded, giving her time to digest the information. She tapped a finger against her lower lip, and he could almost see the wheels of her mind spinning as she tried to make sense of it all.

When she met his gaze, her green eyes flashed in an unspoken challenge. "I confess I'm far less scandalized by my manner of dress than I am intrigued," she said smoothly. "What do you suppose that says about me, Your Grace?"

It told Nash plenty. Bold, beautiful, and witty, Caroline had the power to make his blood thrum in his veins. Which meant she could also disrupt his comfortably predictable and largely isolated existence—making him forget the solemn promise he'd made himself.

But he hesitated for a beat, pretending to ponder her question. Savoring the heat between them. Wondering if she felt it too. At last, he arched a brow and said, "I wouldn't dare hazard to guess."

She rewarded him with a warm, knowing smile—the

sort that seeped under his skin and confirmed what he already suspected. If he wasn't careful, Caroline might easily scale the towering walls he'd built around his heart.

The duke lounged in the armchair beside her bed as though he were relaxing at his gentleman's club. His broad shoulders spanned the width of the chair, and long, muscular legs sprawled in front. His slightly loosened cravat, the shadow of a beard, and the harsh angles of his face conspired to give him a slightly dangerous look— which Caroline found far too appealing.

But this was her chance to ask Nash all that she wished to know. She ignored the somersaulting in her belly and picked up the thread of the conversation. "What reason could I have possibly had to dress myself as a boy?" she asked, hoping he'd have some insight to share.

"I've been asking myself the same question since I first discovered you're a woman," he replied bluntly.

"How, exactly, did you find out?"

"Your hat flew off when you were injured. No man could have hair like yours." His warm amber gaze lingered on the heavy waves around her shoulders.

"I must know the particulars, Your Grace. What happened in the tavern? How was I hurt?" She leaned forward, desperate to know the truth, but also afraid. What if she'd been involved with something nefarious? What if she turned out to be a smuggler or spy?

"You might find the details upsetting," he said, frowning slightly. "Are you sure you want to know?"

"Yes," she replied with conviction, impulsively reaching for his arm. His very hard, masculine arm.

His gaze flicked to her hand clutching the sleeve of his jacket, and she slowly unfurled her fingers. "Forgive me.

It's just I've spent the better part of the day imagining the worst possible scenarios. Right now, I'm wondering if I drank too much, climbed onto a table, and fell off while dancing a jig."

The corner of his mouth quirked. "There were no jigs, I'm sorry to say."

She breathed a small sigh of relief and waited for him to elaborate.

The duke stared at her for several heartbeats, his face impassive. "I'll tell you the story. But you must promise that you'll rest after this. *And* that you will call me Nash."

Those extraordinary eyes of his were giving off a peculiar heat. It danced across her skin and settled low in her belly. "Yes. That is, I will try to do both."

He sat back and rested his clasped hands on his impossibly flat abdomen, staring over her shoulder as though he played the scene in his head. "You were sitting alone in a booth at the Grey Goose, sipping ale and pretending to eat a plate of shepherd's pie."

"Pretending?"

He nodded. "You pushed the food around but only swallowed a bite or two."

Caroline didn't ask why he'd been watching her so intently but filed the knowledge away. "Go on."

"When you stood and headed for the exit, three men tried to steal your bag."

"I carried a *bag*? Good heavens, you might have thought to mention that pertinent detail a bit sooner. Did nothing inside provide a clue as to my identity?"

He casually opened the drawer in the table beside her bed, pulled out a scuffed leather satchel, and handed it to her.

The bag itself was unfamiliar, but it looked like something a messenger boy might carry. Tentatively, she opened the flap, peered inside, and found it empty, save for a few shillings and hairpins that jingled at the bottom. Nothing that hinted at who she might be.

"Please, continue with the story," she urged. She held her breath, waiting to hear if the duke had defended her against the three thieves. She'd hoped she'd had the courage to stand up for herself but had to admit the idea of Nash rescuing her was rather, well, romantic.

"You resisted valiantly," he said, "but you were outnumbered. I stepped in, and, regrettably, you were caught in the middle of a shoving match. When you fell, your cap flew off, your head hit the corner of a table, and you were knocked unconscious. No one in the tavern seemed to know who you were, so I brought you here." He held his palms up as if that was all there was to say—as if he'd wrapped the tale up with a nice bow.

But Caroline had approximately two dozen questions still spinning through her mind. "You fought the men?"

He shrugged modestly. "You looked like a defenseless lad. I couldn't let three brutes bully you."

So, he *had* gone to battle for her. Her belly flipped. "And afterward, you carried me out of the tavern?"

"Yes," he said softly. "To my curricle."

"I see." And she pieced together the rest of the evening. He'd brought her, a complete stranger, into his home. Remained at her bedside all through the night. Reassured and comforted her when she finally woke.

Perhaps it was her imagination, but it seemed the room had grown smaller and warmer. She set aside the bag and boldly reached for the duke's hand, covering it with hers. "I am in your debt. For coming to my rescue at the tavern and for bringing me here."

He flipped over his hand—his very large hand—and gently squeezed hers. Every hair on the back of her arm reacted, standing at attention. She swallowed, craving something more.

As though he were privy to her wanton thoughts, the duke brushed calloused fingertips across her palm, sending a sweet shiver through her body. Her nipples tightened, and she was suddenly very aware that she wore only a nightgown. A thin, white nightgown.

Without releasing her hand, he moved from the chair to the edge of the bed, his hip only inches from hers. "I'm no hero," he said earnestly. His voice sounded unusually gruff and his eyes turned a darker shade of gold. "I behaved as any gentleman would have. You don't owe me anything."

"That's what heroes invariably say," she whispered. Without meaning to, she leaned toward him. Her heart thundered in her chest and her fingers itched to touch the slight stubble on his jaw.

"Caroline." It was a plea and a warning.

At that moment, there was *so* much she didn't know. Who she was. Where she came from. What tomorrow would bring.

But she did know one thing with utter clarity—she desperately wanted to kiss the duke.

# Chapter 6

*"Curiosity about carnal pleasures is perfectly natural, and—contrary to what your mama and headmistress may have led you to believe—nothing to be ashamed of."*

—The Debutante's Revenge

Caroline lifted her hand to Nash's face and slid her fingertip across his forehead, down his cheekbone, over to his mouth. By sheer force of will, he sat frozen beside her on the bed.

She was a young woman with no past and no identity—and, seeing as he'd shoved a man weighing approximately fifteen stones in her direction, he was partly to blame. More importantly, she was a guest in his house.

It was only natural that she'd feel some gratitude, but then, she didn't know the whole story. She didn't know *him*.

And he knew even less about her.

He did know a few things, however. She'd tried valiantly to escape the thugs in the tavern. She was clever and courageous. And she was, without a doubt, the most beautiful woman he'd ever known.

Her gaze tracked the path of her finger as it skimmed across his lower lip and down his chin. "Nash," she breathed. As though her desire matched his own.

A gentleman would bid her good night and leave.

A rogue would lock the door and seduce her.

He found himself lost somewhere between the two extremes.

"You're recovering from a serious injury," he managed.

"I'm feeling much improved." She shifted so close, he could see the pale green flecks in her eyes and the spikes of her lashes. The citrusy fragrance of her hair tickled his nose, and it was all he could do not to spear his fingers through her thick curls and haul her head toward his.

"Anything we do cannot be undone," he said, mostly to remind himself.

"That is true," she said huskily. "What are you thinking of doing?"

He'd shock her if he mentioned half of what he wanted to do. "Kissing you."

She tipped her forehead to his, and their breath mingled in the scant space between them. "I'm thinking of that too."

Shit. He cupped the back of her head in his hand and slanted his mouth—

*Knock.* Nash pulled back just as the door creaked open. Caroline sat up straight.

"Good evening, miss." Molly, Delilah's maid, breezed into the room, quickly took in the scene, and averted her gaze. "Forgive me for intruding. I came to see if you'll be needing anything before bed, miss."

Caroline smoothed a curl behind her ear, quickly regaining her composure. "Actually, I wondered if you knew where my clothes might be. The ones I was wearing when I arrived here."

"I believe they're with the rest of the laundry," Molly said brightly. "A footman is going to polish your boots too. Once everything is cleaned and dried, I'll return your things to you. In the meantime, you must let me know if you need anything."

"Thank you," Caroline said. "You've been so kind. Everyone has."

"I'll leave so you can rest," Nash said, standing. "I'll be gone for much of the day tomorrow, but Delilah will be here. Dr. Cupton assured me he would stop by to check on you."

"I'm sure I shall be fine. Thank you."

"Sleep well." He gave her a tight smile as he walked past Molly, out of the room, and away from temptation. He'd come perilously close to losing control. His intuition told him that kissing Caroline would be like stepping off a cliff. One taste of her lips would send him free-falling, and there'd be no stopping. He'd be gone.

The knowledge that any woman could affect him so was terrifying, but in Caroline's case, it was doubly so. For all he knew, she'd already given her heart, body, and soul to another man.

If she woke up tomorrow with her memory intact, she might walk out Nash's front door and never look back. The thought left him with an odd, hollow feeling—one he didn't care to stop and analyze.

Delilah swept into Caroline's bedchamber as a maid whisked her breakfast tray away.

"I'm glad to see your appetite has returned," Delilah said, her sunny smile instantly brightening the room.

Having eaten nothing but broth the previous day, Caroline had devoured her eggs, ham, and toast. "I enjoyed every morsel," she admitted.

"How did you sleep?" Delilah asked.

"Very well." After Caroline's near-kiss with Nash, she wouldn't have believed it possible that she'd sleep so soundly—but she had.

"That's good," Delilah said cheerfully. "Rest is the best medicine, is it not?"

"I'm afraid I cannot agree." Caroline heaved a sigh. "I think I'll go mad if I remain in bed another day. Or even one more hour." The grand four-poster bed had begun to feel like a prison cell.

Delilah winced. "You must be terribly bored. Why don't I fetch some cards? Or a few books. We could even play chess, if you like."

"May I be frightfully honest?" Caroline asked.

"Yes. I insist, actually."

She shot Delilah a conspiratorial smile. "What I'd truly like is to stretch my legs and perhaps venture out of this room. Would you help me?"

"Let's see. My brother would probably disapprove, and my common sense says we should consult with Dr. Cupton before doing anything so rash." Delilah arched a mischievous brow. "Fortunately for you, I'm willing to ignore both Nash and my usual prudence."

"Thank heaven."

Delilah pressed an index finger to her pursed lips, thoughtful. "But you'll need to wear more than a nightgown if you're going to wander very far."

"True."

"And I feel certain we can improve upon the boys' clothing you were wearing when you arrived here," Delilah said, her blue eyes twinkling.

"You know about my disguise?"

"Of course I do." Delilah smiled and glanced over her shoulder as she flung open the heavy curtains. "I'm the one who changed you into the nightgown."

"Thank you for that." Caroline threw off the bed linens, swung her legs over the edge of the mattress, and nudged herself forward till her feet touched the floor.

Delilah hurried to her side and slipped an arm behind her back. "Let's take it slowly, shall we? A short turn about the room and then we'll see how you feel."

Caroline's knees wobbled at first, and the bedroom floor tilted like a deck of a ship at sea. But, before long, the stiffness in her legs dissipated, and she walked from one side of the room to the other, feeling like a lioness pacing in her cage. "It's a relief to know my body hasn't completely failed me," she said, "even if my mind has."

Delilah clucked her tongue sympathetically. "Don't fret. Your memory will return soon. I feel sure of it." She took a step back, crossed her arms, and assessed Caroline from her wild tresses to her bare toes. "You're rather petite, but I believe I have a few stylish gowns that will fit you."

"I shall be grateful for anything you're willing to loan me," Caroline said, "stylish or not."

Delilah placed her hands on her hips, the picture of determination. "By the time Molly and I finish with you, you shall be ready to glide into any ballroom."

"I'd settle for being able to sit and read in a garden."

"Do not vex me, Caroline," she teased. "Or I shall toss you back into that bed and give you some of my embroidery projects to untangle. As I mentioned, I do not often have the chance to attend grand parties. However, I *do* have ample opportunity to study fashion plates."

Caroline raised her hands in mock surrender. "Very well. I shall place myself in your capable hands."

Delilah rubbed her palms together with relish and headed for the door. "I'm going to have a hot bath sent up. By the time you've dried off, I shall have a dress for you to try." She paused at the threshold and faced Caroline, her expression curious. "Do you have a favorite color?"

It should have been the simplest of questions. As Caroline considered it, an image floated into her mind unbidden. A strikingly handsome face and eyes that shined like—

"Gold," she said firmly. "Gold is my favorite color."

Nash spent the better part of the day boxing at Gentleman Jackson's, reading at his club, and generally avoiding his own damned house. All night long, he'd been haunted by the near-kiss in Caroline's room. In his feverish dreams, they'd both been wild with passion. She'd whispered his name, laced her fingers through his hair, and pressed her lush curves against him. He'd plundered her mouth, hauled her nightgown over her head, and worshipped every inch of her body with his tongue.

It *could* have happened, if the maid hadn't interrupted them—and that knowledge scared the hell out of him. As long as Caroline was living under his roof, he'd have to be very careful. Fortunately, he was something of an expert at avoidance.

He returned home near dusk, just in time for dinner, glad that he'd have a chance to talk with Delilah.

She'd no doubt inform him of any developments where Caroline was concerned and how Dr. Cupton's visit had gone. After dinner he would closet himself in his study until he was certain the entire household was asleep.

It seemed a fine plan.

Until he walked into the dining room and saw Caroline sitting at the table across from his sister.

The sleeves of her shimmering gown barely clung to her shoulders; the daring neckline skimmed the swells of her breasts. Most of her dark, thick hair was piled high on her head, but a few tantalizing curls cascaded down one side of her neck. Luminous green eyes rimmed with sooty lashes blinked up at him.

"So?" Delilah asked impatiently.

He snapped his gaze to his sister's and frowned. "What have you done?" He was starting to have an inkling and didn't like it. Not one bit.

Delilah rolled her eyes. "Isn't Caroline looking well?"

*Looking well?* That was a compliment reserved for a grandmamma sporting a new cap. Or for a spinster aunt after she'd managed to weather a particularly bad head cold.

Caroline, on the other hand, was a *vision*. She could bring a man to his knees and stir something deep and long-forgotten in his soul. Hell, she could make him break every damn promise he'd made to himself.

"You've made quite the recovery," he said warily. "Yesterday you were confined to bed and sipping broth. Now you're dressed for a ball."

"I'm feeling much improved, Your Grace," Caroline said.

Nash sank into his chair and took a healthy gulp of wine. "Am I to assume Dr. Cupton performed a thorough examination and declared you cured? That he gave his blessing for you to flit around the house without regard to your health?"

"No," Caroline said, unapologetic. "But it's torturous to lie in bed all day when one feels perfectly fine. And in my case, the more time I spend doing nothing, the more I dwell on the loss of my memory. I would have gone mad if Delilah hadn't agreed to help me—which she did only because I insisted."

"A head injury should not be taken lightly," he said shortly, sawing the slice of roast on his plate with more force than was necessary.

"Dr. Cupton said a bit of exercise could be beneficial. Perhaps even speed her recovery." His sister paused and sipped her turtle soup. "You must admit there's a certain glow to her cheeks that wasn't there before."

He looked up from his plate at Caroline, luminous in a dazzling gown that might have been molded to her curves. If Nash didn't know better, he'd think Aphrodite herself had waltzed into his dining room and taken a seat at his table. "I'm glad to know that her condition is marginally improved."

"Thank you, Your Grace," Caroline replied, clearly amused by his reaction.

He set down his fork and looked at her and Delilah earnestly. "All I ask is that you refrain from activities which could prove hazardous."

"Oh dear, Caroline," Delilah teased, "I fear we shall have to cancel the boxing lessons we had scheduled for tomorrow. And horseback riding in the countryside. I was so looking forward to jumping hedges with you."

Nash didn't mind that Delilah was having a little fun at his expense. But he did worry that she was far too cavalier about her own safety. "Perhaps you'd like to explore a cave by the sea while you're at it?" he said dryly. "Or walk along the edge of some windblown cliffs?"

Delilah sipped her wine thoughtfully and cast a mischievous smile at Caroline. "I've no doubt we *would* enjoy those things."

Goodness. Caroline twisted the napkin in her lap, wondering how to best calm the tempest that brewed, or if it was even possible. She also wondered if she had siblings of her own to squabble with—and rather hoped she did.

Delilah had treated Caroline like a sister, lending her everything she needed, from a corset to stockings to hair combs. But Nash had shown her kindness too. He'd taken her side in a tavern fight. Stayed with her all night and assured her she was safe. Held her hand like he never wanted to let it go.

She told herself it was best that they'd been interrupted last night. That even the briefest of kisses would have needlessly complicated her already complicated situation. But now, sitting across the dinner table from him, desire stirred in her belly once more. And even though they were in the company of his sister—Caroline's friend—she stared at the hint of a scowl on his full lips. And wondered if she could kiss it away.

For the time being, she would have to settle for lightening the mood with conversation. She took a fortifying sip of wine and addressed Nash. "Delilah tells me you plan to escort her to a ball. Are you fond of dancing?"

Nash's fork froze halfway to his mouth. "Not particularly. Are you?"

"I think so," she said, intrigued by the question. "But it's also possible that I'm hopelessly uncoordinated."

"I cannot imagine that to be true," Delilah piped up. "In fact, I think we should perform a trial of sorts after dinner. I'll play the pianoforte while the two of you waltz. And if Caroline doesn't know the steps, you may teach her." She beamed, delighted at the prospect.

Nash leaned back from the table like a driver pulling on the reins. "I don't think that would be wise."

Probably not. But Caroline could already imagine his hard arms holding her, could already feel the warmth radiating from his amber gaze. "Are you afraid I'll trample your boots, Your Grace?"

He smiled in spite of himself and threw up his hands. "Fine. We'll waltz after dinner—or at least make a valiant attempt." The crinkles around his eyes told Caroline that he didn't dread the prospect nearly as much as he pretended to.

"Tell me more about your day," he said, turning his attention to Delilah. "You've obviously been busy. Where did you find Caroline's dress? It's not one I've seen you wear."

His sister looked at the chandelier, the portrait above the mantel—everywhere, it seemed, but at Nash. "It's just something I found in the back of an armoire."

The skin on the back of his neck tingled. "Whose armoire?"

"I'm shocked the moths didn't feast on it," Delilah replied, clearly avoiding the question.

"Delilah." The look Nash leveled at his sister made Caroline shiver—and she wasn't even in the direct line of fire. "Is it *hers*?" he asked.

Delilah's chin quivered. "Yes," she whispered, her voice hoarse with regret.

Nash went very still. Delilah too. Caroline might have

thought that time stopped and the room was under some sort of unnatural spell, if she couldn't still hear the ominous ticking of the grandfather clock behind her.

Summoning all her courage, she asked, "Whose gown am I wearing?"

The question hung in the air like a thundercloud about to burst. Without saying a word, Nash placed his napkin on the table, stood, and left the room. His footsteps echoed down the corridor, ending with the abrupt *click* of his study door closing.

A wretched sob caught in Delilah's throat, and she erupted into tears. "Forgive me," she said, dashing toward the staircase. Caroline began to run after her, then stopped.

Good heavens. An hour ago, she'd slipped the golden gown over her head, sighing as the silk cascaded down her hips and legs, thinking the dress nothing short of magical. But perhaps, like most magical things, it was also prone to curses.

Caroline was certainly cursing it now.

Clearly, the dress had belonged to another woman— someone who was very important to the duke—and he'd been less than pleased to discover Caroline wearing it. A strange ache blossomed in her chest. It couldn't possibly be jealousy, for she had no claim over him. But it was a pang, nevertheless.

In any event, Nash was the person Caroline needed to speak with. And though he didn't seem inclined to conversation at the moment, she needed answers. Desperately.

Before she could lose her nerve, she smoothed the skirt of the troublesome gown, and marched toward the duke's study.

# Chapter 7

*"Consider sampling stronger spirits for the first time in the company of your female friends. Nick them from your father or brother, if you must, and imbibe them in the privacy of your bedchamber."*
—The Debutante's Revenge

Nash had already managed to down his first glass of brandy and was pouring his second when he heard a knock on his study door.

"Not now," he said flatly. A noxious cocktail of pain and guilt already pumped through his veins, and he'd just as soon spare everyone else from his foul mood. He threw back his drink, relishing the warm tingling in his throat and the knowledge that he'd soon be pleasantly numb.

Another knock sounded. "Nash?"

He froze at the sound of Caroline's voice. "It's not a good time."

"I understand," she said through the door, her tone matter-of-fact. "You'd rather brood alone."

He smiled grudgingly. "How do you know I'm brooding? I could be dusting my bookshelves or cataloging my cigar collection."

"I must see this for myself," she quipped. "I'm coming in."

Before he could formulate a reply, she strode into his study, shut the door behind her, and spun to face him. She folded her slender arms and looked around the room, noting the lay of the land like a spy about to cross enemy lines. Cool and self-assured, her emerald eyes met his as she marched across the carpet and stood toe to toe with him. Her gaze lingered on his open collar, but the subtle twitch of her lips said she didn't give a fig about his discarded cravat or rolled-up shirtsleeves. She was a force of nature swathed in a ball gown—and the most beautiful woman he'd ever seen.

In the far recesses of his mind, a feeble voice of reason cautioned that an unchaperoned visit with a young lady in his study was entirely unadvisable. But that voice was no match for Caroline's commanding presence and the overwhelming power of her personality.

He set the decanter on a shelf beside his desk and faced her. "What are you doing here?"

"Trying to apologize," she said earnestly.

Jesus, *he* was the one who'd acted like an ass. "No. I behaved badly at dinner. I should be asking you to forgive me."

She said nothing but held his gaze, looking deep into his eyes. The air between them seemed to crackle.

He made one last valiant attempt to play the part of a gentleman. "Now that we've settled the matter," he said, "you should probably leave."

"I'm sure I should." She took a leisurely turn about the room, trailing a finger across the spines of several volumes on his bookshelves and pausing to inspect the horse figurine on a side table. "But I've no intention of letting you go back to your brooding." As if to prove her point, she sank onto a cushioned bench in front of his fireplace.

"Shall I fetch you a glass of brandy?" he asked dryly.

Her green eyes twinkled. "That would be delightful, thank you."

Very well. If she could call his bluff, he might as well call hers. He poured a glass, handed her the drink, and ignored every alarm sounding in his head as he sat on the bench beside her.

He watched, transfixed, as she tilted the glass and the amber liquid slid toward her lips.

The delicate muscles in her throat flexed as she swallowed. She narrowed her eyes, thoughtful. "I don't think I've ever tasted this before. The wine at dinner seemed familiar, but this . . ." She stared into her glass and swirled the brandy. "This is new."

The skin between Nash's shoulder blades tingled with awareness. He was flirting with a woman who didn't know her real name. Or maybe it was more accurate to say she was flirting with him. Either way, they were playing a dangerous game. "What are you really doing here?" he asked.

"I wanted you to know that ignoring Dr. Cupton's orders was my idea. I was rather relentless when I begged Delilah to help me. With each hour that passes, I discover more about my personality. Apparently, I am headstrong," she said, impressively unapologetic.

"That is an understatement," he said, smiling. "And I'm not angry with Delilah." He had been at first, but not now that he'd had time to think.

"Ah. Then you're angry with me."

He shook his head firmly. "I'm angry with myself."

"For bringing me here?"

"No," he said, frowning. "I don't regret that."

She set her drink on the side table and scooted closer to him. "Whatever it is, you can tell me."

Part of him longed to unburden himself. To give in to those imploring eyes and tell her everything about Emily, his father, and all the mistakes he'd made before and after he'd lost them both. It would be so easy to confide in Caroline. They'd already forged a connection. She possessed the wisdom and strength of someone who'd suffered a loss and risen above it, and Nash knew, deep in his bones, that if anyone could understand him, she could.

But it didn't seem right to burden her with his troubles. Not while she struggled to find out who she was.

"I shouldn't have lost my temper with you or Delilah. It's a dress, nothing more," he said, feeling exceedingly stupid. "And it happens to look lovely on you."

She slid her hand forward on the bench, and her pinky finger brushed against his in the slightest of touches—a touch he felt somewhere in the vicinity of his godforsaken soul. "Whose dress is this?" she asked.

"Yours," he answered, taking the coward's way out and not caring.

"It belongs to someone you love," she surmised, refusing to let it go. "Your wife or . . . fiancée?"

Good God. He shook his head firmly. "No."

She laced her fingers through his and forced him to meet her gaze. Lifted her chin in a silent challenge that said, *open up to me*.

Damn it all, she was asking him to unlatch the door on a cage of demons that he'd locked away and carefully guarded for five years. He'd known that moving back to London would stir them up—and that a few were bound to escape.

But he hadn't expected that a beautiful stranger with no memory of her past would force him to face his. She wouldn't allow him to take a single memory for granted—even if it was the soul-wrecking variety. He owed her the truth.

"The dress you're wearing belonged to my sister." He closed his eyes and saw her, twirling on a dance floor, laughing. Vibrant as a daffodil blowing in the breeze.

"The gown belonged to Delilah?"

He opened his eyes. "No," he said regretfully. "To my other sister. My twin." He gritted his teeth, preparing to tear open the wound. Forced himself to speak her name. "The dress belonged to Emily."

Caroline swallowed the awful lump in her throat. "I didn't know you had a twin," she said softly. She desperately wanted to understand the duke and sensed she was on the brink.

For a dozen excruciating heartbeats, they sat on the plush bench in silence. She waited, running a slippered foot over the Aubusson carpet. At last he said, "We were very close."

"And?" she asked, even as she dreaded his answer.

He hesitated and looked away. "She died five years ago."

An iron band tightened around her chest. She smoothed the skirt of the golden gown that shimmered unapologetically despite the fact that it had ripped open Nash's wounds. "Will you tell me about her?"

He looked down at their hands, clasped on the bench between them, and let out a long breath before he spoke. "We used to sneak out of our rooms at night and meet in the kitchen," he said, his voice low and faraway, as if he was lost in the memory. "We'd raid the pantry for some fruit or cakes. Then we'd light a candle and talk till our eyelids grew heavy. As children, we plotted ways to terrorize our poor governess. Concocted elaborate schemes to avoid doing our sums." He chuckled softly, the hint of a boyish grin softening the pain that clouded his face. "But as we grew older, we shared heartbreaks and humiliations, things we couldn't talk about with anyone else. I told her about my first fistfight—and black eye—at Eton. She told me about her first ball at Almack's—and how she spilled lemonade on one of the patronesses. Do you know what the most amazing thing was?"

"What?" Caroline asked, humbled by his trust.

"We always felt better afterward. We laughed at ourselves until all our problems sounded stupid and trite. We laughed until the embarrassment wore off and the hurt was gone."

"How lovely," Caroline said, wistful. "You must miss her terribly."

Nash nodded and absently rubbed his chest with one hand—as if he might somehow massage away the pain of losing her.

They sat in silence for several moments while Caroline waited to see if he'd say more, but it seemed as though he'd grappled with the past enough for today.

"Thank you," she said. "For confiding in me." It was a promising start, but she wasn't ready to leave him just yet. She cast a surreptitious glance at their fingers, still entwined in the space between them. His thumb brushed across the back of her hand in a simple caress that turned her knees to mush.

"Nash," she said softly.

He swept a curl off her cheek and gazed at her with heartbreaking tenderness. "We should say good night."

He was undoubtedly right. But she couldn't help sliding a palm across the hard wall of his chest, underneath his waistcoat. "Your heart is beating as fast as mine."

"That's exactly why you should leave," he said gruffly.

"Perhaps," she said slowly, "but first I should like to make one very simple request."

His amber eyes crinkled. "Where you are concerned, Caroline, nothing is simple."

"Kiss me," she said, surprised at her own daring. "Just this one time. No one will know but us, and afterward we can pretend it never happened, if that is what you wish."

Lines creased his forehead and his heartbeat thundered beneath her fingertips. "That is a *horrid* idea."

"Why? Because you didn't think of it?" she countered.

"*No.*" He gave a deep chuckle that vibrated deliciously through her. "Maybe."

"One kiss," she urged, leaning into him. "So that we may rid ourselves of these vexing symptoms."

"And that will be it?" he asked, skeptical. But his heavy-lidded gaze and raspy breaths told her he was on the verge of agreeing to her mad proposal.

"Yes." The word had barely left her lips before his mouth descended on hers. His capable hands cupped her cheeks. The rough pads of his fingers caressed the sensitive skin below her ears, making her entire body tingle. His tongue traced the seam of her lips, and, when she parted them, he deepened the kiss to something altogether different and intimate—taking her through the door to a sensuous new world where only the two of them existed.

She clung to him, pleased that his lack of a jacket allowed her to feel his muscles flexing beneath her fingers. And when even the thin barrier of his shirt frustrated her, she ran her hands along the sides of his neck, hungry to feel his warm skin against her palms.

Without breaking their kiss, he groaned into her mouth and shifted her onto his lap. She gasped, delighting in the feel of his hard thighs beneath her bottom and his strong arms encircling her. Indeed, he seemed to surround her, filling all her senses.

Scents of leather and ink tickled her nose; a hint of brandy danced on her tongue. The shadow of his beard grazed her skin and growls from deep in his throat heated her blood. When she let her eyes flutter open, the sharp angles of his handsome face filled her vision, leaving her even more breathless than before.

And if she was only to be allowed this one kiss with him, she intended to make it last.

She met every thrust of his tongue, matching him stroke for stroke. His hands slid up her sides, and his thumbs grazed the undersides of her breasts. She leaned into him wantonly and speared her fingers through the thick hair at his nape.

He kissed her feverishly. Hungrily. As if he'd never have enough of her.

This was not the measured, deliberate, reserved duke she'd first met. It seemed the reins of his self-discipline had quite suddenly slipped through his fingers—and the knowledge thrilled her.

He caressed her hips, pulling her closer. "Caroline," he murmured against her mouth. "Why can't I resist you?"

Gently, she pulled away, her chest squeezing at the

sight of Nash's heavy-lidded eyes. "For the same reason I find it difficult to resist you. Our lives may have intersected in a strange and unusual way, but I think we came together that night in the tavern because . . . we needed each other."

"Maybe." Nash raked a hand through his hair and shot her an apologetic smile. "But we still don't know who you are, and I was wrong to become carried away. Please forgive me."

"There's nothing to forgive." She'd practically demanded that he kiss her, after all. And she didn't regret it in the slightest. But she supposed that could change tomorrow if she woke and remembered she was engaged or, worse, married.

"What are we going to do next?" he asked. As if she had any answers.

"I suppose we shall go on as we were before and hope that my memory soon returns. If it does not"—she swallowed the knot in her throat—"I shall seek out a different living arrangement."

His forehead creased in concern. "There's no need to rush," he assured her. "No one knows you're here."

"That's part of the problem. I'm invisible outside of this household." She reluctantly eased herself off his lap and stood. "I understand that secrecy is a necessity while I'm here—to protect my own reputation as well as Delilah's. I would never want to risk hurting her."

Nash stood too, reaching for her hands and pressing them between his own. "We'll be careful. You can trust the staff."

"I know, and I appreciate all you and Delilah are doing for me. But being invisible is no way to live."

"You could never be invisible, Caroline." He spoke so

earnestly that it nearly broke her heart. "In a crowd of thousands, you'd stand out."

The sweetness of his words brought stinging tears to her eyes, but she willed them away and attempted a smile. "Yes, well. I have precious few memories, but our kiss is one that I shall never forget—no matter how many times I should bump my head."

"You say that as though we are finished," he said hoarsely. "What if . . . what if we are just beginning?"

"You could find out tomorrow that I am a scullery maid, Nash. And then you would not say such things."

For the space of several heartbeats, he stared at her. "You don't speak or act like a scullery maid. But even if you were, it wouldn't change the way I feel about you."

Perhaps not. But it would make any future for them impossible—and they both knew it.

She let her gaze linger on his handsome face as she moved to leave, wishing she could etch every angle, curve, and shadow in her mind. When she reached the door of the study, she paused.

"Our kiss," she said softly. "You should know that it was gloriously *new*—rather like the brandy."

Nash narrowed his eyes slightly, intrigued. "How so?"

"I can't say how I know, but I'm quite confident I've never experienced a kiss like that before—in this lifetime, or any other."

Before she slipped out the door, he shot her a grin that melted her knees. "Neither have I, Caroline," he said, shaking his head slowly. "Neither have I."

# Chapter 8

*"Pay attention to your physical being. Observe the things that give you pleasure—a kiss on the wrist, the brush of fingertips across your neck, a caress down your spine. Do not be afraid to explore . . . and discover what pleases you."*
—*The Debutante's Revenge*

By the time sunlight began to peek around the edges of the drapes, Caroline had already been awake for an hour. She'd been so hopeful that a decent night's sleep would cure her memory loss, but her mind was still a blank slate. Well, except for the kiss between her and Nash in his study, which she played out in her head over and over, much like rereading a favorite scene from a book. Until a knock sounded on her bedchamber door. Sitting upright, she called out, "Come in."

"Good morning," Delilah said, uncharacteristically sheepish. She held out a pale blue gown draped over her arm. "This is one of *mine*, so you may wear it without fear of starting a civil war."

Caroline shot her a grateful smile. "Thank you."

"I apologize for running off like a ninny at dinner."

"You needn't apologize. It wasn't your fault."

"No? Well, I am embarrassed nonetheless." Delilah laid the pretty dress at the foot of the bed. "How are you feeling today?"

"As confused as ever," Caroline admitted.

Delilah gave her a conspiratorial wink. "That makes two of us, then." Her perfectly coiffed blond hair and smart pink dress brightened the room—and made Caroline feel distinctly unkempt. "I'm certain you have a barrage of questions," Delilah continued, "and I shall attempt to answer them the best I can—over breakfast. But right now, I'm going to send Molly in to help you dress."

"That sounds wonderful." Caroline threw off the covers and had started to unplait her braid when Delilah popped back into the room.

"I forgot to mention—you needn't worry that Nash will be scowling at us throughout breakfast. He left the house after informing Stodges he'd be gone for much of the day."

"That's good to know." An odd combination of relief and disappointment swirled in Caroline's chest. But clearly the duke's absence was for the best. She needed some time to figure out what their kiss had meant to her—and to him. She couldn't stop thinking about the question he'd posed afterward: *What if this is just the beginning?*

After Molly tamed Caroline's thick tresses into a smooth twist and helped her don the fetching blue frock, she found Delilah sipping tea at the breakfast table, a newspaper next to her plate. "What are you reading?"

Delilah's free hand fluttered over the pile. "One of my favorite columns in the *Hearsay*. I thought you might like it, but that's for later. First I must explain why Nash was so upset last night."

Caroline filled her plate with eggs, ham, and toast from the sideboard, sat across the table from her friend, and shot her a sympathetic smile. "I have an inkling. He told me that the dress belonged to your sister, Emily."

"He did?" Delilah gulped. "I haven't heard him say her name in . . . ages," she said hoarsely.

"It clearly pained him." Caroline's chest squeezed as she looked into Delilah's blue eyes, clouded with sadness. "I fear it must be the same for you."

"Yes and no," Delilah said softly. "It hurts. But I long to talk about her. I do not think it is healthy to lock up her room, leave her belongings untouched, and pretend that she is merely away on a holiday."

Caroline frowned. "Is that what your brother is doing?"

Delilah nodded. "He couldn't bear to live in this house after Father and Emily died. We moved to our country estate and stayed away from town for five years. We only returned a few weeks ago, at my insistence," she said, sniffling. "I thought he might take comfort in having something of hers, a memento, to hold close. So, once we were settled here, I offered to sort through her things and freshen up her room. But Nash wouldn't hear of it."

Caroline ached for both of them. "I'm so sorry."

"Nash cannot bring himself to face the memories, but I *long* for them," Delilah said, her voice thick with anguish. "I'm afraid that if I don't talk about Father and Emily, I'll forget how they looked and moved and sounded. Some days I feel like I already am forgetting."

Caroline stood, rounded the table, and hugged Delilah's slender shoulders. "I know it's not much comfort, but anytime you want to talk, I am here to listen."

"Thank you," she replied, dabbing her eyes with her napkin. "It's nice, having someone to confide in. I used to talk to Emily, but when she died, I lost more than just her. I lost a part of Nash too."

Caroline swallowed the huge knot in her throat. "I realize it's none of my business, but may I ask what happened to Emily? I'd like to understand."

Delilah nodded and drew a deep breath. "Five years ago, my sister was in love. I was still a girl at the time, but even *I* could see that she was positively smitten. Her beau was so handsome and kind that I confess to being half-smitten myself. He asked for Emily's hand in marriage, but my father did not approve of the match."

"Why not?"

"He was a barrister. Father said he would be an entirely unsuitable husband for the daughter of a duke."

Caroline nodded sadly. "He wanted her to marry a peer?"

"I suppose so. But Emily and her beau were so happy together." Delilah smiled softly. "And they refused to let my father keep them apart."

"They eloped?"

"They tried." Delilah picked up her teacup and stared into space. "When my father discovered they were on their way to Gretna Green, he chased after them on horseback. They were in his sight when some highwaymen ran their coach off the road . . . and it flipped over."

"Oh no."

"Father was so enraged that he drew his pistol, charged toward the scoundrels, and shot one—but not before the highwayman shot back. Father didn't survive his wounds. And my sister died in the coach accident."

"How awful," Caroline breathed.

"Emily was eighteen. The same age I am now," Delilah added softly, as though the realization twisted the knife that already pierced her heart. "Suddenly, Nash and I were alone in the world. He inherited the dukedom—and responsibility for me—long before he should have. We kept the circumstances around their deaths secret. No one knows that Emily was eloping. They assumed that my father was traveling with her."

Caroline pressed a hand to her stomach as she pictured what that time must have been like for Nash and Delilah. Though she longed to remember her own family and experiences, she did not envy memories as painful as theirs. "I can't imagine what it must have felt like for you, a girl of thirteen, to lose two beloved family members at once."

"I cried for weeks, and when my tears ran dry, I turned to novels as a sort of escape. But my brother didn't have that luxury; he assumed the duties of his new title almost immediately. He was forced to sort through my father's personal belongings but couldn't bear to touch Emily's. When he happened to see a well-meaning maid packing up her hairbrush and ribbons, he ordered her out of the bedchamber, slammed his fist into the vanity's looking glass, and locked the door as he left. He forbade anyone to enter her room from that moment on." Delilah set her teacup down and fiddled with the handle. "Emily was beautiful and witty and headstrong—everything I wanted to be but wasn't."

Caroline reached for her hands and squeezed them tightly. "She sounds positively lovely, and I have no doubt she'd be proud of the woman you are today."

"You remind me of her," Delilah said hoarsely. "And

when you mentioned gold was your favorite color, I couldn't stop thinking about that dress of Emily's. It made me happy to see you in it." Her eyes brimmed, and her nose turned pink.

Caroline pulled her into another hug. "Don't fret. I spoke to your brother last night, and I don't think he's angry any longer."

"Good. I'm used to being at odds with him, but not about Emily. I much prefer it when we're sparring over my lack of social engagements."

Caroline pulled back so she could look into Delilah's eyes. "All I can say is this: When I remember who I am, I hope I'm lucky enough to discover I have a sister like you."

Delilah swiped at her damp cheeks. "No matter who you are, I feel certain we shall remain friends."

Caroline didn't state the obvious—that her true identity could make such a friendship unsustainable. Her relationship with Nash—if it could even be labeled as such—was based on equally unsteady ground.

"It's no wonder your brother is so protective of you."

"He's terrified that something will happen to me and our small family will be snuffed out, just like this." Delilah snapped her fingers to demonstrate. "But sometimes I feel like a princess locked in a tower."

"And your brother would be the fire-breathing dragon?"

"Precisely." Delilah shot her a watery smile. "At least he agreed to let me attend a ball with him. And he brought you here. Both of those are encouraging signs that perhaps, in due time, the dragon inside him can be tamed."

"I hope so," Caroline mused, wondering if she could

play a part in his healing. Or if he might play a part in hers. He *had* opened up to her just a little. That trust and his kisses combined to make a rather promising start.

"Now then," Delilah began. She took a fortifying sip of tea and picked up a newspaper from the table. "Before I turn completely maudlin, I must introduce you to The Debutante's Revenge."

An unexpected shiver stole through Caroline's limbs. "That sounds rather ominous."

"Not at all. It's my favorite column."

"Ah. A gossip column?"

"Not exactly. Rather, each edition arms sheltered young ladies—like me—with indispensable information so that the trials and tribulations of the marriage mart will prove less intimidating."

"How very intriguing." Caroline peered at the newspaper, and a small drawing—a sketch of a young woman sitting beside a handsome gentleman on a pianoforte bench—caught her eye. The couple was depicted in detail that was both remarkable and captivating. Their hands hovered above the keys as though they were poised to play a duet, their pinky fingers barely touching. The sheet music propped on the stand forgotten, the man and woman gazed at one another as though their slight, incidental contact had left them completely shaken. Momentarily stunned.

Caroline blinked away a similar vision—of her and Nash's hands resting between them on the bench in his study. The drawing in the newspaper captured everything she'd felt in that moment. The breathlessness, the giddiness, the glorious anticipation.

"Isn't the sketch lovely?" Delilah asked. "This column is from a few weeks ago, but it's one of my favorites."

Caroline picked up the paper and read the letter accompanying the drawing.

*The Debutante's Revenge*
*Dear Debutantes,*
*Physical contact between a woman and man may*
*cause strange, but not unpleasant, stirrings—*
*even when such contact is of a completely*
*innocent nature. Any thrilling sensations which*
*may result from such contact are not to be*
*ignored, for they are a sign of desire, which may,*
*in turn, lead to more passionate encounters.*
*A young woman must be prepared for those*
*unsettling feelings, in any eventuality.*

Delilah arched a brow expectantly. "What do you think?"

"Delightfully forthright," Caroline managed, even though her whole body tingled oddly. "Who is the author?"

Delilah's mouth curled into a conspiratorial smile. "That's the most delicious part. No one knows."

"An anonymous column written for debutantes," Caroline mused. "I confess I'm intrigued. I should like to read the rest of the columns."

"It just so happens I've saved the entire collection," Delilah said proudly. "Come with me."

Nash flexed his fingers as he strode through a sparsely furnished antechamber into the office of Edmund Drake, his friend and solicitor. Though they were roughly the same age, Drake had already grayed at the temples. Fortunately for Drake, most of London's young ladies found his prematurely silver hair charming and distinguished. Dashing, even.

Drake looked up when Nash entered and waved his secretary away. "We'll finish this up later."

The whip-thin secretary gathered his papers and pushed his spectacles up his nose. "Of course, Mr. Drake." He turned toward Nash and made a halting bow. "Good morning, Your Grace," he said, scurrying out of the office and shutting the door behind him.

Drake's inner sanctum smelled of leather, ink, and cigar smoke. Every surface from the wall of shelves, to the fireplace mantel, to the floor was cluttered with opened books, crumpled papers, and even—unless Nash was mistaken—a discarded cravat or two. The entire room was in shambles, except for Drake's desktop, which was neat and orderly. Meticulously so. Much like the eye of a hurricane, Drake was the calm center in a world of chaos. If there was one thing Nash needed, it was a little serenity, and he knew he could count on his friend to steer him in the right direction.

Nash sank into the seat that the assistant had occupied and leaned forward, his elbows propped on his knees. "I have a problem."

"You have lots of problems," Drake said with a grin. "What's the latest?"

"There's a woman staying at my house, and I don't know who she is. Neither does she."

Drake blinked in disbelief. "You jest."

"I'm dead serious," Nash said—and proceeded to tell him the rest of the story. Except for the part about him being absolutely, inconveniently attracted to her.

When he was through, Drake sat back and rubbed his chin. "You need to find out Caroline's identity, but you also need to be discreet. If anyone discovered she was living under your roof unchaperoned, her reputation would suffer."

"Right. And for Delilah's sake, I'm trying to avoid any whisper of scandal. She'll want to marry, someday." Nash swallowed the lump in his throat, hoping that day was in the distant future.

"I'm happy to help in any way I can," Drake said. "Would you like me to head to the Grey Goose? Make some inquiries?"

"Not yet," Nash replied, grateful for the offer but also hesitant. "I have another idea, but I want to talk to Caroline first."

Drake nodded shrewdly. "Would this mysterious woman of yours happen to be clever and headstrong?"

"How did you guess?" Nash asked, unsurprised. Drake was too perceptive by half.

"Is she also witty and beautiful?"

Nash suppressed a groan and stood. "I'm going to a pub where I can have a pint and something to eat. Are you coming?"

Drake barked a laugh as he grabbed his coat. "Could it be that the man known throughout the ton as Stoneheart is smitten?"

"Hardly," Nash grunted, fairly certain he hadn't convinced Drake—*or* himself.

# Chapter 9

*"Gentlemen are not the only ones entitled to a taste of wickedness."*

—*The Debutante's Revenge*

Caroline trailed Delilah up the staircase to her bedchamber, eager to read more issues of The Debutante's Revenge. The one she'd read at the breakfast table earlier had resonated with her in a way few things had since she'd awaken in the duke's house. Perhaps, like Delilah, she was a devotee of the column. Maybe one of the newspapers in Delilah's collection would provide the spark she needed to regain her memory.

Delilah shut the door behind them and tossed her blond curls behind her shoulder. "Please sit," she said, waving a hand at her bed, which was covered with a counterpane in a spring-like shade of pink. All the room's furnishings, in fact, from the bright yellow curtains to the fresh green wallpaper to the charming landscape of a cottage hanging over the bureau reflected Delilah's sunny personality.

While Caroline settled herself on the edge of the mattress, Delilah threw open the doors of her armoire and ducked her head inside. When she emerged a few seconds later, she held a small stack of newspapers, which she presented to Caroline with unexpected reverence.

"They're in order," she said, "with the most recent issue on top. I'm going to leave you here so that you may read them in peace. Take your time, for while each column is short, it's meant to be savored. Let the words wash over you; let the drawings stir your imagination. Enjoy."

"Thank you," she said, oddly touched. "I shall."

Delilah shot her a wide smile as she glided out of the room and shut the door behind her.

Brimming with anticipation, Caroline kicked off her slippers, stretched out on the bed, and plucked a random paper from the middle of the stack. Her eyes scanned the page, and the image of a man and woman waltzing immediately captured her gaze. His large hand was splayed across the small of her back; her fingers rested on an impossibly broad shoulder. Their chests were only a breath apart, and they looked at each other with such tenderness that it left Caroline breathless. The column beneath the sketch read:

*The Debutante's Revenge*
*Dear Debutantes,*
*While dancing is not inherently scandalous, it does provide ample opportunities for titillating flirtation, passionate glances, and exhilarating contact.*

*Interestingly, a gentleman need not be excessively dexterous or graceful in order to be a good dance partner. Rather, he should move*

*with a natural confidence. He should hold you
with care and respect. He should look at you with
something akin to wonder.*

*If you are fortunate enough to find such a
dance partner, you may wish to consider him as
a potential beau.*

*For expertise on the dance floor often extends
to other key areas as well.*

Goodness. Her fingertips tingling, Caroline sat up and
studied the column again. She agreed with its advice,
but, more importantly, she recognized something within
it. Perhaps she'd had a dance partner like the one described. Or maybe she'd simply read this particular column before.

Vexingly, she had no recollection of either.

Her heart beat fast as she selected another newspaper
from the pile. In this issue, the sketch showed a young
woman from behind as she sat gazing at a lush garden,
her sumptuous gown skimming the stone bench and kissing the ground beneath.

*The Debutante's Revenge*
*Dear Debutantes,*
*There are a great many ways to capture a
gentleman's attention. You may resort to all
manner of tricks, such as wearing a gown
with a shockingly low neckline, pretending to
sprain your ankle, or laughing excessively at
his attempts at humor. All of these tactics, while
tried and true, work only in the short term.*

*If you wish to gain his notice—and keep
it—you must create a more lasting connection.*

*Try asking him a personal question or offering a sincere smile, all while staying true to who you are.*

*If the gentleman responds in kind, you are on your way to establishing a deeper bond.*

*If he does not, you must ask yourself why you are wasting your time with him.*

*Perhaps, instead of desperately seeking to gain a gentleman's favor, you should require the gentleman to seek* yours.

Caroline swallowed, stunned. This advice resonated too. Not only in regard to what it said—but also *how* it was said. The Debutante's Revenge meant something to her—the real her. She sensed it deep in her bones.

Encouraged by the admittedly small development, she proceeded to read all of the columns, in chronological order. She spent hours studying every drawing and rereading each letter, searching for clues, searching for herself.

When a knock sounded on the door, she sat up on Delilah's bed, slightly dazed. She'd been so absorbed by the task that she'd lost all track of time. "Come in," she called.

Delilah strode through the door, and Molly followed with a cart. "We thought you should take a break for tea," Delilah said cheerfully. "You must be famished."

"Thank you," Caroline said. She carefully organized the columns and set them on Delilah's desk. "Tea sounds lovely. You'll join me, won't you?"

"Of course," Delilah replied. "I'm curious to hear your thoughts about the column."

Molly wheeled the tea cart toward a small sitting area

near the window and uncovered a tray filled with small sandwiches, scones, fruit, and clotted cream. "Let me know if there's anything else you need," she said kindly.

"It looks delicious," Caroline said, her belly rumbling in agreement.

Molly clasped her hands in front of her starched white apron and bobbed a curtsy before leaving. Delilah kicked off her slippers, tucked her feet beneath her gown, and gratefully accepted the steaming cup of tea that Caroline had poured. "Did you enjoy the rest of the articles?"

"I did." Caroline nibbled a scone, thoughtful. "But I felt more than enjoyment. I felt a connection to the column."

"I do too," Delilah said. "Sometimes I feel as though the authoress is speaking directly to me." She paused to sip her tea and froze, her cup halfway to her mouth. "Wait. Do you think your connection to The Debutante's Revenge extends beyond that of a reader?"

Caroline worried her lower lip. "Does that make me sound a little mad? Doesn't every person who's taken leave of their senses believe that they're someone talented or famous?"

"You're not mad," Delilah assured her, her voice brimming with excitement. "It's entirely possible that you're associated with the column in some way. Could you have drawn the sketches?"

Caroline pushed the sleeves of her gown up to her elbows. "There's only one way to find out. May I have a sheet of paper and a pencil?"

Delilah sprang out of her chair, rummaged through a desk drawer, and produced a sketchpad and pencil. "Here you are. What will you draw?"

"Not what. *Who,*" Caroline replied with a smile. "You shall be my subject."

"Me?" Delilah hastily attempted to smooth her hair.

"Sit in your chair and relax while I sketch your portrait," Caroline instructed, staring at the blank paper in front of her and wondering where in the world to begin. Maybe a few bold lines. Some subtle shading. She let the pencil glide over the paper, trusting that any talent she possessed would manifest itself on the page.

Alas, it did not.

Delilah must have noticed Caroline's dismay. "How is it looking?" she probed.

"Not good," Caroline said flatly. "I can confidently say that I am not the artist behind The Debutante's Revenge."

"Are you certain?" Delilah said. "Artists are notoriously critical of their own work. Perhaps you should let me judge."

Caroline glanced at the blob she'd drawn, which might have been a passable likeness—if Delilah had been a cross between a mermaid and a sheep.

"No." Caroline tried to snap the sketchbook shut, but Delilah grabbed it and swiftly moved it out of her reach.

Delilah deliberately turned the sketchbook around, then studied the drawing, trying valiantly to keep her face impassive. "Well," she began. "It's not so bad." Pointing to the sheep's tail, she said, "This is obviously my nose."

Caroline rotated the paper one-hundred-eighty degrees. "That's your foot."

Grinning, Delilah handed the pad back to her. "You're definitely not the artist," she agreed. "But you *could* be the writer. You felt a connection to the column, and I think you must trust your instincts."

"My mind hasn't been terribly reliable of late," Caroline replied dryly. "What I need is proof."

"The column is cloaked in secrecy," Delilah said sadly. "And that makes proof difficult to come by."

Caroline blinked. "What day of the week is The Debutante's Revenge published?"

"Fridays. *Oh*." Delilah's eyes grew wide. "If a new letter doesn't appear in Friday's *Hearsay*, we'll know that your instincts are correct. Six days. Not that long to wait."

"I hope to regain my memory sooner, but in case I don't, it's comforting to know we'll have confirmation one way or the other."

"How exciting," Delilah breathed. "I eagerly anticipate every letter, but the next one may turn out to be enlightening on multiple levels. And if we learn that you are behind the column in some way, you have nothing to fear. I would never expose you."

Caroline's eyes stung. "In just a few short days, you've become like a sister to me. And in an odd way, your friendship makes me feel homesick for a place I can't even name. I only know I need to find my family. To discover where I belong."

"You belong," Delilah said firmly. She reached out and gave Caroline's hand a squeeze that she felt somewhere in the vicinity of her heart.

She swallowed the lump in her throat and prayed once more that she wouldn't forever be Caroline, the girl with no real name or family.

"Would you like to hear about my walk in the park?" Delilah's pretty face beamed, and her shoulders lifted as though she'd burst if she didn't share.

"Absolutely," Caroline said, chuckling.

"I happened to meet Lord Brondale as I was strolling along the promenade. He's very charming and witty. Handsome too," she said, sighing. "I think he is fond of me. And I *know* I am fond of him."

"How wonderful," Caroline said. "You deserve to have a dashing beau. Is he courting you?"

"Not ostensibly. That is, he hasn't sought permission from Nash—probably because he knows my brother would disapprove."

A shiver stole over Caroline's skin. "Nash doesn't like Lord Brondale? Why not?"

"He refuses to give specifics—only that he has reason not to trust him." Delilah pushed herself out of her chair and paced her bedchamber. "But I suspect he would disapprove of any gentleman who called on me."

"Your brother clearly adores you, and I'm sure he wants you to be happy. Perhaps I could talk to him about Lord Brondale. Try to persuade him that you are capable of judging his character for yourself."

Delilah faced Caroline and clasped her hands under her chin. "You'd do that?"

"Of course," Caroline replied. "I can't promise that I'll succeed, but I'll try."

"He's eating dinner at his club tonight, so it will just be the two of us," Delilah said.

Caroline tamped down a twinge of disappointment and placed a hand over her full belly. "After all this food, I couldn't possibly eat more. Would you mind terribly if I skipped dinner and retired early tonight?" She needed time to sort through all she'd learned about the column. To try and fit some of the puzzle pieces together.

"Not at all," Delilah assured her. "I shall do the same. Who knows? Perhaps tomorrow, we'll both have a few answers." She gestured toward the stack of newspapers on her desk. "Would you like to take the columns with you?"

"If you're sure you don't mind." Perhaps she'd study them some more after a little rest.

"There's no one I'd rather share them with," Delilah said warmly.

"Thank you." She pulled Delilah into an impulsive hug. "For everything."

Caroline gathered up the newspapers and made her way to her bedchamber, contemplating the earliest acceptable time to change into her nightgown. But when she entered her room, she pulled up short.

Sitting on the chest at the foot of her bed was a neat pile of folded clothes and a pair of boy's boots. She swallowed as she lifted the shirt on top and held the worn fabric against her chest.

Her clothes. The ones she'd been wearing on the night she lost her memory. Besides her bag, they were the only tangible connection to her real life.

Her pulse skittered as she closed the door and loosened the laces of her gown. Perhaps slipping into her old disguise would help her remember the woman she'd been—and who she still was, deep down.

# Chapter 10

*"Most men wouldn't dream of committing to one person for the rest of their lives without experiencing a taste of passion. Why, then, should you?"*
　　　　　　　　　—The Debutante's Revenge

Nash ate dinner at his club and returned home late that night. He'd needed some time away from the house and the bittersweet memories it held.

Last night he'd talked about Emily more than he had in the five years since she . . . left him. Uttering her name had hurt. Like lancing a wound.

Of course, he hadn't revealed the entire truth about Emily and his father. Hadn't told Caroline the part he'd played in that tragedy. The guilt was his alone—his burden to bear, his price to pay. To shrug it off would only compound his sins.

But still, he'd spoken Emily's name, and the earth had not swallowed him whole. If anything, talking about her—however briefly—had released a bit of the anger and pain. Like a geyser venting steam to prevent the earth from cracking open.

Caroline was responsible for that small, temporary

relief. And she'd been on his mind all day. It turned out that the brilliant green leaves rustling in the park were the same green as her eyes. The sunlight sparkling on the river's surface was the same gold as her gown. How the hell was he supposed to *not* think about her?

Especially after the kiss they'd shared. The one that had stirred something deep inside him, making him lose the control he prized above all else.

He'd had an idea, though—a way that they might be able to locate Caroline's family. He intended to talk to her about it at breakfast tomorrow, reasoning that as long as Delilah sipped tea across from them and sunlight streamed through the windows, he and Caroline might resist the temptation to fall into each other's arms again.

Now, as he made his way to his bedchamber, each room he slipped past was blissfully quiet and dark—save Caroline's. A soft light glowed from beneath her door.

He told his feet to keep walking, but they stuck to the floor outside her room. He couldn't pass up the chance to see her briefly. To find out if she'd been as affected by the kiss as she.

So, he knocked softly.

He heard a shuffle on the other side, then her voice, low and slightly breathless. "Who is it?"

"Nash," he answered, his cheek against the door. "Am I disturbing you?"

The door opened a few inches, revealing a narrow swath of Caroline's face—one green eye, the curve of her cheek, and a dark tendril curling around her chin. "Did you wish to talk?"

"Yes," he said earnestly. "But it can wait until morning. I shouldn't have knocked so late."

"No, it's fine," she insisted. "It's just . . . I'm not dressed for company."

"I'm not company," he said with a chuckle. "I don't care if you're wearing a nightgown and robe—unless you do?"

She bit her lower lip. "I'm not wearing a robe. Or a nightgown."

"Oh," he said—momentarily stunned. His blood heated at the thought of what Caroline was *not* wearing.

Before he could articulate a coherent response, she grabbed his wrist, pulled him into her bedchamber, and shut the door. She whirled around, eyes twinkling with mirth as she strode to the center of the room and planted a hand on one hip. "I was trying on my old clothes," she said unapologetically.

Nash swallowed and tried not to gape. Leather boots hugged her legs, snug trousers cradled her bottom, and a billowy white shirt floated around her torso. Her thick tresses tumbled around her slender shoulders and down her back, tickling the nip of her waist. Standing there, so proud and assured, she took his breath away.

"Why?" he managed to ask. "Not that I object to your choice of evening wear. Quite the contrary. But why would you put on your disguise tonight?"

She absently pressed fingers to her temple. "I was try-ing to remember."

"Have you?"

"No," she said, her voice tinged with sadness.

"I suspect it's like trying to swim against the tide. Fighting the currents will exhaust you. But if you can manage to float along for a while, you'll eventually head in the right direction." He shot her a wry smile. "Then again, it's easy for me to be philosophical. I'm not the one lost at sea."

"True." She crossed her arms like she was suppressing a shiver, and he checked the urge to haul her against his chest and comfort her. "You said you wanted to speak with me," she said. "I'd hoped to talk with you as well."

"Would you like to go first?" he asked, his curiosity piqued.

She nodded, sat on the edge of the bed, and patted the mattress beside her. "Please, sit."

He did, wondering if she knew the effect she had on him. That his pulse leapt just from being close to her.

"There's something I'd like to ask you," she began. "It's about Delilah."

At the mention of his sister, his hackles rose slightly, but he nodded. "Go on."

"She told me today that she is rather fond of a certain gentleman—and that you disapprove of him."

"Brondale," Nash growled. "He's no gentleman, and I wouldn't let him within twenty yards of my sister."

Caroline tilted her head. "Why not?"

"I have my reasons." The primary one being that Brondale was one of half a dozen young bucks who'd made a vile wager in the betting book at his club. The first one among them who provided proof that he'd deflowered a virgin would win the pot.

"Don't you think you should share your reasons with Delilah?"

"No," he said firmly. He couldn't begin to imagine how to have that conversation with his sister.

"She's not a child, Nash." Caroline's eyes flashed with

passion. "She's smart. And quite capable of making her own decisions."

"I know," he said, exhaling slowly. "She reminds me daily."

"Then talk to her," Caroline urged. "Tell her your concerns and trust her to listen."

"I'm trying," he said earnestly. "But she needs to trust me too. She was only thirteen when my father died, and, since then, I've been more than her older brother. I've had to be her father and guardian too. I want her to be happy—honestly, I do—but every instinct inside me screams to keep her safe. To protect her from scoundrels who would take advantage of her sweet nature."

Caroline impulsively reached for his hand, and his skin tingled from her touch. "It's difficult to watch the people we love falter and make mistakes. But everyone deserves the chance to make a few of their own. It's how we learn and grow."

Nash swallowed. "My head agrees with you. It's my heart that's stubborn."

Caroline smiled serenely. Maybe even affectionately. "You should tell her that."

"I will," he promised, gazing into her eyes until the air between them seemed to sizzle.

"Good." She blinked and pulled her hand away. "Now it's your turn. What did you want to discuss?"

"I had an idea," he said. "About how we might—" He paused and watched as Caroline repeatedly rubbed her palm over her thigh. "Does your leg pain you?"

"No. Forgive me," she said, frowning slightly. "I just happened to feel something in my trousers. I wonder if there might be something in the pocket."

For the space of several heartbeats, neither of them spoke. But her expression—one part excitement and one part fear—said what they both knew. That the object in her pocket could be the clue they'd been searching for. The one that would take her home.

When he gave her an encouraging nod, she slipped a hand into her waistband, felt around blindly, and withdrew a small, folded paper. Her hands trembled as she carefully opened it. "It's a drawing," she breathed. "Of a man and woman."

She handed him the wrinkled paper, still damp from being laundered along with the trousers. The pencil strokes were smudged and faded, and the sketch appeared incomplete. And yet, somehow, the couple seemed to live and breathe on the page. The man gazed at the woman with unabashed desire.

Nash studied the young woman on the paper, shown mostly from behind, looking for any resemblance to Caroline. There were similarities—the gently sloped nose, the strong chin, and thick curls. It *could* have been her, but it was impossible to say for certain. The mere possibility gave him a sick feeling in his gut.

He gave the drawing back to her. "Do you think the woman is you?"

She shrugged helplessly. "I don't know. It feels oddly familiar, but I have no idea where it came from or who the couple is."

"Could you have drawn it?" he asked, hopeful.

"No. I've already determined I'm a horrid artist." She stared at the picture intently. "But if I carried it in my pocket, it must hold some special meaning."

Not trusting himself to speak, Nash nodded his agreement. Caroline was the first person who'd been able to crack open the impenetrable shell around his heart—and now it seemed likely that she had a beau, maybe even a husband, waiting for her at home.

She carried the sketch across the room to her desk and laid it next to a pile of newspapers. "I'll look at it with fresh eyes tomorrow. Let us continue our conversation now," she said, as though she were determined to put the drawing out of her mind for the moment.

Nash wished he could do the same. Once she'd situated herself on the bed again, he picked up the thread from before. "I thought of a way we could discreetly reach out to your family," he said. "To let anyone who's searching for you know that you're safe and give them a way to contact you."

"How?" she asked, clearly intrigued.

"An advertisement in the *London Hearsay*," he replied. "We could give your description and ask anyone who thinks they know you to contact my solicitor and trusted friend, Edmund Drake. We can even offer a reward for information leading you home."

"That's very generous of you," she said brightly. "And an excellent suggestion. How soon could we place the ad?"

He tried not to take her enthusiasm as a sign that she was eager to leave him. She wanted to find out who she was. He wanted that too. "If we submit it tomorrow, it should appear in the paper the day after next. I don't think we have anything to lose." Except, possibly, the tenuous connection that they'd formed.

"I agree," she said, rewarding him with a smile that warmed his chest. "Thank you for thinking of it—and for coming here tonight."

"I probably shouldn't have," he confessed. "But the truth is that I find it hard to stay away."

* * *

Perhaps it was the deep timbre of his voice or the moonlight casting shadows on his handsome face that suddenly
made Caroline very aware that they were alone. In her
bedchamber. Sitting on her bed. She shivered, not from
fear but from the memory of their kiss and the way he'd
made her feel—like she was soaring above the clouds.

"I should go," he said gruffly.

"Don't," she urged. She wasn't ready to say goodbye.

He reached out and laced his fingers through hers.
"I'm trying to be a gentleman. To give you time."

She stared at their entwined hands, amazed that the
simple pressure of his palm against hers could make her
belly flip in anticipation. "Last night in your study," she
began, "I told you I couldn't be with you until I knew
myself."

"I remember." His eyes glowed like liquid gold.

"But I have reconsidered."

"And why is that?"

"Because I'm realizing that losing my memory comes
with one, glorious silver lining—this time with you. I
may not know my name, but I know what I want. To be
with you."

His gaze dropped to her mouth. "We don't know
what the future holds for us, Caroline. You have a life
beyond these walls—a life that may not include room
for me. The drawing you found in your trousers reminded me of that."

"I know." She curled her hand around his neck, thread-
ing her fingers through the thick curls at his nape. "But
if I was already promised to another, I can't imagine that
I'd feel what I'm feeling for you right now. I care for you,
and I think you care for me too. We should use whatever

time we have together wisely. Show me something of love. Of passion."

Nash went very still. "That sounds like a dangerous game."

"Not a game," she assured him. "We're both adults. We deserve a chance to explore this relationship—and see where it might lead."

"What if it leads nowhere?" Pain, stark and cold, flashed in his eyes, and she sensed in her chest that he was thinking of Emily. "Someone would end up hurt."

"It's always a risk," Caroline said soberly. "But it's one I'm willing to take—if you are."

# Chapter 11

*"Neither oil paint on canvas nor a sculpture made
of marble can do justice to the warm skin, muscled
contours, and primal power of the male body."*
—*The Debutante's Revenge*

Nash hesitated for a heartbeat, then hauled Caroline
closer. He cupped her face in his hands and kissed her—
as though he burned for her.

His kisses filled the emptiness in her chest. The hol-
lowness that had plagued her since her memory loss was
replaced with longing, desire, and warmth. A sense of
belonging.

He paused and searched her face, his breath ragged.
"You must tell me if we move too fast."

"I will," she promised.

"Good." Sandy-brown hair spilled across his brow,
and a wicked smile lit his face. "In any event, I propose
that we begin slowly."

"Slowly?" she said, frowning. *Slowly* didn't sound particularly appealing, given the pounding of her heart and
the ache in her core.

"Slow kisses." He demonstrated with a series of sensuous nips along the side of her neck. "Lingering touches." A calloused fingertip lightly traced her collarbone and left her skin tingling in its wake.

"Oh," she breathed. "Slowly *is* nice."

He skimmed a warm hand up her thigh and around her hip, moaning his approval. She hadn't bothered with feminine underclothes when she'd slipped into her disguise, so the wool of her trousers rubbed against her intimately; the soft fabric of her shirt teased the tips of her breasts.

She leaned into him, reveling in the impossibly hard wall of his chest and the broad span of his shoulders. "We should remove our boots," she murmured.

"That is an excellent idea." After a sweet, knee-melting kiss, he pulled away. "Allow me."

Caroline laid back on the mattress and watched as he tugged off her boots and his. He discarded his jacket before sprawling next to her on the bed. With a heart-stopping smile, he said, "I've never removed a woman's boots before."

She laughed. "I think you mean to say you've never removed a man's boots from a woman."

"That is also true," he conceded with a chuckle.

But their smiles faded as she grabbed his shirt and boldly pulled him on top of her. She savored the weight of his body and the hard length of him pressing between her thighs. An odd but insistent pulsing started there, and she rocked her hips against his. Soon, they were moving together, breathless with need.

He ran his fingers through her long tresses and lightly rubbed her scalp. "I've longed to do this from the first time I saw your hair tumble free from your cap at the tavern. I just knew it would feel this way. Soft as silk."

He grasped a fistful of curls and groaned into her mouth, kissing her deeply.

Tentatively, she wrapped one leg around his, pulling him closer. They moved together perfectly, reaching for something she couldn't even name.

She smoothed her hands down his neck and over the fabric of his shirt, stretched tightly across his muscular frame. His cravat was loose, his waistcoat hung open, and his hair spilled across his brow.

But he'd never looked better to Caroline.

This was a rare glimpse of the man he truly was—not the rigid, brooding Duke of Stonebridge, but *Nash*. The man who rescued defenseless lads from tavern brawls and shared his brandy and played nursemaid all night when necessary. She refused to believe he had a heart of stone.

He lifted the hem of her shirt and slid his hand beneath, cupping her breast and tweaking the taut peak with his thumb. When she arched toward him, he took the hard bud into his mouth, suckling until pleasure radiated to her fingers and toes. "I can't fathom how I ever mistook you for a boy," he murmured against her skin.

"My disguise must have been quite good," she teased. Even as an idea niggled at the back of her mind. "Nash?"

He lifted his head from her breast and shot her a smile that made her thighs clench. "How may I serve?"

Sweet Jesus. She considered forgetting her idea and begging him to resume precisely where he'd left off. But she couldn't waste the chance to talk to him—and make a rather unusual request.

She leaned on an elbow and propped her head in her hand. "I wanted to ask you something."

He sat up and shot her a curious look. "Ask away."

Deciding on a direct approach, she swallowed and said, "Will you take me back to the Grey Goose?"

Nash drank in the sight of Caroline. Her hair was a wild tangle of curls, her lips were swollen from his kisses, and her shirt—rather, a boy's shirt—hung off her bare shoulders. She shimmered with a warmth and intelligence that radiated from within, transcending every traditional notion of beauty.

Still more than a little dazed from their kiss, he cocked his head and made sure he'd heard her correctly. "Why would you want to return to the Grey Goose? Trust me, it's not much to look at."

"I put these clothes on tonight"—she gestured toward her chimney-sweep disguise—"hoping they would help me remember. But maybe the clothes are only part of the equation. Perhaps I need to be back in the place where I was wearing them."

The skin between his shoulders prickled. "A tavern can be a dangerous place for a woman—you know that better than anyone."

"True." Caroline tilted her head, thoughtful. "But I intend to blend into the background."

He couldn't imagine her blending in any more than he could imagine a scarlet-red tulip hiding in a patch of weeds. "Impossible."

She glanced at him from beneath thick lashes. "Not if I'm wearing this disguise."

The image of her, unnaturally still on the filthy tavern floor, flashed in his mind. Made his chest ache. "You tried that before—it didn't end well."

"I was able to fool a tavern full of people," she countered. "Even you."

"Only for a short time," he said, but when her face fell, he reached for her hand and brushed his thumb across her palm. "Help me understand why it's so important to you."

She swallowed then looked up at him, earnest. "I feel as though I'm stuck in a strange purgatory. Until I know my past, I have no future. And I cannot sit idly by while time marches forward. Maybe visiting the tavern will help me remember; maybe it won't. But if I don't *do* something, I fear I'll go mad." She gazed deep into his eyes. "Say you'll help me, Nash."

The sound of his name on her lips made his heart trip. He wanted to help her find her place in the world—and learn if there was room in her life for him.

"If we're going back to the tavern, we'll need to be careful," he said, already aware he'd be kicking himself tomorrow.

Caroline's face split into a smile that warmed the coldest corners of his heart. "Tomorrow night?"

"Tomorrow," he agreed. "But we'll have to modify your disguise a bit. Some of the barmaids and patrons might remember you from the night of the brawl. I should probably wear a disguise too."

"Yes," she agreed, rubbing her palms together. "What did you have in mind?"

He shrugged. "Maybe I'll be a dockworker or a black-smith."

"I like the sound of a blacksmith." Her eyes crinkled at the corners. "I could be your apprentice."

"If you're going to be my apprentice, I'll need you to look more respectable than this," he teased, reaching for the sleeve hanging off her shoulder. A dark brown patch of skin shaped like a small star winked at him, and he leaned closer to look. "Did you know you have a birth-mark here?" He rubbed his thumb lightly over her upper arm, just below her shoulder.

"Yes. It's odd-looking, isn't it?"

"It's distinctive," he said, planting a kiss on her soft skin. "Rather like you."

"Thank you." Caroline beamed. "For the compliment *and* for agreeing to take me to the Grey Goose."

"I must be mad," he said gruffly. But the happiness plain on her face told him he was doing the right thing.

She swept a hand over his cheek and along his jaw. Suddenly, the entire world narrowed to the brush of her fingertips on his face, and he held his breath so as not to break the tenuous spell.

"I can't explain why, but I feel as though I'm getting closer to remembering who I am. Returning to the tavern where I lost my memory could be just the thing I need—to break through the wall that's holding me back." Her heavy-lidded gaze drifted to his mouth, and Nash wasn't sure she was talking about her memory loss anymore.

"The wall will come down," he said. "Probably when you least expect it."

"Well, I intend to give it a good nudge."

He chuckled at that and brushed a wayward curl from her face. "Beware of pushing too hard. I wouldn't want the rubble to crush you, and the truth could be different than what you would have wished." He hesitated, then continued. "What *would* you wish for?"

"A sister like Delilah. A mother and father who care for me. The chance to . . ." She shook her head and looked away. "It's silly. And rather embarrassing to say such things out loud."

"I would never judge your dreams."

"Very well." She swallowed before continuing. "I would like the chance to fall deeply in love. To experience passion. And, one day, to have a family of my own."

"That doesn't sound silly to me. I daresay it's what most people want."

"Is it what *you* want?" she asked, searching his face.

"I used to think so."

She tilted her head, curious. "And now?"

Shit. He sat back and raked a hand through his hair. She deserved to know the truth—at least as much as he could bring himself to admit. "The kind of love you're talking about—that all-consuming, sweep-you-off-your-feet, unbridled emotion—is not for everyone. And I'm afraid it's not for me."

"Why not?" she asked simply.

"I've seen what that type of love can do to a person. It changes them."

"Yes," Caroline agreed. "For the better, I should think."

Jesus, he was in over his head here. "Sometimes, I suppose. All I know is that love often makes people do foolish things. I refuse to be one of those people."

She nodded shrewdly. "You're thinking of Emily."

"Yes," he said, feeling the usual thickness in his throat. "But it's more than that."

"Tell me," she urged.

He clasped her hands between his and kept his voice even and low. He needed Caroline to understand the truth about him. More than that, he needed her to believe it. "Some people aren't meant for that kind of head-over-heels love. We're not capable of it. It's not in our nature."

"I think you underestimate yourself," she said softly.

"I think you give me too much credit."

She leaned close to him and cupped his chin in her hand. "Everyone's capable of love."

Every fiber of his body longed to melt into her, but that would only weaken his argument. "Most people are capable of love," he said slowly. "Others don't—*can't*—feel as deeply. They don't have that emotion inside. They can't give something they don't have."

She held his gaze for several seconds, sadness clouding her eyes.

"You need to believe me, Caroline." If she didn't, she was doomed for disappointment, and the very last thing he wanted was to hurt her.

"Maybe that emotion *is* inside you, buried deep," she whispered. "Maybe you haven't dug down far enough. Maybe you need someone to help you find it."

He shook his head firmly. "Some things are better left buried." He and Emily had planned to follow their hearts. They'd each intended to find the love of their lives. Marry and have loud, happy broods. Live near each other and Delilah so all the cousins could grow up as close as siblings. But none of that was going to happen anymore. Not for Emily, not for him.

For the space of several heartbeats, Caroline was perfectly still and silent, her face impassive. Nash's words echoed harshly in his own head, but he couldn't take them back. They were true. And Caroline deserved to know.

At last, she moved closer, lifted her hand, and brushed a fingertip across his lower lip—a simple touch that he felt in his chest, his gut, and every nerve ending.

Her warm gaze washed over him, and she pressed her

lips to his in a kiss that felt like a promise. "I'm not giving up on you yet."

He wanted to tell her not to waste her time.

That he didn't deserve love and he definitely didn't deserve her.

But he knew Caroline, and she wasn't going to back
down. She'd see the truth for herself eventually. If she
stayed with him long enough, she'd discover that he
couldn't give her what she wanted.

"I'd better go," he said, half regret, half resolve. "Try
to sleep. You'll need to rest before our outing tomorrow
night."

The hint of a smile about her lips said she knew very
well that he'd intentionally changed the subject and that
she was giving him a reprieve—for now. "You'll place
the ad tomorrow?"

"Yes," he assured her, easing himself off the bed and
scooping up his jacket and boots. "Is there anything in
particular you'd like me to include?"

"Just my physical description, I think," she mused.
"Without any mention of the clothes I was wearing."

"Consider it done," he said, relieved to be back in comfortable territory—taking action rather than analyzing
his damned feelings.

She swung her bare feet over the side of the bed. "Wait.
Should we include something about my birthmark? In
the event several people respond, it could help us narrow
down the list to those who actually know me."

"Good idea. We can mention a distinctive birthmark
and see which of the respondents is able to describe it."
He shot her a reassuring smile. "I'll be out much of the
day, but I'll update you on any progress on our way to
the Grey Goose."

She walked him to the door and curled a hand behind his neck, pulling him down for one last kiss, so pure and sweet that he considered carrying her back to her bed. But she broke it off and gently guided him out the door. "Don't forget you're supposed to be a blacksmith tomorrow," she whispered. "Good night, Nash."

# Chapter 12

*"Do not allow anyone to scold you for daydream-*
*ing. If others mock you for being lost in thought, it*
*is likely because they are intrigued by your bliss-*
*ful expression. Let them wonder."*
                            —*The Debutante's Revenge*

As Caroline and Delilah finished up breakfast the next
morning, Delilah set down her teacup and smiled like
a satisfied cat. "I have a little surprise for you," she said.
"Come to the drawing room with me."

Caroline followed her friend, grateful for the distraction. She'd slept well but remained as confused as ever.
She still had no memory of who she was, but with each
day that passed, she became more attached to Nash and
Delilah.

If the ad worked as she and Nash hoped, someone who
knew her would come forward, and she would have to
leave Nash—to return home. What happened between
them after that . . . well, that all depended upon who Caroline was. Whether she turned out to be married, be-
trothed, or single. A proper lady, a genteel companion,
or a barmaid. Her head spun with the possibilities.

Nash claimed he was incapable of a love that was deep and all-consuming.

But she knew differently. She'd seen him stay by her bedside all night. She'd heard the emotion in his throat when he talked about Emily and his father, enjoyed the laughter he shared with Delilah. She'd felt the tenderness in his touch and the passion in his kisses. He *could* love completely—if he'd only let himself.

Caroline walked into the drawing room and sank into a chair beside the hearth where a fire burned, low and inviting. Delilah strode to a mahogany cabinet, pulled something out of a drawer, and hid it behind her as she walked closer. "I was thinking about our conversation yesterday," she began. "And how you felt a connection to The Debutante's Revenge."

"I do," Caroline said. "It's sort of a faint awareness. Like something you half remember from a dream—but everything is terribly murky."

"Well, we concluded that you're not the artist of the column's sketches, but it *is* possible that you're the writer of the column," Delilah said cheerfully.

"It's also possible I'm a princess from a tiny but wealthy kingdom," Caroline countered. "Possible. But *not* likely."

"Perhaps not," Delilah said with a shrug. "But you might as well try your hand at writing." She produced a small, leather-bound journal from behind her back and handed it to Caroline. "What do you think?"

Caroline ran her hands over the fine, supple leather, and flipped through the creamy smooth pages. "It's gorgeous. Almost too pretty to write in."

"Nonsense." Delilah sat in the chair across from Caroline, leaning forward expectantly. "You must write in it if you feel the urge. You could try writing a column, or you could simply keep it as a diary of sorts. One day, when you discover that you *are*, in fact, the princess of a tiny, wealthy kingdom, you will want to remember this particular episode in your life. You will tell the fascinating tale to your faithful subjects, who will pass it down for generations to come until it becomes legend."

Caroline laughed. "Well then, I had better make the story good."

Delilah shot her a wry grin. "If you don't mind, I should like to be described as a fair and gentle maiden."

"With a kind heart and a fiery spirit," Caroline added.

"You see," Delilah said, "I just knew you'd excel at this."

Caroline clasped the journal to her chest, touched. "I shall treasure this always. Thank you." She gave Delilah a fierce hug and swallowed the lump clogging her throat.

"I'm glad you like it," Delilah said warmly. "I hope it gives you some comfort."

"It already has," Caroline assured her. "And you're correct—it can't hurt to try writing a column. Perhaps the words will flow out of me. I have nothing to lose." She hesitated a moment, then asked, "Have there been whispers about the author? Rumors as to who she might be?"

Delilah's sunny face darkened ever so slightly as she shook her head. "Can you imagine the repercussions if the writer of the column was exposed? She'd be shunned. Cast out of polite society and spoken of only in sad, hushed tones. I pray that never happens."

Caroline suppressed a shudder. "What if the column is penned by a man?"

"I daresay the consequences would not be so dire for

him," Delilah replied dryly. "But after studying every issue of The Debutante's Revenge at great length, I'm confident it's written by a woman. She comprehends the nuances and pitfalls of the marriage mart and accurately portrays them—from the female point of view."

"I tend to agree," Caroline said. "That narrows the field of possibilities to half the population of London."

Delilah's bright blue eyes twinkled. "Speculation has been rampant since the very first column, but I do have a theory."

Caroline sat down again, listening intently. "Please, go on."

"It must be someone who has access to grand balls, esteemed drawing rooms, and aristocratic parties. But I suspect she exists somewhere on the fringes—not spurned exactly, but certainly not embraced to the bosom of London's elite."

"Yes, that does stand to reason." Caroline thought about the columns she'd studied the day before and smiled. "Anyone who encourages young women to nick brandy from their fathers and brothers does not adhere closely to society's strictures."

Delilah's face split into a mischievous grin. "She also recommends sultry gazes, forbidden books, and day-dreaming. It's no wonder she's gone to great lengths to conceal her identity."

"I certainly have no wish to expose her, but I can't escape the feeling that she somehow is key to discovering who I am." Caroline marched to the window, swept aside the plush curtains, and looked out over the square. Gentlemen walked along, swinging their canes. Nannies chatted as they pushed their prams down the pavement. Ladies on their way to the milliner's shop twirled pretty parasols. Beyond the walls of the duke's town house, life progressed at its usual, brisk pace.

Everyone seemed to be sailing somewhere exciting and new while she was marooned on the shore, no boat in sight.

As Nash and Caroline rumbled through the dark streets of London in a hackney cab, he enumerated in his head all the ways their plans could go awry.

Delilah could awake and discover he and Caroline were gone.

One of the Grey Goose's patrons could see through his or Caroline's disguise.

They could end up in another tavern brawl.

But, if he was honest with himself, the real source of his worry was how Caroline would respond to returning to the scene of her injury. She desperately wanted her memory back, and he . . . he wanted that for her too. But he couldn't help wondering what that might mean for him and for their unconventional courtship—if it could even be called that.

There hadn't been any formal introductions or ballroom dances or walks in the park. He didn't know her surname, and neither did she. But after spending less than a week with her, he was already having difficulty imagining a future without her. A dangerous development, that.

He glanced over at her gazing out the window on the seat beside him. Remembered it was her first time out of the house since she'd hit her head. "Does anything look familiar?" he asked.

She continued staring at the passing houses, shops, squares, and streets as though they might disappear if she took her eyes off them. "Not in the sense that I can recall being in specific places, but . . ."

"But?" he prompted.

"I do sense that I belong here. Does that make any sense at all?"

"It does." He longed to tell her that perhaps her instincts were telling her she belonged with *him*, but instead, he reached between them and held her hand, wishing they weren't both wearing rough leather gloves.

"Remember," he said, "anything that compromises your disguise puts you at risk. So try not to talk. Stay close. And, for the love of God, no smiling."

Predictably defiant, she beamed at him. "From the moment we step out of the cab, I promise to stay by your side, silent and sullen."

"You'll need to if we're going to have the slightest chance of fooling anyone." He scowled at her long lashes and elfish chin. "Let's hope the taproom is dimly lit and the clientele are pleasantly drunk."

As the cab rolled to a stop, she took a deep breath, gave his hand a little squeeze, and released it. "Here we go," she said, all her hopes and fears for the evening plain on her lovely face.

"Everything will be fine," he said. "Trust me."

It took every ounce of restraint he possessed not to grasp her waist as she hopped out of the cab or place his hand at the small of her back.

For the next half hour, they were blacksmith and apprentice. He pulled his cap low over his brow and strode to the door of the taproom. "Let's go."

Caroline followed at Nash's heels, taking in the exterior of the Grey Goose. Large mullioned windows, cloudy with smoke, flanked either side of a black door sporting a tarnished brass kickplate. Above the door, the tavern sign hung from an iron brace, swinging slightly in the night breeze.

None of it looked familiar in the least.

But she stepped over the threshold, undaunted. Perhaps something inside would jar her stubborn memory.

Nash led the way through the sparsely populated taproom to a booth in the corner, and she slid onto the wooden bench opposite him. In the center of the room, one table of men played cards, another sang bawdy songs and ogled the waitresses. The acrid smells of liquor, smoke, and urine filled her head, and she fought back a wave of nausea.

"Are you all right?" Nash asked softly.

She opened her mouth to reply, then, remembering her vow of silence, clamped her lips shut and nodded.

A barmaid sauntered over and gave Nash a slow, seductive smile. "Drinks, gentlemen?" she asked, not sparing a glance for Caroline.

"Two ales, please," Nash said.

The barmaid pursed her red lips and stared over her shoulder at him as she walked away, bottom swaying.

Nash turned to Caroline and shot her an apologetic glance. "This is the booth where I first saw you that night," he said. "You were sitting alone in that exact spot, looking much as you do now."

Caroline shifted on the hard bench, wondering how it was possible that she had no recollection of being there just a few days before. She placed her palms flat on the table, letting her fingertips trace its grooves and gouges, waiting for a memory to take root. But none did.

"The room was more crowded, then," Nash elaborated.

"It was earlier in the evening, and scores of men poured through the door, looking like they'd come straight from the docks."

The barmaid returned, setting their glasses on the table with a *thunk* that made ale slosh over the rims. But instead of leaving them to their drinks, she snaked her arm around Nash's neck and whispered in his ear. He gave a curt shake of his head, and she retreated, pouting.

Caroline took a healthy swig of ale.

Nash shot a pointed look at her glass and arched a brow.

In response, she lifted her glass, silently toasted him, and drained half. In no time at all, the bitter ale warmed her belly and loosened her limbs.

Nash held his mug in midair and stared at her across the table, his expression impassive. Then his amber eyes crinkled at the corners and his mouth split into a grin. "Cheers," he said, before raising his glass and drinking.

His charming manner melted her insides, and she felt her own mouth curling into a smile.

"Don't," he warned under his breath. "Your smile is what betrayed you last time."

Her smile?

Reading the question in her eyes, he continued. "I stepped in, taking your side, and you smiled at me. That's when I knew that you weren't who you seemed."

She frowned and tried to remember. Tried to imagine herself doing the things Nash described. None of it seemed real—and somehow that frightened her more than his account of what had happened.

"Hearing this and not remembering must be upsetting," he said softly. "I'm sorry." His tortured expression made her desperate to rise from her seat, perch on his lap, and kiss him on the mouth. If she hadn't been dressed as a boy, perhaps she would have.

But blending in and escaping detection was essential, so she settled for surreptitiously extending a leg beneath the table and brushing her knee against the outside of his thigh. His warm gaze snapped to hers and the current between them raised the hairs on the back of her arms.

Suddenly, she couldn't wait to leave the tavern. She'd thought that it would hold answers for her, but the crass jokes, pungent smells, and raucous music felt as foreign to her as another language.

She believed Nash when he said she'd been there.

But that didn't mean she *belonged* there.

She flicked her eyes toward the door and shrugged one shoulder in a silent plea.

"Ready to go?" Nash asked.

When she nodded, he slapped a few coins on the table and eased himself out of the booth.

She endeavored not to stare at his broad shoulders and powerful back as she followed him toward the door. She could scarcely wait to reach the relative safety of a hackney cab, where she would be free to speak and smile and—

A warm, clammy hand grasped at Caroline's wrist, stopping her in her tracks and whirling her around.

"I recognize you." A tall barmaid with overly rouged cheeks held Caroline's forearm tightly and moved closer—till their noses were only an inch apart. "You're the same boy—nay, *girl*—who was knocked out cold a few nights ago."

Blast. Caroline swiveled her head, looking for Nash, who was almost to the door, unaware that she'd been detained. Swallowing, she turned back toward the bar-maid and shook her head in a feeble denial.

"No?" the barmaid drawled. "Then tell me your name, lad."

Caroline yanked her arm loose, attracting the atten-tion of a couple of burly men at a nearby table who must have assumed she'd been harassing the waitress. They stood, blocking her path.

Dash it all, where was Nash?

She was about to make a run for it when he angled his way between the two oafs, wrapped an arm around her shoulders, and pulled her through the men, rushing her out the door. "I can't turn my back on you for even a minute?" he whispered in her ear.

"One would think you'd learned your lesson by now," she retorted, tripping along as fast as she could in her oversized boots.

When they reached the street, Nash looked over his shoulder, his expression grim. "Looks like they're chas-ing us. Can you run?"

"Absolutely." She had no specific memory of being a capable runner, but her leg muscles knew exactly what to do—and she couldn't wait to stretch them out. "Try to keep up," she said, winking at him.

She set off at a brisk jog, which was the best she could do in the ill-fitting boots. Nash stayed right behind her, shielding her from the men in pursuit.

A potent mixture of fear and excitement kept her legs churning and her arms pumping. But after several blocks, the sole of one boot separated from the foot, and she slowed down.

"We've almost lost them," he said.

She turned to him, gasping for air. "My boot broke."

Nash frowned and looked down the street at the men still bumbling after them. "We should be able to find a cab on the next block." He planted his hands on his knees and crouched beside her. "Hop on."

"I beg your pardon."

He jabbed a thumb over his shoulder. "Wrap your arms around my neck and jump on my back. I'll carry you."

"You must be mad."

Behind them, the men from the tavern began to close the distance. "We don't like goose chases," one of them shouted, slurring his words a bit.

"I won't drop you," Nash said solemnly. "I would never let anything happen to you."

A warm feeling spread through Caroline's chest. "Very well." She flung her arms around his neck, and he lifted her knees as he stood.

Before she could even adjust to the view from above his shoulders, he was sprinting down the block, and she was bouncing along with him . . . and laughing.

Perhaps it was the breeze on her face or the fact that her legs were wantonly wrapped around his waist. Maybe it was her disguise and the thought of how they must appear to anyone who saw them.

But deep inside, she knew she was laughing because she was with Nash and, for that night at least, they were gloriously free—living an adventure neither of them would forget.

When he rounded the corner, Caroline spied a hackney cab just a stone's throw away. "There," she called out, pointing.

Nash flagged down the cab, and Caroline dismounted, climbing into the conveyance while he gave instructions to the driver. Seconds later, Nash slid onto the bench beside her and slammed the cab door. "We made it," he said as the vehicle lurched forward. "Are you all right?"

She took off her cap and leaned her head on his shoulder. "I'm more than all right."

"And your memory?"

She shook her head. "I had such high hopes, but I'm afraid I didn't recognize anything or anyone in the tavern."

"I'm sorry," he said.

"Don't be." She nuzzled his neck and brushed her lips across his jaw. "Because while we were fleeing from the tavern, I realized something. When I'm with you—no matter what I'm doing or where I am—I feel like I'm right where I belong."

# Chapter 13

*"The male form is widely portrayed in classical art, and therefore, you could be forgiven for thinking you have seen it all. But until you have . . . you have* not.*"*

—*The Debutante's Revenge*

Nash had never been so happy to see the inside of a hackney cab. From the moment he and Caroline had become separated, his heart had been pounding. First from stark fear that something terrible had happened to her, and then from their sprint through the streets of London.

But now Caroline was leaning into his side, talking about belonging, her brilliant green eyes gazing up at him like he was some sort of hero. Which he wasn't. Still, sitting there, basking in her radiant glow, he could almost believe he was.

"I wish tonight hadn't been a disappointment for you," he said. But perhaps a small part of him *was* glad that her memory hadn't come rushing back at the sight of the tavern. Because when she discovered her identity, she would have to go home.

"How could it be a disappointment?" Caroline asked.

"I dressed as a boy, drank ale in a tavern, and—with a little help—outran a couple of drunken thugs."

"And you lived to tell the tale," Nash teased.

She chuckled. "I'm not certain it's a story I shall pass down to my grandchildren, but yes—I survived."

"I would never have let anything happen to you."

She slipped her hand into his. "I know."

They didn't speak for the rest of the ride. But whenever he squeezed her hand, she smiled dreamily. When he traced circles on her palm with his thumb, her lips would part. And each time she pressed her trouser-clad thigh against his, he instantly grew hard.

The cab rolled to a stop at the corner Nash had specified—a block from his town house. In case the driver noticed anything unusual about his two roughly dressed passengers, Nash didn't want him connecting their activities to the Duke of Stonebridge.

He and Caroline hopped out onto the deserted street, stretching the tightness out of their legs. "You might be sore tomorrow," he said.

"It will have been worth it," she said confidently. "To feel the thundering of my heart and the burn in my muscles. To feel . . . *alive*."

"I think I know what you mean," he said. But the truth was, he felt alive whenever he was with her. Even if they were simply eating breakfast.

He led her to the back of his house, pausing just outside the garden gate. "If anyone encounters us, our disguises would be hard to explain," he whispered.

"Then we should take care to avoid detection." Grinning, she leaned against the exterior wall and pulled off one boot, then the other.

He took them from her, tucked them under an arm,

and led her into the house, up the back staircase. He held his breath as they slunk down the corridor to his bed-chamber and didn't release it till Caroline was safely inside.

The moment the door closed behind them, he dropped the boots and Caroline flew into his arms. Her hands clung to his shoulders. Her hips rocked against his. Their mouths crashed in a kiss that was primal and fierce. He lifted her, and she wound her legs around his waist as she speared her fingers through his hair and let her tongue tangle with his.

"Caroline," he murmured against her mouth. "We shouldn't become too carried away."

She broke off their kiss and looked directly into his eyes. "I *want* to become carried away. With you. I know this isn't permanent—it can't be. But if our days together are numbered, I don't want to waste them."

Holy hell, she was difficult to resist. He let her slide slowly down his body, placing her gently on her stock-inged feet. "How carried away do you wish to be?" he asked.

She leaned into him and skimmed a fingertip over his lower lip. "I want to see your body and feel your skin against mine. I want to experience passion and . . . plea-sure."

He swallowed, humbled by the trust she was placing in him. "You're sure about this? Even though you still don't have your memory?"

"I know enough about me. And I know enough about you." She placed a palm on his chest and searched his face. "I can't explain exactly what's happening between us, but I need this. I think you do too."

"Maybe I do." Nash's blood heated. He did need Caroline—in more ways than he wanted to admit.

Caroline drank in the sight of Nash's handsome face, thrilled at the heat in his gaze. "We're going to need to remove our clothes," she said matter-of-factly.

"We will." His chuckle vibrated through her, wickedly deep and promising. "But there's no hurry."

"There isn't?" she asked, not bothering to hide her skepticism. Her whole body pulsed with need.

"Trust me." He shot her an amused smile and turned her so that her back pressed against the wall of his chest. As he tugged the tails of her shirt out of her waistband, he trailed kisses down the side of her neck, the scruff of his beard scraping lightly over her skin.

His large, warm hands found their way under her shirt and up her torso, caressing the sensitive skin of her belly and cruising over the bands of silk that bound her breasts.

She wanted to tear off the binding *and* his clothes—to remove every barrier between them. But he wanted to go slowly. And so she would, despite the temptation to rush to the best parts.

She melted into him, sighing as he inched the hem of her shirt up past her navel, past her breasts, and over her head. He tossed it aside with a satisfied growl and spun her around to face him. Everywhere he looked—her lips, her shoulders, her hips—heated under his blatantly appreciative gaze.

"Now it's my turn," she said, sliding her hand over the hard planes of his chest and under the collar of his jacket. With deliberate slowness, she pushed the jacket off his broad shoulders, molding her palms to his muscles and flesh. Coyly, she circled behind him, nipping at his neck while she tugged the coat off his arms.

When she would have removed his shirt, he lightly grasped her wrists. "Your trousers are next."

"Very well." She looked directly into his golden eyes as she unbuckled her belt and slid it off. Removing the trousers took a bit more of her attention, but she managed to undo the buttons and shimmy the waistband over her hips while stealing glances at Nash. The rough fabric grazed her thighs and knees, then puddled around her ankles. Smiling shyly, she stepped out of the trousers and was rewarded with a molten kiss.

At last, she lifted his shirt, admiring every inch of skin she exposed. The fuzzy, taut flesh above his waistband. The contoured muscles of his abdomen. The smooth planes of his chest, and his dark, flat nipples. She discarded his shirt and traced the ridges of his torso with her fingers, tasted his salty skin with her tongue.

Meanwhile, Nash pulled the pins from her hair, letting it cascade over her bare shoulders and arms. She couldn't wait to lie with him on the bed, to tangle her legs with his, but he sat on a chair and pulled her close, so that she stood between his thighs.

He reached behind her and pulled the end of her binding free. "I've been waiting all night to do this," he whispered, with something akin to awe. Slowly, he tugged on the silk strip, winding the fabric around his fist as he unwrapped her—like she was a rare and special gift. She spun before him, feeling the cool air and his hot gaze on her increasingly naked skin. With every turn, the binding grew looser, and her breasts felt fuller . . . till the last bit of silk fell away.

"You are gorgeous, Caroline." Nash's face was level

with her breasts, and he greedily took the tip of one into his mouth. He wrapped his arms around her waist, holding her steady despite her wobbly knees.

Her hair fell in a dark curtain around them, and the rest of the world faded away. All that remained were their almost-naked bodies, their fast-beating hearts, and the glorious feelings they stirred in each other. Every time he drew her nipple in his mouth, she arched toward him, wanting more.

As if he felt the same, he effortlessly scooped her into his arms and carried her to his massive bed. They sprawled across it, and he propped his head on an elbow, gazing down at her. "There's no need to rush into anything. We could just lie here, together, for a while."

"We could." She imagined him holding her, kissing her, and playing with her hair. She'd derive hours of enjoyment from that—and from the magnificent view of his handsome face and sculpted torso. "But one thing I've learned from my injury is that we never know what the next day may bring. If you're always waiting on the future, it's easy to miss the joy of the present. I hope that we shall have a few more nights together, but I don't want to waste a single one."

To further argue her point, she arched her breasts to his chest and captured his mouth in a kiss. He growled and flipped onto his back, deftly rolling her on top of him. Her thighs straddled his hips, and even though he still wore his trousers, she felt the hard length of him between her legs. Once she recovered from the shock of sitting astride him, she found it deliciously empowering. And arousing.

He seemed to drink in the sight of her, his languorous gaze lingering on her breasts. With a wicked smile, he grasped her hips and showed her how to move against him, stoking her desire every time she rocked. The fabric of his trousers teased her wet, swollen flesh, increasing the ache in her core. She tried moving slowly, then faster, till she found the rhythm that felt best.

Nash's low moans spurred her on. Neither of them spoke, but their eyes met and locked as their hips moved together. Her hair fell softly around her, tickling her shoulders and the tops of her breasts. He brushed away the long curls and cupped the mounds in his hands, his palms grazing her nipples every time she rocked.

When the pleasure became almost too much to bear, he gently rolled her onto the bed. While she tried to catch her breath, he kissed a path down the side of her neck to the sensitive undersides of her breasts. With his tongue, he traced spirals around the taut peaks, closer and closer, till, at last, he took one nipple in his mouth. He lightly pinched the other, driving her mad with desire.

"Nash," she murmured, desperate to ease the ache inside her. As she ran her fingers through his impossibly thick hair, he moved lower, kissing her belly and circling her navel with his tongue. He settled his body between her thighs, nudging them farther apart. Warm, sure fingers touched her entrance and parted the folds, making way for his mouth.

She gasped at the first pressure of his tongue, sighed with every seductive stroke. She'd never even dreamt that Nash might kiss her there, and shocking as it was, she gave herself up to the pleasure, thrilled that he seemed to enjoy it almost as much as she did.

His low moans vibrated through her in the most delicious way. His fingers filled her as his mouth tasted and teased the spot that seemed to be at the very center of her need. Her thighs clenched, and her body arched as though it were reaching for something very sweet. Something very close.

Suddenly, the pulsing in her core grew stronger and faster, tipping her over the edge of a beautiful precipice. She bit the back of her hand to muffle her cries and surrendered to the inevitable power of it—from the first glorious contractions to the last blissful echoes.

Nash held her tightly through it all. Telling her how lovely she was. Soothing her with warm kisses on the insides of her thighs.

Afterward, he smiled a bit smugly. With his sandy hair adorably disheveled and the stubble on his jaw broodingly dark, he looked every inch the charming rake. And for tonight, he was hers.

He peeled back the counterpane and tenderly lifted her, placing her head on a pillow and tucking her under the blanket—as if he knew that her limbs were loose and heavy. But she was not ready for bed. Or rather, she was not ready for sleeping.

"Will you join me?" she said, surprised by the purr-like quality of her voice.

He grinned and started to slip between the covers. "Of course."

"Wait," she said, frowning slightly. "You're still wearing your trousers."

"That's easily remedied." He quickly unbuttoned them and took them off, revealing narrow hips, tight buttocks, muscular legs—and the hard length of his arousal.

She sat up and met him on the edge of the bed, eager to touch him and give him the pleasure he'd given her. "You're magnificent," she murmured, savoring the sight of him standing naked before her. "May I touch you?"

"Anywhere you like," he growled. "Anytime you like."

She ran her hands over the sculpted contours of his buttocks. Glided her palms over the rock-hard muscles of his thighs. Trailed her fingertips over the ridges of his abdomen. His body was so different from her own. Pure power. Coiled strength.

Tentatively, she curled her fingers around his shaft and glided her palm down, over its smooth, hard length. She paid close attention to the signals Nash gave her. Low groans in his throat. Eyes closed in ecstasy. Involuntary thrusts of his hips.

Confident she was on the right track, she stroked faster, with the pressure and rhythm he seemed to like best—and was rewarded with a muffled curse. "Caroline," he said raggedly. "That feels . . . too good."

Encouraged, she lowered her head and slowly licked the top of his shaft. Took him into her mouth.

"Jesus, Caroline." He moaned and gently caressed her scalp as she tasted him, alternately licking and sucking till she discovered what pleased him most. "You are incredible," he said, gasping. "But you don't have to do this."

Of course she didn't—but she wanted to. And she didn't stop. Not when she heard him utter an oath. Not when she felt his body tremble on the edge of release. And not when he cried out in pleasure.

Spent, Nash climbed into bed, curled his body around hers, and pulled the covers over them. He planted tender kisses along her neck and across her shoulder, sending delicious shivers down her spine. Tucked in their own intimate cocoon, they held each other as their eyelids grew heavy and their breathing slowed.

He'd warned her he was incapable of a deep and abiding love. But this . . . this felt awfully close.

Tomorrow she'd go back to wondering and worrying. He'd go back to sparring and avoiding.

But tonight, everything had felt true and perfect and right. And Caroline wouldn't ever forget it.

# Chapter 14

*"If you truly care for him, you will notice more than his broad shoulders and handsome visage. For few qualities are more desirable in a partner than a beautiful mind."*
—The Debutante's Revenge

Nash stretched and rolled over, reaching for Caroline. The mattress beside him was still warm, and her sweet scent still lingered on the sheets. But she was gone.

Holy hell—he'd slept too long. He'd planned to wake in the wee hours of the morning and carry her back to her bed. Instead, he'd slept the deep, blissful sleep of a child on a long coach ride.

He wished that Caroline had woken him before leaving his bed. So that he could have given her a kiss—a kiss to say everything he couldn't.

That last night had meant something to him.

*She* meant something to him.

And though he could never be the man she deserved, or love her the way she needed him to, they had something special. Maybe her memory would return; maybe it wouldn't. Either way, surely *some* sort of future was possible for them.

He bounded out of bed, scooped up both their disguises from the chair where he'd left them, and wadded everything into a ball which he stuffed into the bottom drawer of his bureau. Eager to shave and dress, he rang for his valet. Hopefully he'd see Caroline at breakfast before he set out for the day—and he was already mentally making plans to meet her again tonight. Secrecy was a necessity, unfortunately, but he was determined to win her over.

And find a way they could be together.

A half hour later, he walked into the breakfast room where Delilah sat, eating alone. "Good morning," he said, taking a seat and pouring himself coffee. He took a bracing gulp of the hot, bitter brew and gestured toward the empty chair at the table. "Where's Caroline?"

"Still abed," Delilah said brightly. "I'm glad she's resting so well. Sleep is surely the best thing for her."

"No doubt," he said, tamping down a niggle of guilt. He and Caroline had been awake till the wee hours of the morning, but at least she was resting now. "I'm glad to have you to myself this morning. I've been wanting to talk with you."

"Really? About what?" She tossed several ringlets of blond hair behind her shoulder, signaling she was already on her guard.

"About my tendency to be protective of you." Delilah arched an expressive brow at that, and he smiled. "Very well. My tendency to be overly protective," he corrected.

She set down her fork and looked at him earnestly. "You were eighteen years of age when you became responsible for me—barely an adult yourself. And I was a girl in the schoolroom. In many ways, you've been more of a father to me than our father ever was."

Nash pressed his lips together. Their father had been controlling but aloof. Never talking or laughing or hugging. Chances were, Nash would turn out the same way. "I've made a lot of mistakes, but all I've ever wanted was to keep you safe and make you happy. After we lost Emily and Father, moving away from town seemed like the best option. We needed that time—to grieve and gather ourselves together without being under the scrutiny of the ton."

"Yes," Delilah agreed. "That makes perfect sense."

"But the longer we stayed away, the less I wanted to return. This house is so full of memories. I climb the stairs and see Emily sliding down the banister. I walk through the garden and hear her laughter." He shrugged helplessly. "So I avoided coming back—and that wasn't fair to you."

Delilah's blue eyes shone with understanding. "Well, we're here now. That's the important thing. All I ask is that you allow me to make my own decisions—and not just about my reading material or the style of my gowns," she added. "I deserve to spend time with the gentleman of my choosing."

Nash's jaw clenched out of sheer habit, and he counted to three in his head before speaking. "I agree, actually. There's nothing that would make me happier than if you were to fall in love and settle down with a good and decent gentleman."

She stared at him through narrowed eyes. "Why do I feel as though there's a *but* to follow?"

"Because finding a good and decent gentleman in

this town could take a while," he said dryly. "I would rather that you not rush into anything. Take a couple of seasons to meet all the eligible bachelors—and to learn their true natures. We've been away from society for a long time, and you've yet to see its underbelly."

"It almost sounds as though you're encouraging me to experience London's darker side," Delilah said warily.

"Not at all," he said firmly. "But I *would* wish for you to go into the marriage mart with your eyes wide open. Men are not always who they seem to be, and there are many who would take advantage of a kind and generous young woman like you."

"I'm not naïve, Nash." She crossed her arms, clearly insulted.

Jesus, he couldn't say anything right.

Delilah continued, her chin lifted and her tone firm. "I am a fairly good judge of character and would never give my heart to a man who didn't deserve it."

He exhaled slowly. "I am glad to hear that."

"But Lord Brondale has given me no reason to distrust him," she argued. "On the contrary. He's courteous, attentive, and respectful—and yet, you don't approve of him."

"I do not," Nash ground out. "I'm sure he puts on a good face in front of you. But there are aspects of his character that you don't know about."

Delilah rolled her eyes in frustration. "Then why don't you tell me what you know? Give me all the pertinent information and allow me to decide for myself whether or not Lord Brondale is deserving of my affections."

Nash pushed his chair away from the table, stood, and paced the length of the breakfast room. Caroline had urged him to be honest with his sister, and he would.

Even though learning the truth about Brondale might break her heart. Better for her to hear it now, before she fell deeper.

"He gambles far too much and is deep in debt," Nash began.

"That describes at least three-quarters of the men in London," Delilah said with a shrug. "Go on."

"He regularly jests that he plans to maintain a life of debauchery as long as he possibly can before taking a wealthy bride," Nash said.

Delilah's face clouded at that. "Perhaps it is simply a jest, as you yourself just said."

"I don't think so," Nash said regretfully. "Brondale is involved in a very unsavory wager. The terms are spelled out in the betting book at my club, and his signature is there, plain for all to see. It's clear from the nature of this bet that he has a complete lack of respect for women."

Delilah's forehead creased. "What sort of wager?"

Nash hesitated. "Suffice it to say that he's a cad for even contemplating it."

"I see." She set her napkin on the table, and Nash detected a slight tremor in her hand.

"I'm sorry, Delilah. It must be hard to hear," he said.

"You've given me plenty to consider," she said softly. "I think I'll go to my room and rest for a bit."

"I'm going out but will return in time for dinner," he said. "Do you have plans?"

"I'll keep Caroline company most of the day. And I have a visit with the modiste this afternoon. I require a few adjustments to the gown I'm wearing to the ball this week." She cast a sideways glance at him. "You haven't forgotten about that, have you?"

"Of course not," he said, only half fibbing.

Delilah shot him a smile that said he wasn't fooling her. "I'm glad we talked, Nash." She rounded the table and pressed a kiss to his cheek before leaving the room.

All in all, the conversation had gone more smoothly than he'd expected.

There'd been no tears, no shouting, no hurling of objects.

He should have felt better—but he didn't.

He had the distinct feeling that, where Delilah was concerned, trouble lay ahead.

It was late morning by the time Caroline rose and dressed. She couldn't stop thinking about her night with Nash. The excitement of escaping the thugs at the Grey Goose. The thrill that shot through her limbs when he reverently unbound her breasts. And, most of all, the hours of pleasure they'd shared in his massive bed.

The whole night had been a grand adventure—one she'd cherish forever.

She made her way downstairs for a light breakfast of tea and toast, then stopped in the drawing room, expecting to see Delilah—but the room was empty. Assuming that she'd find her friend in her bedchamber, Caroline made her way toward Delilah's room—and found it empty too.

A young maid with flaxen hair bustled down the hall carrying a stack of linens. "Miss Delilah went for an early walk in the park," she explained with a smile. "And she's going to the modiste's shop this afternoon. My name's Winnie. Molly asked me to check on you and provide anything you need."

"I'm fine, thank you," Caroline said. "I'll be in my bedchamber if anyone is looking for me."

But as she closed the door to her room, she realized the stark truth.

No one was looking for her. Or, if they were, they had no idea she was staying with the Duke of Stonebridge. But the ad Nash placed yesterday could remedy that.

She opened the door, darted back into the hallway, and saw the maid dusting a small table near the staircase landing. "Actually, Winnie, there *is* something I need. Would you happen to have a copy of this morning's *Hearsay*?"

Winnie cocked her head, thoughtful. "I believe we do, miss. Give me a few moments, if you please, and I'll fetch it for you."

"Thank you," Caroline said sincerely before returning to her room.

Resolved to make the most of her morning, she went directly to the desk, opened the drawer, and pulled out the journal that Delilah had given her. She located a pen, dipped the nib in the ink pot, and stared at the first, creamy page.

The very *blank* page.

How to begin? The first entry in a journal had to be special—for it set the tone for everything that followed. Delilah had encouraged her to write about her memory loss and the feelings Caroline was experiencing as a result, but she was free to write a story or a poem or even a shopping list instead. She let her gaze travel around the room, looking for inspiration, until the stack of papers on her desk caught her attention. Delilah's copies of The Debutante's Revenge.

An odd tingling washed over her skin, and suddenly,

she knew just how to start. She may not have known who she was, but, thanks to the evening she'd spent with Nash, she knew something of love. And, as Delilah had suggested, what better way for Caroline to determine if she was connected to the column than to try her hand at writing one?

*Dear Debutantes,*
*The delight one takes in giving a gift is often as sweet as the joy in receiving one.*
    *And so it is with love.*
    *Seek a partner who is generous—with his time, attention, and affection. Someone who puts your pleasure before his own.*
    *Strive to be equally generous. For nothing is quite so satisfying as seeing a sensuous, sated smile on your partner's face.*

Caroline set down her pen and blinked at the entry she'd written. It had flowed out of her quite easily, but it proved nothing, except, perhaps, that she was rather good at imitating the style of the columns that she'd studied the day before.

Still, it *was* possible—however unlikely—that she was the authoress.

A brisk knock sounded at the door, and Caroline slammed her journal shut. "Come in."

Winnie bustled into the room, a copy of the *London Hearsay* in her hands. "Here you are, miss. Enjoy, and let me know if you'll be needing anything else."

"Thank you, Winnie." Caroline carried the newspaper to the bed where she stretched out and turned to the advertisements.

One ad sought a dog—a setter—who'd strayed from an inn.

Another reported a missing wife described as "thick-set" and "shabbily dressed."

Caroline shuddered, dismayed that her best hope for being reunited with her family hinged on an ad sand-wiched between sad notices about stray dogs and run-away wives.

But there, near the bottom of the page, she found the ad that Nash had placed.

Found: a female of approximately two and twenty years, of average height, with dark brown hair, striking green eyes, and a distinctive birthmark. Due to a head injury, she does not know her name but is otherwise of sound body and mind. Anyone who knows her and can provide proof of her iden-tity shall be handsomely rewarded. Please direct inquiries to Mr. Edmund Drake, Solicitor, Oxford Street.

Caroline pushed aside the paper, rolled onto her back, and stared at the ceiling, fighting to keep tears at bay. There was nothing wrong with the ad Nash had placed. It was exactly as they'd agreed. And yet, reading the ad had felt like a kick to the gut.

She'd been reduced to a scant few lines of text—age, height, hair and eye color, and an odd birthmark. Surely, there was more to her than that.

But as long as she stayed with Nash and Delilah, she was isolated from the rest of the world. Maybe the ad would work as intended, and she'd be home in a day or two. But if it didn't work, she needed a plan.

# Chapter 15

*"It is easy for a gentleman to hang about when all is well. Seek a man who will remain by your side when everything goes awry."*
—*The Debutante's Revenge*

Nash strode into Drake's cluttered office, called out a greeting, and helped himself to a glass of brandy. He'd never seen Drake take a drink himself, but the solicitor kept a decanter at the ready for his friends and clients.

Nash took healthy gulp from his snifter, and without preamble asked, "Have we had any replies to the ad?"

Drake arched a brow and pushed a tidy stack of papers from the center of his desk to the side. "We've had three queries."

"Anything promising?" Nash asked, navigating his way around the stacks of books on Drake's dusty floor. He sank into one of the leather chairs across from his friend's desk, his thoughts jumbled. He wanted Caroline to discover her identity—but he didn't want her to leave.

Drake withdrew a paper from the top right drawer of his desk and consulted a neatly written list. "One is from a vicar who believes the woman might be his daughter, Trudy."

Nash arched a brow. Caroline didn't look like a Trudy. But then, he couldn't imagine her as anyone but Caroline. "Did the vicar provide a description?"

Drake gave a curt nod. "His daughter is with child. About six months along."

Nash gave a firm shake of his head. Ignored the wave of relief that washed over him. "We can rule out the vicar. Who else responded?"

"A couple who owns an inn. They suspect the young lady you described could be a barmaid who worked for them. She went missing a week ago," Drake said, "after stealing all the money in their safe box."

Nash tried to picture Caroline committing the crime and couldn't. "Did they mention her birthmark?"

"They said their barmaid has a dark mole next to her nose."

"Definitely not Caroline." Nash exhaled, glad for the proof that his instincts had been correct. "Who's the last reply from?"

"An elderly baron who claims that, for reasons unbeknownst to him, his governess suddenly abandoned her post." Drake cleared his throat, signaling his skepticism. "Reading between the lines, I'm guessing that the baron had a difficult time keeping his hands to himself."

Nash's thoughts had run along the same lines. So much so that his blood simmered and his fists clenched. "Even if Caroline *were* his governess, I wouldn't tell him. But it might be worth investigating if it helps us discover who her family is. Does he have any evidence?"

"He said he wasn't aware of a birthmark," Drake said.

"It's on her shoulder," Nash admitted. "He wouldn't see it if she routinely wore long-sleeved gowns or shawls."

Drake nodded, thoughtful. "The baron claims to have plenty of samples of her handwriting that we could compare to Caroline's."

"I'll talk to her and see if she wants to pursue the lead. Otherwise, we'll wait to see who else replies."

"Here you are." Drake folded the paper containing all his notes and handed it to Nash. "If we receive any other responses to the ad, I'll notify you at once."

Nash threw back the rest of his drink and balanced the empty snifter on his thigh. "Is it awful of me to admit that I'm not eager for Caroline to remember who she is?"

Drake winced and shot him a sympathetic smile. "It's a little awful of you. But I think I understand. You have feelings for her and don't want her to go."

"It's not that simple," Nash grumbled. "She could recover her memory tomorrow and walk out of my house—my *life*—never to return again."

"Ever the optimist, aren't you?" Drake ribbed. "Of course, there's the possibility that Caroline will leave. But no matter who she turns out to be, she'll be more likely to stay if she knows how you feel."

Nash muttered a curse. "What if *I* don't know how I feel?"

Drake chuckled. "You might need to dig deeper, my friend."

Nash shook his head firmly. "I don't have the luxury of losing my head over a woman. I have responsibilities to my estate and to Delilah. For her sake, I need to be steady and solid. I'm the only family she has left, and I can't—won't—risk doing something foolish, even if I am drawn to Caroline." Look where all-consuming passion had gotten Emily. She and their father were dead, and Nash and Delilah had an awful, gaping hole in their lives.

"You're right to be cautious," Drake said. "But though I haven't yet met Caroline, I have the sense she's special. I've never seen you like this. Perhaps she *is* worth the risk."

Nash shook his head, grim. He could try to make her happy. He could try to convince her to stay. But he couldn't give her his heart without dredging up demons.

Demons that were best left alone.

At dinner that evening, Caroline endeavored not to stare at Nash but was not entirely successful. A deep green jacket stretched across his broad shoulders and his amber eyes sparked in the candlelight. The dark slashes of his brows seemed more expressive than usual, and every glance he sent her held the promise of wicked delights—which made it difficult to focus on her steaming bowl of clam chowder.

Earlier that afternoon, he'd stopped by her room briefly on his way to dress for dinner. He'd said there had been no credible replies to the ad but promised to tell her more that night when they were alone. The stab of disappointment she felt was eased with the hope that more people would reply in the days to come. In the meantime, she had another evening with Nash to look forward to, a deliciously wicked thought that heated her blood.

She fanned herself with her napkin and took a fortifying sip of wine before looking across the table at Delilah, who wore a fetching pale green dress and an effervescent smile.

"How was your outing to the modiste?" Caroline asked.

Delilah's cheeks glowed pink. "Lovely. My gown will be ready the day after next—just in time for the ball."

"I can't wait to see you in it," Caroline exclaimed.

"I wish that you could join us," Delilah said. "I shall feel awful going out, knowing you are left here alone."

"You mustn't give me a second thought," Caroline replied. "I plan to spend a pleasant evening reading in the library—and perhaps writing in my journal."

Nash glanced at her from across the table, curious. "You have a journal?"

"Delilah gave it to me," Caroline said, smiling. "I've been writing a bit, hoping it will help jar my memory."

"That's excellent." Nash's voice was deliciously low and smooth, and yet, Caroline had detected a hint of hesitation. "Delilah and I will definitely miss you at the ball. But, with my sister on my arm, I'm sure I'll be the envy of every man there."

A strawberry stain crept up Delilah's neck. "That reminds me," she said, fluttering one hand over her chest. "While I was out today, I happened to see Lord Brondale, and he asked whether he might be permitted to call on me tomorrow."

Nash's fork froze halfway to his mouth. "And you told him *no*." It was half question, half statement.

Delilah shrugged her slender shoulders and winced. "Actually, I told him that he would be welcome."

Nash's knife clattered on his plate and a chill slithered up Caroline's spine. "Damn it, Delilah. What were you thinking?"

"That it might be nice to have a gentleman caller for once," she retorted. "That I'd enjoy experiencing the sorts of things that other young ladies do—like entertaining a handsome beau."

Nash's brows shot halfway up his forehead. "I warned you about Brondale. Explained why he's not right for you. And now you're telling me he's your *beau*?"

Delilah threw up her hands, flustered. "Perhaps. I don't know. The point is that I would like to find out."

"What about the wager?" Nash demanded.

"For all I know, he made that bet months ago—before he met me. People are capable of change, you know."

Caroline knew better than to step into the middle of a sibling argument but couldn't help herself. She turned to Nash, confident he'd listen to reason. "It's admirable that you wish to protect your sister, but surely no harm would result from a brief, chaperoned visit by Lord Brondale."

"And you know this because of your own vast experience?" he asked dryly.

Her stomach sank. "I don't pretend to be an expert on such matters."

"It certainly seems that way." Nash unleashed the force of his golden gaze on her, but she refused to cower.

"I merely presented another point of view," she said deliberately. "In an effort to contribute to the discussion."

"And I appreciate it," Delilah chimed in. To Nash, she said, "If I'm not permitted to have callers, I shall never have suitors. And if I never have suitors, then . . ."

Nash blinked slowly and inhaled as though trying to rein in his temper. "Do you want to know what I think?"

Caroline straightened in her chair. "I feel sure you are about to tell us, Your Grace."

"You and Delilah have been spending too much time reading that column—'The Vengeful Debutante.'"

Caroline swallowed hard, momentarily speechless. For reasons she couldn't explain, his disdain for the column felt intensely personal—like a dagger to her heart.

"It's called The Debutante's Revenge," Delilah corrected.

"Call it what you will. It's filled your head with fanciful, romantic notions."

"So what if it has?" Caroline ventured. "Is it so terrible—to long for a bit of romance or passion in one's life?"

"*Yes*, actually," Nash shouted, rattling the crystal. He pressed his lips together, regaining a thread of composure before continuing. "It *is* terrible. And worse, it's dangerous."

Caroline made fists so tight that her fingernails bit into the flesh of her palms. "That is the most ridiculous thing I've ever heard."

"I have half a mind to burn every last column that Delilah has stashed away in her bedchamber."

Delilah pinned him with her gaze. "You wouldn't."

"Don't test me, Delilah. Brondale will *not* enter this house," Nash ground out. "And I forbid either one of you from speaking his name or discussing this matter further."

Caroline's hackles rose. *Forbid?* How dare he.

"Am I understood?" he demanded.

Delilah tossed her hair over her shoulder and glared. "Perfectly."

"Caroline?" he prodded.

Her throat constricted and her hand trembled as she set down her fork. She'd thought she could trust Nash—not only with her body but also with her heart.

Now, during the course of their one and only real

argument, he'd disparaged the column—the same one she felt strangely connected to. He'd ridiculed her beliefs—the very same ones that had driven her into his arms. Belittling the idea that women should be free to seek love and expect to be equal partners in their relationships.

And he'd stubbornly refused to debate the matter with her.

She wanted to scream, and now he was waiting for her to meekly accept the edict he'd issued. But she'd be damned before she capitulated.

"I understand you quite well," she said, her voice raw and raspy but still dripping with sarcasm. "You do not think that Delilah is capable of choosing her own beau. You mock a column that aspires to empower young women. You expect blind obedience from the women who live under your roof." She glared at him while she caught her breath. "Have I missed anything, Your Grace?"

Nash crossed his arms, stretching the fine fabric of his jacket to its limits and looking vexingly handsome despite his infuriating pompousness. "That's not fair."

"What's not *fair* is your utter arrogance. And neither Delilah nor I will tolerate it." She stood, tossed her napkin on the table, and rushed from the dining room before he could see the tears spilling down her cheeks.

She'd thought she knew Nash. But perhaps she'd only seen the side of him she wished to see. Maybe the injury to her head had impaired her judgment along with her memory.

Because she could never be with a man who mocked the ideas that meant so much to her.

And after all they'd shared, she couldn't stay. She was leaving Nash. Tonight.

# Chapter 16

*"If you go in search of the perfect gentleman, you
are destined for disappointment. Look, instead, for
the man who is perfect for you."*
                                    —*The Debutante's Revenge*

Nash scrubbed the back of his head as Delilah stormed
out of the dining room, right on Caroline's heels.

Bloody hell. One minute they'd been discussing Delilah's trip to the modiste, and the next he'd spun out of
control and ended up looking like a complete ass.

Probably because he'd been acting like one. Shit.

He'd spent the afternoon trying to plan the perfect
night for him and Caroline.

And instead, he'd spoiled everything. She *and* Delilah detested him.

He waited a quarter of an hour, figuring everyone
could use some time to cool off. But he'd made the
mess, and now he needed to fix it—somehow. Since he'd
lashed out at his sister first, he began by knocking on her
door.

"Go away." Delilah's voice was muffled, like her head
was buried under a pillow.

"We need to talk," he said.

"You mean *you* want to talk. And you expect *me* to listen." She wasn't wrong, damn it.

He hesitated. "What if I promise to listen too?"

For several seconds, she didn't reply. Then, he heard her shuffling toward the door, sniffling and hiccupping, making him feel approximately two inches tall. She opened the door, revealing her splotchy face and red-rimmed eyes. Hell. The sight of her—so sad and defeated—was a punch to his gut. This was Delilah, his irrepressibly cheerful sister. The one who could brighten any room just by smiling.

And he'd made her absolutely miserable.

"May I come in?"

She nodded and stepped aside.

"I'm sorry," he said.

"About what?" She spun toward him and planted her hands on her hips. "That I'm no longer a little girl you can keep locked up?"

He shot her an apologetic smile. "It was easier, then."

She paced the length of her bedchamber, fuming. "You're convinced it's such a big, bad world out there."

"It can be." He knew better than anyone.

"I don't believe that it's all bad. I know you still miss Emily. I do too." Delilah's voice cracked with emotion— an ache that echoed in his chest. "But do you think she'd want to see us arguing like this? Do you think she'd want us to live our lives by half measures? Because I think that nothing would have made our sister sadder." She sank into a chair and held her head in her hands.

He lowered himself onto the footstool opposite her, so that they were at eye level. Her sleek hair twist appeared to have lost its fight with her pillow and her dress was wrinkled. With her fair curls falling around her face and her eyes puffy from crying, she looked younger than her eighteen years.

But she was right. About everything.

"For the last five years, it's been only you and me." He reached for her hand and sandwiched it between his. "I suppose I wanted things to stay that way, even if I knew they couldn't."

"I know you want to protect me. It's only natural that you would after we lost half our family."

He swallowed the lump in his throat. "Do you remember the way Emily hummed to herself while she worked on her needlepoint?"

"It drove you mad," Delilah recalled. "She knew that, of course. It's why she did it."

"You remind me a little of her," he admitted. "Like you, she said exactly what she was thinking, and her face showed everything she was feeling. Did you know she cried every time she went to the opera? She never took her own handkerchief with her, so she'd steal mine right out of my pocket. I'd grumble about it, but the truth was . . . I loved that she counted on me. For the little things and the big things." He paused, waiting for the pounding in his head and heart to subside. "I miss her," he choked out.

"I know. I do too." Delilah leaned forward and pulled him into a hug. "But I'm not her, Nash. I'm not going anywhere."

"You mean until you fall in love and marry."

"You needn't sound so morose," she said, chuckling through her tears. "In case you haven't noticed, I have no suitors at the moment. Zero."

"You will have plenty," Nash said dryly.

She sat back and shot him a watery smile. "Even after I'm married, I'll need my brother. And I will always be here, should you need me."

"You really *have* grown up, Delilah." He pressed a kiss to the back of her hand. "I'm sorry it's taken me a while to realize that."

"Better late than never. At least I'm not on the shelf yet."

He grinned at her. "No, I don't think you're destined for spinsterhood." More soberly, he added, "I still don't approve of Brondale, and I've told you the reasons why."

"No one is perfect, Nash. And people can change— especially when they find someone worth changing for." She looked at him from beneath her tear-spiked lashes. "Maybe Caroline is that person for you."

He rolled his shoulders, wishing Delilah weren't so damned perceptive. "I'm a lost cause," he said, only half jesting. "But I *will* try to be reasonable about where you go and who you see."

"Does that mean that Lord Brondale may call on me tomorrow?" she asked, transparently hopeful.

An image of the betting book containing Brondale's vile wager loomed in Nash's head. Every instinct screamed for him to forbid the marquess from visiting his sister. But he'd made a promise. "He may call on you *if* you have a chaperone. But, Delilah, I know in my gut he's not the right man for you. I'm asking you to trust me on this."

She stared at him for several heart-wrenching seconds, then blew out a long breath. "Very well. Let us hope that I meet a few eligible young men at the ball on Wednesday. And then, let us pray that there is at least *one* among them who is acceptable to you and not abhorrent to me."

"I feel certain we'll be able to find some common ground." He kissed her forehead and stood.

"Have you talked to Caroline yet?" Delilah worried her lower lip.

"No. You were at the top of my list of apologies. She is next."

Delilah yawned, exhaustion plain on her face. "I'm going to ring for Molly and turn in early tonight. But I hope you can make things right with Caroline. I adore you both and hate to see you feuding, but if I am forced to pick a side . . ."

"Traitor." He gave her a wink before heading to the corridor and closing the door behind him. He'd managed to patch things up with Delilah. Surely, he could do the same with Caroline.

When he reached her bedchamber, he found the door slightly ajar but paused to straighten his cravat and gather his wits. He couldn't mess this up, damn it.

He blew out a long breath and knocked softly.

When she didn't respond, he tried again—a bit louder.

Still no answer.

"Caroline?" He pushed the door open a few inches and peered into the room. The bed was perfectly made. The desk immaculate.

He burst inside, scanning every nook.

Caroline was gone.

His stomach dropped through his knees. She hadn't left a note on the desk or the bed. Surely, she wouldn't have left without saying goodbye. No, she was probably downstairs in the library. Or maybe she'd gone looking for him in his study. That would be just like her—to seek him out so she could give him the dressing-down he deserved.

Yes, he'd wager Caroline was in the library, plotting all the ways she was going to make him miserable until he begged for forgiveness. He wouldn't even mind. The truth was, there was no one he'd rather have torture him than Caroline.

He took two strides toward the door, then drew up short next to her bedside table.

She had only one possession from her prior life, and it was in the drawer of that nightstand, unless . . .

Heart racing, he pulled open the drawer. Found it empty.

She'd taken the bag with her, which meant she wasn't in the library or even the study.

Caroline was gone.

Caroline swiped at her eyes as she walked down the street, clutching her bag to her chest. She'd only walked a few blocks, but the enormity of what she'd done had already begun to sink in. She was a young woman with no name, no money, and no home, walking through the streets of London. Alone.

She should have asked Delilah if she could borrow some money, but she would have begged Caroline to stay, and refusing those pleading blue eyes of hers would have been far too difficult. So Caroline had grabbed the few coins she possessed and slipped out of the back door, determined to find a boardinghouse where she could stay until she found some sort of position—as a companion or governess or maid. The neighborhood was as unfamiliar to her as the rest of her life, so she would have to ask a stranger about possible places to stay.

For now, however, she walked, taking long, sure strides that helped her burn off her anger while also putting distance between her and Nash. She cursed him for not being the man she'd hoped he was, and she cursed herself for being so naïve. For giving him her heart.

Leaving him was no doubt the best course of action. But the ache in her chest made it difficult to breathe. Night had fallen, and a chilly breeze raised the goose-flesh on her arms. She hadn't brought a shawl—it was bad enough that she'd run off wearing Delilah's gown. All Caroline had with her was the bag containing a few coins and her journal.

Half a block ahead, two elegantly dressed women and a tall gentleman ambled down the pavement toward an awaiting carriage. Dressed in evening finery, they looked as though they were heading to a ball or the opera. Caroline walked a little faster as she debated whether to approach them. Chances were, they would take her in for the night, and that was all she really needed. In the morning, when her head was clearer, she'd begin looking for a place to stay and for some sort of work.

A footman opened the door of the carriage, and the trio began climbing in. Caroline opened her mouth to call out to them, then stopped. If she ran away, she'd be doing exactly what she'd accused Nash of doing—avoiding the pain and refusing to do the work of healing and growing.

Blast. She paused and leaned against a brick wall, inhaling deeply.

"Caroline!" Nash's voice shot through the night air, lancing her heart. He'd come searching for her. And after all they'd shared the night before, she couldn't turn her back on him. Not without hearing what he had to say.

She pushed herself off the wall and walked toward him slowly.

His boots slapped the pavement as he ran closer, gasping for air. When he stopped beside her, his expression was a mix of anguish and disbelief. "Where are you going?"

She gazed into his amber eyes, determined the vulnerability she saw there wouldn't weaken her resolve. "I had no specific destination. I only knew I couldn't stay with you."

He flinched as though she'd slapped him. "You have no place to go. It's not safe for you to be walking around town on your own."

"I'm grateful for all you and Delilah have done for me. But we both knew that I would eventually have to leave."

"Not like this," he countered. "You have no plan and no money."

"You are not responsible for me," she said evenly. "You've fulfilled any obligation you had."

He swallowed, his face sober. "Is that what you think, Caroline? That you are an obligation?"

"I don't know what I am to you," she tossed back, lifting her chin.

He drew in a deep breath. "Look, before, at dinner— I was an ass. I've already made amends with Delilah. Return to the house with me. Give me the chance to apologize and tell you how I feel and how . . . you're changing me."

She knew how difficult those words had been for him, but the ones he'd spoken at dinner still echoed in her head. "I'm not certain anything you say can make a difference," she said sadly.

"Please," he said, his voice ragged. "If you still want

to leave in the morning, I'll take you to a damned board-inghouse and pay your first month's rent. But I hope you'll change your mind."

His honey-colored eyes warmed her from the inside out and melted her traitorous heart. "I'll go back to the house," she said softly. "And I will listen. That's all I'm promising."

# Chapter 17

*"Friendly games (such as cards, cricket, and cro-
quet) provide welcome opportunities for the sexes
to mingle. Never hide your skills in an attempt to
boost a gentleman's pride. No matter the contest,
you must play to win."*

—*The Debutante's Revenge*

Nash's nerves buzzed throughout the walk back to his
town house. When he offered Caroline his arm, she refused it, clutching her bag to her chest like she was
headed to the gallows. He needed to find the right
words—to apologize and convince her to stay. But since
he was approximately as skilled with words as he was
at needlepoint, it wouldn't be easy. And a part of him
knew it shouldn't be.

Neither he nor Caroline spoke during the several-
block walk, but the tension between them was palpable—
a mixture of anger and hurt laced with a dangerous dose
of attraction.

When they reached his front step, he ushered her
through the front door and waved away his curious but-

ler. "Thank you, Stodges. That will be all for tonight."
To Caroline, he said, "Come with me?"

She nodded serenely and followed him to the first floor
and down the corridor to his study. Tucked in a back corner of the house, the room afforded a measure of privacy and a view of the garden.

He paused at the threshold and turned to her. "I
prepared a few things earlier today. It may seem presumptuous of me. Hell, in hindsight, it was *entirely*
presumptuous, but well . . . you'll see." He opened the
door and watched as she entered the room, trying to
view it from her eyes. Moonlight streamed through the
open curtains, bathing everything in a bluish glow. A
thick quilt covered the floor in front of the dormant fireplace. A heap of jewel-toned silk pillows spilled over
one side of the quilt and a large picnic basket sat on the
other.

Caroline took two steps into the room and stopped.
"What is this?"

"It was meant to be a surprise. For you," he added, in
case it wasn't absolutely clear.

She nodded, but her body seemed coiled and ready to
spring.

"Why did you leave?" he asked.

She shifted her gaze away from him, set her bag on a
table, and crossed her arms. "You know why."

He paced behind her, wishing he could see her eyes.
"I know I behaved like a boor at dinner. I shouldn't have
spoken so harshly, and I owe you an apology."

"An apology won't change anything. Your view of the
world is too different from mine."

He rubbed the back of his neck. "How do you know?"

"Based on the way you treat Delilah. You wish to control her."

"I wish to *protect* her," he corrected.

At last, she spun to face him, her green eyes sparking. "Isn't it the same thing? You don't trust her to make her own decisions, which means you wouldn't trust me to make mine, and I . . . I cannot be with someone who doesn't trust me."

Nash muttered a curse, slumped into one of the chairs beside his desk, and gestured toward the other. "Will you sit? Please?"

She carefully navigated her way to the chair, skirting around his legs as though any incidental contact might burn. She lowered herself onto the seat and stared at him, her beautiful face impassive.

"I want to tell you something." He rubbed the back of his neck and rolled his shoulders as if he were preparing to run the gauntlet. "It might help to explain why I'm so protective of Delila."

She nodded, encouraging him to go on.

"Five years ago, Emily and I were the same age as Delilah. I've already told you how close we were. Even during the years I was away at school, she wrote to me regularly, keeping me apprised of all her adventures."

"What sorts of adventures?"

He smiled, ignoring the tightness in his chest. "Once, at a musicale, she played a different song from the rest of the quartet, just so Father would despair of her ever becoming an accomplished violinist and allow her to cease her lessons."

"Did it work?"

"It did." He chuckled. "Another time, when she was supposed to be confined to her room, she snuck out of her window, climbed down the trellis, and met her friend at Gunter's for ice cream."

"I think I would have liked her," Caroline said with a smile.

"Everybody did. Wherever she went, there was lively conversation—and, usually, spirited debate. She received countless invitations and accepted most of them. She was friendly with men and women, young and old alike. Many gentlemen vied for her hand . . . but she only had eyes for one."

"Delilah told me about Emily's beau—and that your father didn't approve of him because he was a barrister."

"Right." Nash blew out a long breath. "Emily confided in me and told me about her plans to elope—every detail. I didn't like the idea of her running away. I knew our father would be irate, and I was always trying to make peace between them. Even so, I didn't attempt to discourage her; I knew it would be pointless."

Caroline sat forward, leaning her elbows on her knees. "Probably so."

"The night before she was going to elope, my father became suspicious that something was afoot. Emily had been less argumentative than usual and had passed up a night at the theatre saying she wanted to rest. He called me into his study—where we're sitting now—and begged me to tell him what she had planned." Nash swallowed the knot in his throat. "He pleaded with me to reveal what I knew. Told me that Emily's entire future hung in the balance and that if I loved her, I would help him stop her from making a terrible mistake."

"Oh, Nash." Caroline reached for his hand and squeezed it.

"I laughed and said I didn't know a thing." Nash hung

his head and continued in a hoarse whisper. "I told him he was imagining things and that she'd never do something so reckless. I lied to him."

"You were trying to protect her," Caroline said, in a valiant attempt to comfort him. But nothing could absolve him of his guilt. Nothing could bring Emily and their father back. He'd lived with that pain for five years. It was as much a part of him as an arm or a foot—and it never went away.

"I knew about the rash of highway robberies going on at that time but convinced myself that no harm would come to her. She'd wed the man she loved and return to London; eventually, Father would forgive her. But it didn't turn out that way."

Caroline's eyes welled. "I'm sorry."

Now that Nash had started to tell the story, he felt compelled to finish it—no matter how agonizing it proved. "Emily left in the middle of the night. The next morning, when my father found the note she'd left, he charged out of the house, determined to catch her before she reached Gretna Green. When I learned he'd set out after her, I saddled my horse and went after him."

"Delilah didn't tell me that part."

Nash shook his head. "That's because she doesn't know. By the time I caught up to my father, one highwayman was dead, the rest were fleeing. My father was shot in the stomach, taking his last breaths. He used every ounce of strength he had left to speak, and he asked one thing of me—he begged me to leave him and rescue Emily from the overturned coach."

Caroline caressed his cheek, her eyes reflecting his pain.

"She was alive when I pulled her out of the coach." He closed his eyes as if it were just that easy to erase the memories of mangled bodies and twisted wreckage. "I held her and told her I was taking her home. She smiled and said she couldn't stay. I didn't know what the hell she was talking about. Or maybe I did and didn't want to believe it. She said that her Henry was gone, and she had to go too. She asked me to forgive her and then . . . she faded away."

A tear trickled down Caroline's cheek. "I'm so sorry."

"If I'd told my father the truth about Emily's plans, they'd both still be here. Maybe he'd have eventually permitted her to marry Henry and they'd have a babe or two by now."

"Don't. You mustn't torture yourself." Caroline ducked her head, forcing him to look into her soulful green eyes. "I can't imagine how much you miss your father and Emily. But you are *not* to blame for what happened to them."

"I disagree." Nash dragged his hands down his face and sighed. "But now, I'm Delilah's guardian. She is full of the same romantic notions that Emily was at her age. That's the reason I go to such extremes."

"It's understandable—and admirable—you'd want to keep her safe," Caroline said. "But Delilah is her own person. The more control you attempt to exert over her, the more she'll struggle to be free."

Nash stood, paced the length of the study, and stopped in front of the window, where tiny drops of rain ran down the glass. "I know. Delilah said something similar. I told her I wouldn't stop her from seeing Brondale, and I won't. But I don't have to be happy about it."

"That's true," Caroline said sympathetically.

"It's no excuse for the way I behaved tonight, though." He turned to face her again. "I'm sorry."

She nodded, thoughtful. He was doing his best where Delilah was concerned, and what he lacked in parenting skills, he was trying to make up for with sheer effort and brotherly love. But his treatment of Delilah was only half of the problem.

"Why do you hate The Debutante's Revenge?" she asked.

"I don't," he admitted. He walked to his desk and sat on the edge. "Not really. It's fairer to say I resent it."

"Why would you resent a newspaper column?" she asked, incredulous.

"Because it seems Delilah trusts it more than she trusts me," he said bitterly. "She'd rather take advice from the anonymous author of an advice column than from her own brother."

"I'm sure that's not true." Caroline stood and leaned against the desk, so close that their shoulders brushed lightly. "Perhaps she values both points of view."

"Maybe so," he said, doubtful. "But the truth is that all I can do is tell her how I feel."

"Without losing your temper," Caroline added.

"Or acting like a prig," he said with a wry smile. "Which, you must admit, is a pretty tall order."

Her face softened, and she leaned into him. "I feel certain you're up to the task."

"Does that mean you forgive me?" he asked, hopeful.

She hesitated for a heartbeat. "Yes. And I'm glad you told me about Emily. I'm glad we're talking about . . . everything."

He exhaled as though a sack of grain had been lifted

off his chest. He'd told Caroline the truth, and she was still there. At least for now.

But there was so much unresolved, so much unknown. "We had a few responses to the ad today," he said, noting her slight gasp. "Nothing promising, though. One man thought you could be his runaway governess and requested a handwriting sample, but I'm thinking there was probably a good reason his governess fled."

Caroline nodded sadly. "True. If he returns, we could request that he leave a sample with us. That way we could conduct our own test to see if there's a match rather than trusting his word."

"A good plan," Nash said, impressed that she'd thought of a way to confirm or disprove her potential connection to the man without revealing herself. He hesitated a moment, then added, "Even if you *did* happen to be his governess, I wouldn't let him force you to return to his employ. You don't need to go back to any life that you're unhappy with."

"I'll remember that," she said, gratitude shining in her eyes. "But I'm not sure any of us can truly escape the past. I'll find out who I am eventually—and then I'll need to face that reality, whatever it is."

"I'll be here to help," he said sincerely, "if you want it."

Caroline gazed at Nash's face, which somehow looked even more handsome now with a hint of vulnerability flashing in his eyes. He'd opened up to her and given her a glimpse of the guilt and sorrow he'd been carrying on his shoulders for five long years. No wonder he was protective of Delilah.

She tilted her head, thoughtful. "May I ask another question?"

"Of course."

She waved a hand at the inviting quilt and pillows on the floor. "What's all this?"

"It was meant to be a romantic evening." He looked down at his boots, charmingly unsure of himself. "I thought that after being cooped up in the house for several days, you might enjoy a picnic."

"Oh." Her heart fluttered.

"I'd planned for us to take everything out to the garden, but it's started to rain. Not surprising, considering the way my evening has gone."

"Why don't we have the picnic here?" Caroline ventured. "I bet if we opened the window a bit, we'd be able to feel the breeze without letting the rain in. We might even be able to smell the rosebushes."

Nash inclined his head and smiled. "You might be right," he said, before crossing the room in three strides and opening the window.

She slipped off her shoes, sat next to the basket, and stretched out her legs. "You *can* feel the breeze. It's lovely."

"I want you to know something, Caroline." He remained in front of the window, where the moonlight threw his handsome face into sharp relief. "Last night meant something to me."

Her belly flipped. "It meant something to me too."

"I know that you plan to leave here eventually," he said, his voice unusually gruff. "But will you promise not to leave without saying goodbye?"

He looked so earnest, so hopeful, that she couldn't deny him. "I promise."

"Good," he said, stretching out on the blanket beside her. "Now we can relax and enjoy my first ever indoor picnic."

Caroline shivered in anticipation. A light breeze ruffled the wisps of hair at her neck, and crickets outside chirped a seductive lullaby. If she ignored the ceiling and walls and the furniture in the study, she could imagine she and Nash were in a field, lying under the stars.

He lit a lantern, turned the flame low, and set it to the side of the quilt. "Are you going to open the basket?" he asked, his eyes crinkling in amusement.

"Yes!" She rubbed her palms together and flipped open the basket's hinged lid. A soft checkered cloth covered the contents, so she pushed it aside before reaching in.

On top was a small bunch of yellow and white wildflowers tied with an emerald green ribbon. She held them to her nose and inhaled deeply. "They're lovely."

He shot her an uncharacteristically sheepish smile. "The ribbon matches your eyes."

"Very observant of you, Your Grace," she teased. She carefully pulled out a wine bottle and two glasses and handed them to Nash. Next, she retrieved an endless variety of fruits, sandwiches, and cakes. "This is more than we could eat in a week."

He shrugged. "I included a little of everything."

"It all looks and smells delicious. Thank you," she said, touched.

"There's more." He inclined his head toward the basket.

She reached into the basket once more, pulling out a small box. "A gift?" she asked, not bothering to hide her surprise.

"I wanted you to have something your own," he explained. "Something that's not borrowed, but just for you."

"That's very sweet." Her fingers tingled as she opened the box. Inside, a breathtakingly beautiful silver necklace glistened on a bed of blue velvet. Suspended from the delicate chain was a graceful swan.

"Nash," she whispered. "It's exquisite."

"It's meant to remind you of our night at the tavern," he said softly. "Except instead of a grey goose, it's a silver swan. I suppose that's cheating a bit, but you and I will know what it represents. Do you like it?"

She nodded, not trusting herself to speak.

He helped her put it on, and she fingered the beautiful swan as it rested against her chest. "I love it even more now that I know it's a goose. Thank you, Nash. For everything."

With a knee-melting smile, he uncorked the wine, splashed some into the two glasses, and handed her one. "To indoor picnics," he said, raising his glass. "And second chances."

Caroline clinked her glass to his and took a sip, resolving to enjoy the rest of the night.

"Let's play a game," he suggested.

She arched a brow. "What kind of game?" Nash wasn't exactly the sort to play charades.

He chuckled and held up a hand like he'd been falsely accused. "Nothing wicked. I promise."

"I'm listening," she said, amused.

"I propose we slice up all the fruit and take turns feeding bites to each other."

She gave him a knowing smile. "I fail to see how that qualifies as a game."

"Whoever's tasting the fruit has to close their eyes and guess what kind it is." His amber eyes glowed with an enthusiasm that was contagious.

"Very well. Challenge accepted."

Despite Nash's assurances that the game would not be wicked, it wasn't at all proper—definitely not the sort of parlor game that respectable matrons would have approved of.

When Caroline closed her eyes, Nash brushed a juicy peach slice across her lips; but when she would have eaten the fruit, he moved it away. And when he brought it back to her mouth, his fingers lingered near her lips, tempting her to nip at him. Likewise, when he closed his eyes, Caroline deliberately squeezed the ripe strawberry she lifted to his mouth. And when juice dripped down his chin, she licked it off.

Before long, the game turned into a kiss so sweet and tender that it curled her toes.

"I'm glad you came back," he murmured against her cheek.

"I am too," she said truthfully.

"Do you feel better now?"

"Yes. Just tired," she replied. "Tired, but happy."

"You know," he mused. "One of the best parts of picnicking is the post-meal nap."

"Is that so?"

"Absolutely." He set aside their wineglasses, wrapped up the remaining food, and moved the basket off the quilt. Then he tossed a couple of silk pillows behind them and patted one. "Lie down."

The plump pillow looked too inviting to refuse, and she sighed as her head sank into the softness. Nash rested his head next to hers, mirroring her pose.

"Now we'll play the nap game," he whispered.

"What are the rules?" she asked with a yawn.

"Your lack of knowledge regarding picnic games is

appalling," he quipped. "The first one who falls asleep is the winner, of course. You receive bonus points for snoring."

"I think I shall excel at this particular game." Her eyelids were already growing heavy.

"I like a formidable opponent." He pulled a corner of the quilt over her and gently brushed the hair away from her face. "While you're beating me at the napping game, I shall protect you and our picnic basket."

Her eyes fluttered shut, and she smiled against the smooth satin pillow. "From what?"

"Everything." He ran his fingers through her hair, lightly caressing her head. "Ants, squirrels, bears . . ."

"Bears?" she said with a yawn.

He kissed her forehead. "Good night, Caroline."

# Chapter 18

*"Enjoy the occasional lapse in propriety—share a delicious secret, dance in your nightgown, throw caution to the wind."*
                                        —The Debutante's Revenge

The next afternoon, Delilah peeked out of Caroline's bedroom window onto the street below. "Lord Brondale's on the doorstep now," she said, cheeks glowing with excitement. "Are you sure you won't join us in the drawing room? I'd love for you to meet him."

Caroline shook her head regretfully. "I wish I could, but the fewer people who know I'm here, the better. There are many who'd judge me harshly for staying here unchaperoned. And they'd judge you harshly too, just by association."

"That seems rather petty, considering the injury you suffered." Delilah made a face as she checked her hair in the looking glass and smoothed her sprigged muslin gown. "But I'm sure you're correct. Molly will be with me downstairs—I promised Nash that Lord Brondale's visit would be very proper, and so it shall. I'll tell you all about it later."

"I can't wait," Caroline said, smiling.

"How do I look?" Delilah asked, uncharacteristically nervous.

"Beautiful—as always. Enjoy yourself."

Delilah squeezed her shoulders gratefully and headed toward the drawing room, leaving Caroline alone—and free to dwell on her night with Nash.

After a rocky beginning, she'd had a lovely evening with him. But there was still much she needed to say to him. And more she needed him to reveal to her.

Today, Nash was meeting with his friend Drake, and he'd promised to share any new responses to the ad when he came to her later that night. She was eager to hear any promising leads—but nervous too. Her relationship with Nash was new and fragile as a blossom, and it wouldn't take much of a storm to scatter its petals to the wind.

She told herself that if she and Nash were meant to be together, they'd find a way—no matter who she was. And that made her feel slightly better about the decision she'd made—to leave soon, whether she'd regained her memory or not.

Making the decision had been difficult, but she sensed that telling Nash would be even more so.

Feeling at loose ends, she went to the desk, pulled out her journal, and began to write.

*Dear Debutantes,*
*Romantic relationships consist of more than*
*breathless waltzes, moonlit gardens, and tender*
*kisses. They require an equal measure of*
*heartfelt talks, sincere apologies, and second*
*chances.*

*In short, sometimes your handsome prince
may behave like a toad.*

*Occasionally, you (the fair princess) may act
like a witch.*

*But, if you are willing to face the dragons
together, you just might reach your happy ever
after.*

Caroline stared at the passage, amazed that the salu-
tation and the rest had poured out of her effortlessly. Once
again, she'd instinctively written a letter in the style of
The Debutante's Revenge.

Of course, it was entirely possible she was merely
mimicking the columns she'd read.

But it was *also* possible she was the authoress.

A new column was scheduled to appear in the paper
three days from now. But if the column wasn't there as
expected, it could be a clue.

Specifically, a clue that the authoress had failed to
meet her deadline. Illness or a holiday could be to blame,
or the lapse could be due to something rather more
unusual—such as memory loss.

Nash knocked softly on Caroline's bedroom door just
before midnight.

She opened it wearing a long, white nightgown—so
soft and ethereal that it stole the breath from his lungs.
Her long dark hair hung over her shoulder in a thick
braid, and her curious gaze flicked to the cloak draped
over his arm. "Nash," she breathed. "Come in."

He closed the door behind him and offered her the
cloak that had belonged to his sister. "Would you like to

go for a walk? I've never been to the park at night, but I imagine we'll have it all to ourselves."

"That sounds lovely." She flashed him a warm smile as she took the cloak and ran her fingers over the fine silver-braided trim. "Where did you get this?"

"It was Emily's." Opening the doors of her armoire had been like releasing a floodgate of emotions, both happy and sad—but at least he was feeling *something*, for a change.

Caroline gazed at him with sympathetic eyes—as if she understood. She flicked the cloak around her shoulders, and he gently pulled the hood over her head. "I'm glad you're here," she said simply.

"I have some news from Drake—about the ad," he explained.

"I have something I want to tell you too," she said, and the wistful note in her voice made the skin on the back of his neck prickle. "But why don't we wait and talk at the park?"

He nodded and took her hand, leading her down the back staircase and out the door that opened into the garden. They wound their way around the fragrant rosebushes, beneath the ivy-laden trellis, and through the creaky garden gate. Neither of them spoke till they had walked two more blocks and crossed the street into Hyde Park.

"Do you know this place?" he asked.

"Yes. Hyde Park," she said—as though she'd surprised herself.

"Maybe that's a good sign," he said hopefully. "Maybe people and places will become a little more familiar each day. Let's walk along the Serpentine and throw bread crumbs for the swans."

Her fingers absently went to the pendant he'd given her, and she smiled as she traced the swan's neck with a slender fingertip. He gently tugged on her hand and led her down the winding path.

Moonlight glinted on the river, and the evening breeze stirred small ripples on the otherwise glassy surface. The sounds of gently lapping water and insects punctuated the silence, and it seemed he and Caroline were the only souls for miles.

As they rounded the first bend, he pulled the heel of a loaf of bread from his jacket pocket and gave it to her. She laughed as she tore off small pieces and tossed them onto the shore, oblivious to the way the starlight caressed her face and danced in her eyes. He fought the impulse to slide his hands inside her cloak and pull her body against his.

"So," she began, pausing to tear off a morsel of bread. "What did you learn from your friend Drake today?"

"We've had a few replies to the ad," he said. "Most of them dead ends. But there was one interesting response today." He pointed to a bench a bit farther up the path. "Shall we sit?"

Caroline nodded and tossed the rest of the bread into the Serpentine where it landed with a plop near a bevy of grateful swans. She and Nash walked to the bench and sat, their knees only an inch apart. He stretched his arm, resting it behind her and barely resisting the urge to pull her close and kiss her senseless.

But even in the relative darkness, he could see the mixture of hope and apprehension in her eyes, and he knew that what she needed now was information—at least as much as he could provide. "This morning a slender woman, maybe thirty or forty years old, walked into Drake's office," Nash began. "She wore a black veil and wouldn't give her name, but, based on the physical description we gave in the ad, she thought she might know you. She said that if you were the woman she knows, you'd have a diamond-shaped birthmark on your shoulder."

Caroline sat straight up, and her heart thudded in her chest. "Someone knows who I am," she said, incredulous. "Did she tell you my name?"

"No." Nash's golden eyes glowed with regret as he leaned forward, propping his elbows on his knees. "She didn't want to give her name or yours until she'd confirmed your identity. She insisted on meeting you face-to-face."

Caroline sprang to her feet and paced in front of the bench. "We can see her tomorrow," she said eagerly. "Right after breakfast."

"Drake suggested that, but the woman said she couldn't return until Friday."

Her belly sank through her knees. "But that's . . . that's three days away."

"I know," Nash said softly. "I'm sorry."

She strode across the pebble path, the silver cloak swirling about her legs. "Why all the secrecy? If the woman truly knows me, why wouldn't she just tell Drake my name? At least then we'd have some information to work with."

Nash went to her and placed his hands gently on her shoulders. "Drake said she was very concerned with maintaining her anonymity."

"I don't like it." Caroline suppressed a shiver. "What if she's merely involved in a scheme to claim the reward?"

He arched a dark brow and looked at her earnestly. "She made a point to say that she doesn't want it."

Caroline pondered that for a moment, then leaned her forehead against his hard chest. He reached for her trembling hands and held them tight. "Are you all right?"

"Yes," she said. "It's just frustrating. To be so close to knowing . . . and not know."

"Hopefully you'll have your answers on Friday morning," Nash said soothingly. "And I'll be there with you."

They stood by the river for a while, Nash's strong arms encircling her as she listened to the leaves rustling overhead. Someone out there knew her name. Maybe. "There's always the possibility that this mysterious woman is mistaken," Caroline said—more as a reminder to herself than to him. "That she doesn't know me after all."

Nash impulsively lifted her hand and pressed a kiss to the back. "Or she could be the key to discovering who you are."

"I hope so," she choked out.

"You need to know something," he said. "No matter what, I will stand by you. It doesn't matter to me if you're highborn or not, wealthy or poor. I *know* who you are, Caroline, and I like you." He cupped her cheek in his palm. "Very much."

The desire in his eyes made her belly turn cartwheels. He hadn't mentioned love or marriage, but those things were almost too much to hope for.

"You said you had something you wanted to talk about too," he said.

"Yes," she said, reluctant to leave his embrace. "Let's sit." She led him back to the bench and faced him, wondering how to begin. "I've realized I cannot stay in your house indefinitely. Somewhere out there, my family could be looking for me, wondering where I am."

"I know," he said. "That's why we placed the ad. And, fortunately, it seems to have worked."

"I'm hopeful the woman knows me," Caroline said. "Or, perhaps I'll wake up tomorrow and remember everything. But just in case neither of those things proves true, I need a plan."

Apprehension flicked across his face. "What sort of plan?"

"For a start, I think I must find another, more suitable living arrangement."

He swallowed hard. "Where would you go?"

"I thought I might seek a position as a lady's maid."

"A maid?" he repeated. "Caroline, you don't need to do that."

She raised her chin proudly. "I can't rely on your generosity forever. No matter how much I adore Delilah and . . . you."

His gaze snapped to hers for a heartbeat. "I don't want you to go," he said hoarsely.

"It might be hard for you to understand, but it's important for me to make my own way in the world."

"I respect you for wanting to," he said, frowning slightly. "But making your own way is fraught with hardship and danger. Cramped living quarters. Long, hard hours. Employers who would think nothing of taking advantage of a pretty, young maid. I would spare you all that if I could."

Her chest squeezed. "I know. But I can take care of myself."

"You don't have a reference," Nash argued. "You have

no details about your education or upbringing. How will you convince someone to hire you?"

"I'm not afraid of hard work, and I can be quite persuasive. Besides, I have little choice."

"You could marry someone." The words hung awkwardly in the air between them while Nash sat opposite her, looking like he couldn't quite believe what he'd said.

She hesitated. "Even if a gentleman were to propose to me—a scenario that is unlikely to occur—I could never agree to marry without knowing who I am."

He stood and paced in front of her. "Please promise me you won't do anything rash."

"I can't remain with you, hoping someone will miraculously learn of my existence and present themselves on your doorstep to claim me. I can't abide feeling so helpless." She leaned forward, willing him to understand. "I must *do* something."

"All I ask is that you give yourself—and me—a little more time. There's a good chance you'll know more about your situation on Friday. Will you at least stay till then?"

She went to him and slipped her hands around his waist. "I will."

He hauled her against him, sending delicious shivers through her body.

All she and Nash really had was the present—right now.

His golden eyes melting her insides like butter. His fingers running through her hair. Her heart thumping like a bass drum.

He cradled her face in his hands. "Can I kiss you, Caroline?"

She took a few seconds to reply, only because she wanted to soak in every detail of the moment and imprint it in her memory. The stillness of the park. The faint mist rising off the water. The moonlight glinting on Nash's thick curls.

But mostly she wanted to remember the way he was looking at her.

"You can kiss me, Your Grace," she said. "Right here, in front of the swans. In fact, you can kiss me anytime you like."

# Chapter 19

*"Gentlemen may try to goad you into betting on
anything from whist to the weather. Enjoy the
thrill of the game if you wish—but never make a
wager you don't want to pay."*
                                    —The Debutante's Revenge

Nash released the breath he'd been holding. Caroline was
going to stay for at least a few more days. As he led her
back to the park bench, her green eyes glowed with desire and affection. Maybe even something more.

"Come here," he murmured, pulling her onto his lap.
He slanted his mouth across hers and teased the seam
of her lips with his tongue. When she opened to him, he
deepened the kiss, pouring everything he felt for her
into it.

In one short week, she'd burrowed her way into his
barricaded heart. In spite of her current predicament,
she'd shown courage and compassion. She'd seen him at
his absolute worst . . . and she was still there.

Her soft bottom rested on his thigh, and he slid a hand
over the tantalizing curve of her hip. "I will never have

enough of you," he growled. "If we stayed just like this for a hundred years, it would feel too short."

She leaned into him and sighed. "What you just said—it's what I've always wanted to hear. And you're saying these things without knowing who I really am."

"I know enough," he said gruffly. "I know that you're brave and independent and loyal—and that I'm a better person when I'm with you."

She tilted her forehead to his. "Whatever the future may hold for us, I will treasure this night. And I want you to know that no matter who I am, my feelings for you could not be more real."

Her slightly ominous tone raised the hairs on the backs of his arms, but he refused to be anything but optimistic about Caroline and him. If she cared for him half as much as he cared for her, it would be enough.

Cradling her face in his hands once more, he pressed his mouth to hers. He slid his hands inside her cloak and over her curves, nibbling his way down the side of her neck. She sighed and wriggled closer, pressing a thigh against his cock and making him harder than he already was. She speared her fingers through his hair and moaned into his mouth.

"It feels very wicked to do this in public," she whispered. "Especially when I'm wearing only a nightgown under my cloak."

"Wicked? Or exciting?"

She shot him a sultry smile. "Both."

He slid his hand beneath the hem of her nightgown and caressed her calf. Traced circles around her knee. Skimmed his palm over her inner thigh.

"Nash." She parted her legs and grasped his shoulders. "Someone could see."

"No one's around," he assured her. "But I'll stop if you want me to."

"No," she breathed. "Please don't."

He moved his hand higher until he found the spot that made her breath hitch and her eyes flutter shut. She was wet and warm, and the mewling sounds she made in his ear drove him wild. He continued stroking her as he spoke softly.

"You can trust me, Caroline. I may have disappointed you before, but it won't happen again. I'm not going anywhere. And I pray to God you don't either."

Her breath came in rasps, and her head lolled onto his shoulder, as if she lacked the strength to hold it up. "You're difficult to resist, Your Grace. Especially . . . right . . . now."

She clutched at his jacket and cried out as she climaxed, coming apart in his arms. And in that moment, the moonlight shined brighter, the air smelled sweeter, and his worries felt lighter. Everything was right with the world.

Caroline was his, and he was hers.

Nothing on earth could change that.

The next evening, Caroline threaded a silver ribbon through Delilah's hair, taking care not to disturb the curls she'd just pinned into place. The effect was dazzling, if she did say so herself.

Delilah stared into the looking glass on top of her dressing table and smiled at Caroline's reflection. "Please don't take this the wrong way, but based solely on your talent for styling my hair, it's quite possible we shall discover you are a lady's maid."

"Maybe I *am* a lady's maid," Caroline mused, "or

maybe I have a houseful of sisters who constantly demand my services."

"Either way, I'm glad you're here now." Delilah turned her head, admiring the spirals that dangled from her crown.

"You'll be the belle of the Delacamp ball," Caroline said.

"I wish you could come with us," Delilah said, pouting. "I've been so eager for this night to arrive, and now that it's here, my knees feel wobbly. It would be different if you were with me."

"Nash will take excellent care of you."

Delilah rolled her eyes. "That's what I'm afraid of. He won't let me out of his sight. Lord Brondale and I barely had a moment alone when he visited. But we did talk privately in the garden, and I feel as though I'm falling for him."

Recalling all of Nash's objections about Brondale, Caroline frowned slightly. "What is it about him that you're drawn to?"

"Beyond his charming manners, winning smile, and perfectly sculpted backside?" Delilah quipped.

Caroline grinned. "Yes. Besides all that."

Delilah rested her chin in her hand, pondering the question. "He listens to me. He cares about what I think. And he makes me laugh."

"Those are encouraging signs," Caroline admitted.

"Yes. But that's not all." Delilah stood, leaned her back against a bedpost, and smiled mischievously. "Sometimes he whispers in my ear, saying things that make my heart beat wildly. It's the most delicious, heady feeling. Have you ever felt like that?"

Caroline perched on the vanity stool and faced Delilah. "Yes." Her whole body tingled, remembering the moments she'd shared with Nash in the park. "I think I have."

"I know that love and desire are not the same thing," Delilah said.

"No. They are not."

"But perhaps they are two sides of the same coin," Delilah said, thoughtful. "He wants to kiss me, and I hope that we'll have the opportunity at the ball tonight."

Caroline swallowed. She wanted to tell Delilah to be careful and guard her heart—but it would have been the height of hypocrisy. "I want you to be happy," she said. "Just be sure that Brondale is deserving of your affections."

"I will."

"Good." Caroline gestured to the beautiful silk concoction laid out on Delilah's bed. "Shall I help you into your gown?"

"No, Molly will be in shortly. But, please stay—I'd like your opinion on which earrings to wear." Delilah walked to her dressing table and opened her jewelry box.

"What will you do while we're gone?"

"I'll probably write in my journal and read." And await Nash's return. Last night, after their passionate encounter in the park, he'd walked her back to the house and to her bedchamber. Neither one of them had wanted to say good night, so she'd invited him into her room. He'd carried her to bed and crawled in behind her, still mostly clothed.

He'd held her close all night long, stroking her shoulders and arms. By the time the sunlight peeked through her curtains, he was gone.

But on the pillow beside her, he'd left a sprig of lavender.

The notoriously grumpy Duke of Stonebridge had snuck down to the garden and clipped fragrant flowering herbs to leave on her bed. Romantic and thoughtful, it was the sort of gesture that could melt her heart—and make it exceedingly difficult to leave when the time came.

A time that was approaching much too fast.

Molly scurried into the room, pulling Caroline from her thoughts. Upon seeing Delilah's hair, the maid clasped her hands beneath her chin. "How lovely!" she exclaimed. "Miss Caroline, you must teach me how to do that sometime."

"I'd be happy to," she said, chuckling. She and Molly worked as a team to dress Delilah, fluffing, smoothing, and lacing her beautiful white gown. They helped her select her jewelry and reticule and gloves, and a half hour later, Delilah was ready.

She spun before a full-length mirror, craning her neck to admire the pretty sash at her waist and the square-cut back of her dress.

"You will steal many hearts tonight," Caroline predicted, and Molly murmured her agreement.

Delilah's eyes sparkled like the dazzling aquamarine necklace she wore. "There's only one heart I wish to steal." She tugged on Caroline's hand. "Come downstairs with me. We can tease Nash about having to wear an evening jacket."

Caroline swallowed, mentally preparing herself. If Nash had taken her breath away dressed as a blacksmith, the sight of him in formal attire might well make her swoon.

By the time she and Delilah reached the stair landing, he was already waiting at the bottom, looking supremely dashing, assured, and slightly impatient. He consulted his pocket watch, then looked up, meeting Caroline's gaze.

"Good evening, ladies."

Delilah hurried down the stairs and did a twirl for Nash's benefit. "What do you think?"

"That you shall have far too many eager dance partners," he said dryly, but then his eyes crinkled at the corners. "You look lovely."

Caroline descended slowly, soaking in the scene. Delilah's palpable joy, Nash's brotherly teasing, the rightness of it. A wave of wistfulness washed over her. How she'd miss this.

Nash's arresting eyes met hers, and the tenderness in his expression made her throat tighten painfully. "I'm sorry you can't join us tonight," he said. "But one day soon, after your memory returns, I hope you'll attend a ball—and that you'll allow me to claim a dance with you."

Delilah raised a brow, incredulous. "Nash! You sounded rather . . . *charming* just now. If you continue with that sort of talk, your reputation as a brooding, unapproachable duke shall be in jeopardy."

Nash rolled his eyes. "Let's be off," he said, offering Delilah his arm before turning to Caroline. "Enjoy your evening."

Caroline hugged herself happily. Because Nash's eyes had said what he couldn't—that he'd come to her that night. And her whole body thrummed at the prospect.

The ball wasn't quite as onerous as Nash had feared. Lady Delacamp had been delighted to take Delilah under her wing and introduce her to the other guests, which left Nash free to escape to the far side of the ballroom. He preferred to maximize the distance between him, the dance floor, and the matchmaking mamas.

From his vantage point by the open terrace doors, Nash could enjoy his drink, keep a watchful eye on Delilah, and relish the evening breeze at his back. The brandy was fine and the orchestra tolerable, but he was really just counting the minutes till he could see Caroline.

He hoped that she'd wait up for him, but he owed this ball to Delilah and wouldn't ask her to leave the festivities too early. She'd been beaming since they arrived, and he couldn't recall the last time he'd seen her so happy. She deserved to be part of the social whirl, and if that meant he had to endure a couple of balls or soirees or trips to the theatre each week, then so be it. Her brilliant smile made the stuffy crowds, loud music, and small talk worth it.

Nash suspected Brondale was also partially responsible for his sister's giddiness. Across the room, he bowed over Delilah's hand, and Nash clenched his jaw, not inclined to fall for the gallant gentleman act. Still, he supposed it was *possible* that Brondale had changed, and little harm could come to Delilah as long as she remained in the ballroom. He blew out a long breath, rolled his shoulders, and took a healthy swig of brandy, pleased to see Drake in the crowd, making his way over.

"I confess I'm shocked that you're here." His friend sidled up beside Nash, oblivious that he drew the eyes of half the females in the room with him. Thanks to his athletic build, graying hair, and fine manners, ladies from eighteen years of age to eighty routinely flocked to him.

"When I stopped by your house earlier, your butler told me where I could find you."

The skin on the back of Nash's neck prickled. "You have an update regarding Caroline?"

"I do." Drake kept his expression impassive as his gaze drifted around the room. "Shall we discuss it out on the terrace?"

Nash scowled at the dance floor where Delilah waltzed with Brondale. He held her too close, and Delilah's cheeks were too flushed, damn it. "I can't leave my sister unchaperoned. Let's move to the corner." Nash gestured toward a triad of potted palms. "We're less likely to be overheard."

Once they'd found a quiet spot, Drake spoke. "The mysterious woman sent a note about Friday's appointment. She said she'll be at my office at noon and looks forward to meeting the young woman described in the ad."

Nash rubbed his jaw, more curious than ever. "Did she sign the note?"

Drake shook his head. "No. And she didn't bring it herself. It was delivered by a middle-aged woman in a gray cloak. I asked Herbert to trail her and see where she went, but he lost her in a crowd that had gathered to watch a boxing match."

"Damn." Nash dragged a hand through his hair. "At least we know she'll be at your office on Friday. Which reminds me," he jested, "if we're going to meet in your office, you really should have Herbert tidy it."

"Over my dead body."

Relieved to have the details of the meeting set, Nash chuckled, sipped his brandy, and looked out onto the dance floor, automatically scanning the room for

Delilah's white gown. He spotted several young ladies wearing white—but none of them happened to be his sister. "Bloody hell."

Drake flinched. "What's wrong?"

Nash clunked his glass on a nearby table. "I need to find Delilah."

"Wasn't she with Brondale earlier?" Drake asked. "The one who made that vulgar wager about being the first to bed a—"

"Check the main entrance for me, will you? I'm going to look out on the terrace."

Drake gave an understanding nod and strode off, proving that while he was a damned good solicitor, he was an even better friend.

Nash stuffed his hands in his pockets and headed for the terrace as fast as he could without alarming anyone. If Delilah happened to be in a compromising situation, he didn't need scores of guests following him outside to witness the spectacle.

At last, he stepped out onto the flagstone terrace, finding it darker than expected. A sitting wall surrounded the large patio, and lanterns had been placed several yards apart on top of it, but much of the terrace remained in shadows, where it was too dark to see anything but silhouettes.

Along the north wall, one couple sat close, leaning their heads together. He strolled over and coughed loudly, sending a man and woman—not Delilah, thank God—scurrying back inside.

He was making his way to the opposite wall when Delilah approached, Brondale at her heels. "Nash, is that you?" Even in the dim light, he could see the deep blush staining her cheeks.

"Go inside," he ground out, shooting a death glare in Brondale's direction. "I want to talk to him."

She nervously glanced around the almost deserted terrace and placed a palm on Nash's chest. "There's no reason for you to be upset. We came out here one minute ago for no other reason than to escape the noise."

Nash gave a skeptical grunt. "Inside," he repeated. "I'll meet you there in five minutes."

Brondale smiled bravely at Delilah and gestured toward the ballroom doors. "Go. I'll be fine," he said, his delivery less than convincing.

Delilah lifted her obstinate chin. "Very well, but do not allow my brother to persuade you that we have done anything wrong. If escorting a young lady onto a moonlit terrace for a stroll is a sin, then I daresay he has committed much worse."

Nash flinched. She had a point. He remembered the promise he'd made to himself and to Delilah. He'd give her room to make her own decisions—and maybe even a few mistakes.

But in the meantime, he could have a word with Brondale. And strike a little fear in his heart.

Delilah held her head high as she glided back into the house, leaving him alone with Brondale. Nash's fists involuntarily clenched, and he had to cross his arms to keep himself from hoisting the blackguard by the collar.

Nash stepped forward till his chest was only an inch from Brondale's. "I know about your wager," he said through gritted teeth. "Whatever scheme you have to seduce my sister will not work. You don't care about her, and I won't let you hurt her."

Brondale chuckled nervously. "The bet is just a farce. I don't deflower virgins for sport."

"Glad to hear it." Nash casually cracked his knuckles. "If that's true, you should go directly to the club and strike the wager from the book."

The scoundrel frowned and shifted his eyes toward the ballroom like he couldn't wait to escape the terrace. "I can't undo the bet. It's a matter of honor."

Nash gave Brondale's shoulder a satisfying push, almost daring him to throw a punch. He'd have loved an excuse to start an all-out brawl. "If you had any *honor*, you wouldn't have made the bet in the first place."

"That sort of thing is done all the time," Brondale retorted.

"Maybe. That doesn't make it right." Nash counted to ten in his head before continuing. "Let me tell you what I know. You're up to your ears in debt, and creditors are knocking down your door. You've slept with half the widows and married women in this town. And while my sister isn't your usual type, you think she's just naïve enough that you'll be able to seduce her, win your vile bet, and force her into marriage. But you underestimate her. She's too smart to fall into your trap. I'm telling you right now. It will. Not. Happen."

"We'll see about that," Brondale said with a sneer. "You might be surprised to learn that your sister was the one who suggested we repair to the terrace."

"You're despicable," Nash spat. "If you harm Delilah, I'll meet you at dawn."

The color drained from Brondale's face. "You're as mad as they say."

Nash arched a brow and smiled menacingly. "Don't test me," he said, before turning on his heel and returning to the ballroom. Delilah was on the dance floor with another partner, but her eyes darted around the room as though she were looking for him and Brondale. When she finally spotted Nash, he gave her a tight smile.

She really was a remarkable young woman, and he'd been unfair to her. Not tonight, because Brondale truly *was* a cad. But for the last five years, Nash had been determined to keep her in a cocoon, solitary and safe. And he couldn't keep holding on to her so tight—not unless he wanted to lose her completely.

As he watched her twirl around the dance floor, her blond hair shining in the candlelight, his throat constricted. He wished Caroline were here; somehow, he knew she'd understand the odd combination of brotherly pride and dread that filled his chest.

They'd only been apart for a few hours, but he missed Caroline.

Couldn't wait to see her tonight.

# Chapter 20

*"It may be of interest to note that representations
of the male anatomy in classical art, while quite
beautiful, are notorious for their disproportion-
ately small depiction of a certain appendage."*
—The Debutante's Revenge

*Tap, tap.* The knock at Caroline's bedchamber door woke
her from a light sleep.

"It's me," said a muffled voice in the corridor outside.

*Nash.* She rubbed her eyes and smiled to herself.
"Come in."

"Did I wake you?" he asked, closing the door softly
behind him.

"I might have dozed a little." She stretched sleepily.
"How was the ball?"

"It could have been better." He gestured toward the
edge of her bed. "May I?"

She nodded and moved her legs to make space for
him. "Tell me what happened."

He sat beside her, the low light of the lamp illuminating the sharp lines of his face and the weariness around

his eyes. "Brondale and Delilah went out onto the terrace alone, and I lost my temper."

"Oh no. Please say you didn't hurt him."

"I wanted to," he admitted. "But I didn't."

She exhaled, relieved. "That's good."

"I apologized to Delilah again," he said flatly. "But she barely talked to me on the ride home."

Caroline shot him a sympathetic smile. "Maybe her mind was elsewhere."

"Maybe," he said, skeptical. "All I know is I missed you."

"I missed you too." She reached for his hand, tingling from the slight pressure of his fingers grazing her palm.

"I saw Drake at the ball tonight too. The woman who responded to our ad is going to meet us at his office on Friday at noon."

"That's . . . wonderful." But it was also a reminder that her time with Nash would soon come to an end. She'd spent an hour that evening looking through the newspaper for positions she might apply for. There was one for a companion that sounded tolerable, and another for a lady's maid. She'd be fortunate to land either one of them.

"Let's hope she knows you—and that she'll reunite you with your family." He gave Caroline a bolstering smile that didn't quite reach his eyes.

"Two more days," she said, lacing her fingers through his. "We shouldn't waste a minute."

Without saying a word, he released her hand, locked the door, and took off his clothes. She watched, mesmerized as he shed his starched cravat and formal jacket and tailored trousers—the trappings that made him a formidable duke. But underneath it all, he was sinewy muscle and hard flesh and primal male. Underneath it all, he was Nash. *Hers.*

His heavy-lidded gaze raked over her as he stripped down to his drawers, which did little to hide the hard length of his arousal. The knowledge that she could affect him so made her body thrum.

He turned the lamp a little lower, then lifted the corner of the sheets and slid into bed, reaching for her. His warm hand cruised over her bare hip then froze. "Jesus, Caroline. If I'd known you were naked under here earlier, I wouldn't have been able to form a coherent sentence."

She chuckled and tangled her legs with his. "You're doing pretty well right now."

He cupped her face in his hands and stared into her eyes. "There's something so *right* about this—about the two of us together. No matter who you are and no matter where you go when you leave here, I know we'll find our way back to each other."

Her chest squeezed. "I hope so."

She brushed her lips over his, in the tenderest of kisses. He speared his fingers through her hair, massaging her scalp.

With his mussed hair and sleepy eyes, he looked younger—almost vulnerable. "Tell me you feel it too," he murmured, nipping at her shoulder.

"I do." Her limbs had turned to jelly, and she tingled from her head all the way to her toes.

He slipped an arm around her waist and hauled her body against his. Slowly, thoroughly, they explored each other. He cupped her bottom and stroked the backs of her thighs. She ran her hands over the lean muscles in his shoulders and back. They twined their legs and moved together till they were both breathless with longing.

He might have been one of the most powerful men in England, but in that moment, he belonged completely to her, and she to him. Deep inside, she knew this was all she'd ever wanted—to have someone to hold at the end of every day. Someone who looked at her as though the sun rose and set on her smiles.

"I want to be with you," she said. "I want us to be as close as two people can possibly be."

He swallowed and gazed deep into her eyes. "You're certain?"

"Absolutely." She knew it, felt it, deep in her bones. "I can't make promises about the future without knowing who I am, and neither can you. But tonight, I am all yours. And you . . . you are all mine."

Their mouths collided in a kiss that chased every rational thought from her head. His tongue probed the warm, soft recesses of her mouth; she nibbled at his lower lip. She rocked her hips against his, pressing her core against his hard length.

He let out a growl as he grabbed her bottom and rolled her on top of him, gazing at her face and body as though he were committing every freckle to memory. Her hair fell around them in a curtain, tickling her breasts and his chest. Nash showed her how to move against him, heightening her own arousal. And when she was aching with need, he encouraged her to take the lead, even as he stoked her desire.

With sensuous caresses.

And wicked promises.

And heart-stopping kisses.

Her whole body seemed to be swept up in beautiful

song, its tempo rapidly accelerating toward one glorious final measure. Nash's amber eyes looked up at hers, warming her from within. With every thrust, he teased out the pleasure building inside her, letting it gradually crescendo until there was nowhere left for it to go.

Her release unfurled—unexpectedly powerful and impossibly sweet. Her back arched and a whimper escaped her throat as pleasure transported her. For an interminable moment, she was ethereal as a melody, floating softly in the night.

Nash held her through it all, watching her with tenderness and awe.

And afterward, when it seemed her neck could scarcely support her head, he deftly rolled her onto her back while remaining inside her.

Pleasant little pulses echoed within, and she smiled up at his handsome face, her heart swelling.

"I understand you have doubts," he said breathlessly, "and I don't blame you. But I don't need to know your surname or your family or your background to know *you*. To know that we belong together."

Oh God. Her eyes stung, and she pulled his head down for a slow, sultry kiss.

With a low groan, he started moving again, thrusting in a mesmerizing rhythm. His broad shoulders blocked out the rest of the room. His muscular arms were braced on either side of her head; his powerful body covered hers. She ran her hands over the smooth planes of his chest and back, reveling in his appreciative moans.

Before long, pleasure spiraled inside her again, mirroring his. They came together, clinging fiercely to each other. When he would have pulled out to avoid spilling his seed inside her, she wrapped her legs around his hips, urging him to stay. Perhaps it was foolish of her. Perhaps she'd regret it in the morning. But she wanted all of him.

He pressed his forehead to hers throughout his climax, kissing her and murmuring her name like it was his salvation. "You have my heart, Caroline. Don't break it."

All night long, Nash held Caroline close. Nuzzling the spot at the base of her neck that made her sigh. Inhaling the light, intoxicating scent of her hair. Wondering at the perfect fit of their bodies.

He dozed off for a while, then woke to find Caroline kissing his face, her breasts brushing against his chest. "I want more of you," she whispered, making his heart pound wildly.

"Take what you want," he said hoarsely.

Boldly, she reached for his cock, curling her fingers around him and purring when she felt the slick bead of semen at the top. She stroked him surely, and when he moved toward her, she shook her head. "Lie back and relax," she said, tracing the shell of his ear with her tongue. "And let me please you."

He did as she asked—or at least tried to. But everything she did drove him mad with desire. Nipping at his neck, trailing her fingertips down his torso, moving her supple body against him. And he knew he couldn't wait another second to bury himself inside her.

He lifted her and flipped her back onto the mattress. Covered her body with his. Positioned his hips between her thighs.

Her eyes shining with emotion, she gazed up at him and wrapped her legs around his waist. "This feels like a dream," she said. "I don't want it to end."

But Nash knew it wasn't a dream. It was better.

He thrust slowly at first, but she tilted toward him, pulling him deeper. He pressed his forehead to hers as they set up a rhythm. Soon they were both panting, their bodies slick with sweat. "Are you all right?"

"Don't stop." Her dark lashes fluttered, and she licked her kiss-swollen lips. "It feels . . . too good."

God, he loved that she was so passionate. He reached between their bodies and touched her, listening to every telltale hitch of her breath, every soft whimper. Kept thrusting till her body was coiled tight. Felt her release begin. She arched toward him, crying out as she came undone.

He held off as long as he could, but the feel of her body pulsing around him was more than he could take. Release raced toward him like a flame gobbling up the fuse on a firecracker.

He grasped her hips and groaned into the curve of her neck as he came, inhaling the citrusy scent of her hair and tasting the salt on her skin.

And he wished they could stay, just like that, forever.

"Jesus, Caroline," he murmured at last. "That was amazing."

"Mmm." She nuzzled against his side, and when he'd recovered sufficiently to move, he grabbed the corner of the quilt, tucking it around her to keep her warm.

He liked the feel of her silky hair on his chest and the weight of her lithe leg on his thigh. He savored the little puffs of air she blew against his neck and the even sound of her breathing as she drifted off to sleep.

Bedding Caroline, a woman with no identity, was without a doubt the most reckless thing Nash had ever done. And tomorrow they would face a whole host of complications. But for now, he was utterly content. For the first time since Emily's death, he felt a measure of peace. And if it wasn't quite happiness . . . well, it was pretty goddamned close.

"I've brought something for you." Delilah breezed into the drawing room the next morning wearing a pale blue gown that matched her eyes. She smiled mischievously, hiding something behind her back as she marched up to Caroline.

Caroline sat on the settee, staring at the rough sketch she'd been carrying in her pocket on the night she'd lost her memory. She hadn't been able to stop thinking about it and what its significance might be. Did she know the couple in the drawing? And why had she been carrying it in her pocket? She tucked it inside the front cover of her journal and exhaled slowly.

Delilah tilted her head thoughtfully. "You seem a million miles away."

"Forgive me." Caroline set her journal aside and patted the settee cushion beside her, inviting Delilah to sit. "You caught me daydreaming, but *you* are the one who's been wearing a secretive smile. The ball must have been more fun than you let on," she teased.

Delilah shrugged mysteriously. "Every girl should be permitted a few secrets."

Caroline felt an odd tingling in her chest. "Is that a quote from The Debutante's Revenge?"

"It is," Delilah said, unapologetic. "Now, aren't you curious to know what I'm hiding behind my back? You might at least *feign* a bit of interest. Try to guess."

Caroline crossed her arms, all too happy to play along. "A horse."

Delilah narrowed her eyes. "Smaller."

Caroline pretended to ponder the clue. "Pony?"

"You're incorrigible," Delilah said, grinning as she propped a hand on her hip. "Try again."

"Very well." Caroline schooled her face into a serious expression. "A toad."

"Parlor games are *not* your forte," Delilah said, shaking her head with mock sadness. "Remind me never to side with you in charades."

"I give up," Caroline exclaimed. "Tell me what you have there."

Delilah shot her a triumphant smile as she produced a folded newspaper from behind her back. "Today's edition of the *Hearsay*."

"The Debutante's Revenge column doesn't come out until tomorrow."

"I know. I can scarcely wait," Delilah said smoothly, handing Caroline the newspaper. "But there's something else that I thought might be of interest."

Caroline scanned the top of the folded paper. "The advertisements?"

Delilah nodded excitedly. "There are two new listings for governesses. Of course, you may prefer to join an agency, but nevertheless, it's interesting to see what positions might be available. And there's an ad for a companion as well. You'd be wonderful with children or older people . . . do you have a preference?"

Caroline stared at the paper, touched. "Thank you for this," she said sincerely. "I've been perusing the listings too. I'm not sure what I'll do. But I think I'll wait until Saturday to begin my search in earnest. I'm still hoping that the woman who responded to our ad will be able to tell me who I am."

"Forgive me," Delilah said. "I didn't mean to rush you. Nor did I mean to imply that I'm anxious for you to leave—on the contrary."

Caroline quickly set the newspaper on the table and gave Delilah a hug. "Trust me, I know you're only trying to help, and I appreciate it more than I can say."

"Good. And I hope you know I was only jesting about the parlor games. I'd choose you for my partner over Nash any day. You and I might not always win, but we'd have more fun." Delilah fiddled with the fringe on a pillow. "I must admit, though, Nash has been more fun since you came to stay with us. I can't believe he's taking us out tonight."

"I'm looking forward to spending the evening with both of you," Caroline said. At luncheon earlier, Nash had proposed that they all do something special in honor of Caroline's last night with them. Delilah had immediately suggested Vauxhall Gardens, and Nash had readily agreed. They could blend into the shadows at the venue and even wear a mask if they wished to mingle in the crowd without being recognized.

Delilah impulsively squeezed her hand. "I know you must be nervous and frightened about tomorrow—and the days after that," she said. "If it helps, you should know that I don't care who your family is or where you live. I will remain your friend, no matter what."

Caroline's throat grew thick. "Thank you. It does help."

"Good." Delilah sniffled. "Now that we've settled the matter, we should go upstairs and choose a gown for each of us to wear tonight. Something daring, I think."

Caroline smiled at her friend. "Daring sounds perfect."

# Chapter 21

*"Wearing your favorite gown into a crowded ball-
room does wonders for your confidence—and that
confidence allows your true beauty to shine."*
                                    *—The Debutante's Revenge*

Caroline gazed into the looking glass in her bedchamber as she adjusted her swan necklace above the bodice
of the exquisite ruby gown she'd borrowed. Tiny puffs
of sleeves barely clung to her shoulders, and delicate
beaded trim skimmed low across her breasts. Rich red
silk glistened in the candlelight and caressed her skin as
she moved.

She imagined Nash's face when he saw her in it and
smiled.

Tonight, quite possibly their last night together, would
be bittersweet, but she resolved to enjoy it as much as she
could.

"There you are," Caroline said, looking up at Delilah as she entered the room, still wearing her dressing
gown. "Why haven't you changed?"

Delilah sat on the edge of the bed and shot her an

apologetic smile. "I came down with a bit of a headache after lunch."

"Oh no," Caroline said, frowning. "I know how much you were looking forward to Vauxhall, but no matter. We can just as easily enjoy a quiet evening at home."

"Absolutely not," Delilah said firmly. "I'd be miserable if you changed your plans to stay with me. And if you want to know the truth, it makes me happy to think of you and Nash having a romantic evening." She gave Caroline a playful wink. "Go. Have a wonderful time, and I will see you in the morning. We can read the new edition of The Debutante's Revenge together."

Caroline's chest warmed. "I want you to come, you know. Nash does too."

"I know," Delilah said, grinning. "But I've seen the way you and Nash look at each other. You need this time together—to sort out how you feel."

"I know how I feel," Caroline said. Just thinking about Nash made her heart flutter. "But even if he felt the same, I wouldn't be able to commit to a future without knowing who I am."

Delilah nodded. "You and Nash have some difficult decisions to make." She stood and tightened the sash of her dressing gown. "I do too."

Caroline's fingertips tingled ominously. "Decisions involving Brondale?"

"Yes," Delilah admitted. "It would be so much easier if Nash liked him."

"Give your brother a little more time," Caroline urged. "Maybe he'll come around."

"Maybe," Delilah mused. "But in the end, I think I must follow my heart."

Caroline swallowed. "I suppose that's all any of us can do."

"Does any of this feel familiar?" Nash asked. Caroline held his arm as they walked along a quiet, winding path lined with verdant shrubs and illuminated by festive lanterns.

Her green eyes shone with wonder. "No. It seems like everything is new."

It seemed new to Nash too. He'd been to Vauxhall years ago, but now he was seeing it through Caroline's eyes. The tranquil fountains and artificial ruins. The talented minstrels and raucous bands. She delighted in all of it, and the rapture on her face filled his chest with a warm glow.

They ate supper—savory ham and fresh salads—in a richly appointed private box. Caroline insisted they try mixing their own punch, and the result was a delicious, if potent, blend that included rum, lemons, and pineapple. While she sipped the brew, he drank in the sight of her.

Dark curls cascaded from her crown and framed her beautiful face. Her gown revealed the swells of her breasts and the creamy skin of her shoulders. The red silk was the perfect complement for her fearless and passionate nature, and he already anticipated peeling it off her later that night.

She sat next to him on a small settee and shot him a half-drunk smile over the rim of her glass. "Thank you for this evening. I've loved every minute."

"The night isn't over yet," he said soberly. "*We* aren't over yet."

She set down her drink and leaned into his chest. "Let's not think about tomorrow," she said softly. "When the sun comes up, we can worry about what comes next. Till then, let's just be with each other. In the moment."

He caressed her cheek lightly and gazed into her eyes. For once he didn't try to hide what he felt for her. Didn't deny it, even to himself. Her courage and compassion had moved him. Changed him. And all the emotion he'd buried deep inside bubbled to the surface and lodged in his throat.

She'd become the center of his world.

She swallowed hard and blinked up at him, eyes wide as the color drained from her face.

"Are you all right?" he asked, slipping an arm around her shoulder and lightly caressing the birthmark there.

She frowned slightly. "I'm fine. But the way you looked at me just now . . . It reminded me of something. I'm not sure what or how, but it made me feel rather odd inside. As though I'm on the brink of remembering."

"That's good," he said too brightly, like he was trying to convince himself. "Do you want me to take you home?"

"No," she said without hesitation. She nestled closer, draping a silk-clad leg over his thigh. One of her sleeves slipped down her arm, exposing the ripe curve of her breast, and his heart started beating double time. "I'm not ready to go."

He tilted his forehead to hers. "Then we will stay. We can visit the colonnade, go to a concert, or even dance. It's up to you."

She arched a brow and threaded her fingers through his hair. "If it is up to me, then we will stay here. Just the two of us. Like this." She brushed her lips across his in a whisper-soft kiss that quickly morphed into something deeper.

He ran his hands over her breasts and hips. Slid a hand under her dress and up the inside of her thigh. Touched and teased at the juncture of her legs until she panted and writhed on his lap.

Outside their supper box, fireworks rocketed into the sky and thundered through the night. In the brilliant flashes of light, Caroline's skin glowed and her gown shimmered. Nash gazed at her, committing every detail to memory.

Her smiling at him with heavy-lidded eyes and flushed cheeks.

Her fingers grasping his shoulders and her hips rocking against his.

Her soft, blissful cries mixing with the booms of rockets soaring through the air.

The sun's first pale rays peeked through Nash's curtains the next morning, kissing Caroline's luminous skin. Her back was to him, and the sheets bunched around her hips revealed the perfect hourglass of her body. He nipped at her bare shoulder and slid an arm around her waist. "Good morning."

With a sleepy moan, she rolled into him, nuzzling her face against his chest. "I cannot agree."

He chuckled and planted a kiss on the top of her head. "No? And why is that?"

"I should like to stay like this—for a few more hours at least." She rubbed a smooth, lithe calf against his thigh.

"Mmm," he said, entirely of the same mind. "We can't steal more hours, but I know how to make the most of the minutes we have left."

She pressed her naked body against his and rolled on

top of him. "Perhaps the morning has something to recommend it after all."

A half hour later, she was shooting him a sleepy, sated smile. He reached for her dressing gown where it lay at the end of his massive bed and held it open for her as she reluctantly tossed back the sheets and padded toward him, slipping her arms into the sleeves.

"We'll leave for Drake's office in a couple of hours," he said. "Are you nervous?"

"Yes. About the meeting and about leaving here afterward," she admitted.

"You don't have to leave today," he said, damn near close to begging. "You could stay another week."

She cinched the tie of her dressing gown and looked at him with sad eyes. "Would it change anything?"

He knew what she was asking. Would he ever be able to give his heart to her completely and without reservation? Would he ever be able to love her the way she deserved to be loved? And he owed her an honest answer.

"No," he said simply. "I wish I could be the man you deserve."

A tear trickled down her cheek as she turned to leave. "I wish you could see that you are."

Apparently, Delilah had a Friday morning tradition that revolved around The Debutante's Revenge column—and this week, Caroline was invited to participate. The custom involved sleeping later than usual and taking breakfast in Delilah's bedchamber. As soon as the new edition of the *London Hearsay* was delivered, the butler presented it to Delilah, who proceeded with her first, ceremonial reading of the column.

Delilah had insisted that Caroline come to her room

in her nightgown and crawl into bed beside her while they waited for breakfast. When Molly arrived, bearing a cart laden with silver serving platters and delicate china, they bounded out of bed like perfect heathens. While the delicious aromas of tea, scones, ham, and eggs wafted around the room, they sat in a pair of comfortable arm-chairs flanking a window, filled their plates, and dove into their feast with gusto.

Caroline would have adored the coziness of the morning—if she hadn't known it was her last in that house.

When the butler knocked on the door with the news-paper tucked under his elbow, Delilah set down her teacup and rubbed her palms in anticipation. "Thank you, Stodges."

She waited for him to leave, then turned to Caroline. "Ready?"

Her heart beating wildly, she nodded. Of course it was *highly* unlikely she was the authoress of the column, but a small part of her still thought—even hoped—that she might be. If The Debutante's Revenge appeared in the paper as expected, however, she could put that theory to rest. Because the only columns she'd written in the past week were the ones in her journal.

Delilah opened the paper and smoothed it across her lap. "Here it is."

Caroline tamped down the disappointment that nig-gled inside. So, she wasn't the authoress. She'd been foolish to think she could be.

She and Caroline both took a moment to admire the accompanying sketch of a couple sitting beneath a para-sol, gazing at each other as though they were on the verge of sneaking a kiss.

Then Delilah cleared her throat, and, blue eyes gleaming with anticipation, she raised her chin like a town crier preparing to read a royal proclamation.

*The Debutante's Revenge*
*Dear Debutantes,*
*When it comes to matters of the heart, every maid, miss, and matron considers herself an expert. But for a young woman on the marriage mart, no opinion is more important than her own. She is likely to have many well-meaning relatives and friends offering her advice or cautioning her against certain gentlemen. In the end, however, she is the only one who can determine which suitor is the best match for her.*
*This life-altering choice should not be made based on a gentleman's fortune or rank or even his manners. Instead, a debutante should look for someone who makes her days brighter and her sorrows lighter. She should seek a man who can make her pulse race with a simple glance and who appreciates her not in spite of her foibles, but because of them.*
*If you are fortunate to find a love so rare, grab hold of it. Refuse to let go.*

For several seconds after Delilah finished reading, neither she nor Caroline said anything.

Caroline felt that odd tingling sensation again—the one that she'd been having more frequently lately. The one that made her feel like she might be on the verge of remembering.

Delilah's gaze flicked over the paper again, as if she

were slowly devouring every word—for a second time. When she looked up, her expression was unusually sober. "What do you think of the column?" she asked Caroline. "Do you agree?"

She nodded, thoughtful. "I do. If I was lucky enough to fall in love . . ." she paused to swallow past the knot in her throat, ". . . I would do everything in my power to protect that love. To nurture it and let it grow."

"That's what I think too." Determination sparked in Delilah's eyes. "Sometimes the right advice makes everything seem clear."

Caroline frowned. "You're not planning to do anything rash, are you?"

"Don't worry about me. You have enough on your plate as it is. Which reminds me," she said with a mischievous smile, "I have something for you."

She set down the paper, strode to her armoire, and pulled out a stack of three neatly folded gowns. Handing them to Caroline, she said, "These are the most practical, serviceable dresses I could find in my wardrobe—perfectly suitable for a companion or governess. Take them with you when you go to the boardinghouse."

"Oh, Delilah," Caroline said, deeply touched. "I couldn't."

"Nonsense," Delilah countered. "I know you want to make your own way, but everyone needs a little help getting started. Nash is going to pay your rent for the first month and give you some spending money."

"You've both been so good to me. And so generous," Caroline choked out. "I promise that I'll write to you and let you know as soon as I secure a position. And I'll try to visit you if I can."

"You'd better," Delilah teased, but she was sniffling

too. Glancing at the clock, she added, "You should go now and dress for your meeting with the mysterious woman. I'm hoping that she'll know who you are and take you home so that you'll be able to forget all about your plans to live in a boardinghouse."

"I hope so too," Caroline said. But the truth was, it didn't matter to her whether she lived in a cramped attic room or a royal palace.

Any future that didn't include Nash was doomed to be bleak.

# Chapter 22

*"A gentleman needn't always agree with you, but he must always respect you. Never apologize for who you are or what you believe in."*
                    —*The Debutante's Revenge*

An hour later, Caroline sat beside Nash in his elegant coach as it rumbled through the streets. "I should warn you about Drake's office," Nash was saying. "Imagine a study where there are more books on the floor than on shelves. Odd pieces of furniture and knickknacks placed randomly around the room. Stacks of paper piled everywhere—except the desk. *That's* what Drake's office is like."

Caroline smiled at Nash's attempt to calm her nerves—and perhaps his own. "It sounds charming."

"Hardly." He squeezed her hand. "We'll be lucky if we can round up the necessary chairs for our meeting." Turning serious, he added, "No matter what happens, I'll be right there with you."

"I know," she said. "Thank you."

"How are you feeling today?" he asked.

"I feel fine." Physically, at least. Inside, her heart was breaking. "I'm a little worried about Delilah, though."

His forehead creased. "Why is that?"

Caroline hesitated. "There was a new edition of The Debutante's Revenge in the paper today, and after she read it, she—"

*Bam.* The coach suddenly lurched to the left, and Caroline's head slammed into the window. Pain exploded behind her eyes. Radiated down her neck.

"Caroline!" Nash cradled her head in his hands and searched her face. "Are you all right?" His voice was threaded with panic.

She blinked up at his handsome face. Saw a mix of fear and concern swirling in his golden eyes. "What was that?" she asked, wincing.

"We must have hit a rut in the road. I'm surprised we didn't lose a wheel." Nash gently moved his fingers, inspecting her head. "Let me see if you're bleeding."

The coach had continued rolling along, and Caroline felt every jostle in her skull, but the pain was already receding into a dull ache.

"You have a lump right here," he said, gently touching a tender spot above her left ear. "I'm going to tell the driver to take us home. We should have Dr. Cupton examine you."

Caroline frowned. She was so close to meeting the veiled woman. So close to discovering her own identity. "No." She clasped his wrist and pulled his hand away from her head. "It's just a little bump, and I'm fine."

Nash arched a dark brow, clearly skeptical. "Are you certain?"

"Yes." She pasted on a smile and brushed a stray

tendril away from her face. "I'm not as fragile as I look," she joked.

Nash's shoulders relaxed slightly, and he pressed a light kiss to her forehead. "Very well. We'll be at Drake's office in a few minutes, but you must tell me if the pain worsens."

"I will," she promised.

She laced her fingers through his and stared out the window, mentally preparing herself for the meeting ahead. But as the houses, storefronts, and offices rushed by outside the coach, a strange sensation took root in her chest. Wrapped its tendrils around her heart. Refused to let go.

Blaming her frazzled nerves, she took a deep breath, closed her eyes, and resolved to distract herself with pleasant thoughts.

She remembered the night in Nash's bedchamber when he'd slowly unraveled the strip of cloth binding her breasts. The heat in his honey-colored eyes had made her belly flutter. She saw the scene behind her eyelids, but she felt it too. Like a dream. But more real.

Silk slid against her skin as she spun away from him, but instead of growing looser, the bands grew tighter with each turn. She couldn't stop spinning. The cloth squeezed her rib cage too tightly. She tried to take a deep breath but couldn't. She was gasping, desperate for air—

And suddenly, she stood in front of a mirror, breathing quite normally and running her hands over her bound torso. She hauled a boy's shirt over her head and stepped into a pair of trousers—only she wasn't in Nash's room anymore. She was in another place. Not home, exactly, but close.

And before she could properly analyze *that*, she was back in the Grey Goose.

The tavern teemed with people, and this time, Nash wasn't at her side.

He *was* there, though. Sitting across the room, observing her as though her disguise hadn't quite convinced him. His scrutiny had been so unsettling that she decided to leave.

And then two men were blocking her path. Or perhaps it was three men.

Yes, it was definitely three. One of them demanded she give him her bag.

*Oh God.*

She saw it all.

Her futile attempt to distract the men and run away.

Them catching her, sneering down at her with their nostrils flared.

Nash stepping in and the knock-down fight that ensued—ending with *her* slamming into a table.

Pitiful moans. Blinding pain. Blackness.

Her eyes flew open. Her mouth was dry, her skin was clammy, and her heart raced like she'd climbed a mountain. But she was still in Nash's coach, and he was sitting beside her, holding her hand and grounding her in the present like an anchor.

What on earth was wrong with her? She pressed a hand to her chest, willing her heartbeat to slow. She'd just had some sort of breakthrough—she was sure of it. The scenes that had played out behind her eyelids weren't just random thoughts. They were . . . memories.

She was almost scared to believe it in case it wasn't true, but it seemed that, finally, snippets of her life before the injury were coming back to her.

But the most central question remained. Who *was* she?

"We're here," Nash announced as the coach rolled to

a stop in front of a brick building with a blue arched door. He turned toward her, and the bolstering smile on his face evaporated. "You're very pale, Caroline. Are you sure that you want to do this right now? We could reschedule the meeting."

"I don't want to put it off," she said firmly. "I'm simply a bit dazed because just now I . . . I think I remembered something. Something that happened before I lost my memory."

"My God." His gaze snapped to hers, and his eyes glowed with a mix of hope and apprehension and . . . tenderness. A tenderness that made her whole body thrum. "What do you remember?" he asked soberly.

"That night at the Grey Goose. The first time we were both there," she said haltingly, piecing it all together. "Before I knew who you were."

A footman opened the door of the cab, and Nash waved him off. "Give us another moment, please, Thomas." To Caroline, he said, "Go on."

"I was in trouble, and you came to my defense," she said, picturing it again in her head. "You were holding your own against the men . . . until I smiled at you."

Nash's golden eyes gleamed. "You *are* remembering," he said, his voice low with awe.

Caroline nodded. "It's a start." She couldn't help thinking that remembering the night she'd hit her head was like finding the end of a thread. The hardest part was done. Now she merely had to follow that thread, wherever it might lead. "I still don't know who I am, but I do know this—I'm closer than ever to finding out."

Nash escorted Caroline up the walkway to Drake's office, relieved to see that after the bump to her head she was still clear-eyed and steady on her feet. Drake's secretary, Herbert, greeted them in the antechamber. "Good afternoon, Your Grace," he said. Bowing in Caroline's direction, he added, "Miss Caroline." He waved a lanky arm at the door behind him. "Mr. Drake and his guest are waiting for you inside."

Nash leaned close to her ear. "Everything will be all right," he assured her.

She stared at the closed door and swallowed. "How do you know?"

"Because I know *you*." He gave her hand one last squeeze and led her into Drake's office.

The solicitor sat behind his desk, and a slender woman dressed in black perched on a chair across from him, her back to Nash and Caroline.

Herbert had apparently cleared a path through the cluttered office to a pair of empty chairs, also near Drake's desk. As Nash and Caroline walked toward them, Drake and the woman stood and faced them.

"Miss Caroline," Drake said warmly. "Stonebridge has told me much about you. It's a pleasure to finally meet you."

Caroline smiled back. "I've heard a lot about you as well. Thank you for your help with the advertisement."

When Caroline turned to face the woman, Drake cleared his throat. "Allow me to introduce Miss Serena Labelle."

Nash blinked. He'd heard the name before but couldn't say where.

Serena hesitated, then lifted her veil and placed it on top of her hat. She had dark hair laced with gray, a pointed chin, and hazel eyes that seemed strangely wistful as she looked at Caroline. "When I read the description in your ad, I thought I might know you. And I do."

"I don't recognize you." Caroline searched Serena's face. "Have we met?"

The woman shook her head. "Not really. Mr. Drake told me you are suffering from memory loss. Aside from that, are you well?" she asked anxiously.

"Yes," Caroline said. "And I'm starting to remember. Little things. But I still don't know who I am."

"I imagine this is all rather nerve-racking," Serena said, sympathetic. "Would you care to sit?"

"No," Caroline said evenly. "Please, tell me what you know about me."

Serena clasped her gloved hands in front of her. "Your name is Miss Lily Hartley. Your parents live several blocks from here in an elegant town house. Your sister, Fiona, is married to the Earl of Ravenport. And you . . . you are an heiress."

Nash watched Caroline's face—that is, Lily's face—closely. The relief that shone in her eyes matched his own. She wasn't married. Her family lived here in town. Maybe he wasn't mad to think there might be a future for them.

As if she were privy to his thoughts, she silently reached over the arm of her chair and laced her fingers through his. That simple touch told him everything—that she wanted him with her, whether she was Caroline or Lily.

"My name is Lily Hartley," she repeated to herself before turning to Nash, her beautiful face awash with joy. "Yes. That sounds right. My name is Lily."

He took her hand and pressed a kiss to the back of it. "I'm delighted to meet you, Miss Hartley."

She cast a soft smile in his direction before turning to Serena. "Are you a friend of my parents?"

Serena shook her head. "Not really."

Lily took a deep breath, and then her smile faltered. "My poor family. They must be sick with worry."

"I thought the same thing," Serena said. "So I made some discreet inquiries over the last few days. Apparently, your parents and sister are out of town. Perhaps that's why they haven't been frantically searching for you. They may not even know you're missing."

Caroline took a step back and slowly sank into the chair behind her. "That would explain a lot." She looked up at Serena. "But you haven't told me how you know me or how you knew about my birthmark."

Nash had been wondering the same thing. He began repeating the woman's name over and over in his head, hoping to jog his own memory. Vaguely recalled hearing her name whispered in his club.

And then it hit him. The mysterious, veiled woman who knew Lily wasn't merely Serena Labelle.

She was *Madam* Serena Labelle.

Proprietress of the most infamous brothel in London.

# Chapter 23

*"If you have questions of a delicate nature, seek answers from those you trust. Consider turning to an older sister or a married cousin—someone who won't call for her smelling salts at the mere mention of a gentleman's anatomy."*
—The Debutante's Revenge

Lily's head was spinning. From the moment Serena had uttered the name *Lily Hartley*, snippets of her life flashed through her mind.

Mama and Papa. Their comfortable house. Her cozy bedroom. Fiona and Gray. Her dear friend Sophie.

The tangle of memories was working itself loose, freeing her mind from its binding.

But she still didn't understand her connection to the woman dressed in black who sat across from her—Serena Labelle.

"How do you know me?" Lily asked again.

Serena deliberately stepped back and sat in the chair adjacent to Lily, clasping her trembling hands in her lap. "I knew you when you were a babe," she began. "Your birthmark is rather distinctive, and though I only saw it when you were very young, I remembered the shape of it."

"Are you a family friend?" Lily asked.

The woman shook her head. "Not really."

"A relative?" she pressed.

Serena swallowed. "It's rather complicated, and you're already overwhelmed with information."

Lily pressed her fingertips to her temples. "I want to understand."

Serena gazed at her with compassion. "Go home to your family. Make sure they know that you're safe." She flicked her eyes to Nash and added, "Listen to your heart."

"I intend to," Lily said, frustrated. "But I must have the whole picture. Whatever it is that you're keeping from me—I deserve to know it."

Two small lines appeared between Serena's eyebrows. "You're right. You do deserve to have all the facts." She reached into her reticule, pulled out a tiny baby bootie, and pressed it into Lily's hands. "Here. This may not mean anything to you right now, but it will, eventually. Take time to sort through your feelings. After that, if you still wish to talk, I would love to meet with you again. But if you'd rather not further our acquaintance . . . I understand completely."

Serena stood and nodded politely in Drake's direction. "I am grateful for your assistance, Mr. Drake." Turning to Nash, she said, "And thank you, Your Grace, for taking good care of Lily."

Finally, she faced Lily and looked deep into her eyes. "I hope to see you again, but in case I don't, please know that I wish nothing but the best for you. That's all I've *ever* wanted for you."

With that, she pulled the veil over her face and glided out of the office, her head held high.

Nash slipped an arm around Lily's shoulders, and she leaned into the comforting solidness of his chest.

Drake stood and circled around his desk. "I'll leave you two to talk," he said kindly. "Take all the time you need."

When Nash and Lily were alone, he sat, pulled her onto his lap, and pressed his forehead to hers. "I wonder how many times I'll slip and call you Caroline."

She wound her arms around his neck and nuzzled his cheek. "I don't mind if you do. I think I'll always carry a little of Caroline with me."

"If you'd like, I can take you home directly," he offered. "Or, we could send word to your family that you're safe and will be home later tonight. That would give you time to gather your things and say goodbye to Delilah."

"There's no rush to notify my parents or Fiona." She closed her eyes and recalled her last evening at Fiona's house. "My parents are in Bath for another week or so, and Fiona and her husband are in Scotland. My dear friend Sophie is visiting her aunt." She shrugged. "I think we should go home to Delilah and tell her the news."

Nash frowned slightly. "That reminds me. In the coach on the way here, you were going to tell me something about her."

"Yes," Lily said. Her mind was still a mush of memories, recent and old. "She mentioned that after reading the latest edition of The Debutante's Revenge, she finally knew what she had to do."

"That sounds ominous," Nash mused. "What was the column about?"

"Let me think." She shook her head to clear the cobwebs. And then she remembered the drawing that Delilah had shown her that morning, of the man and woman sitting on a bench, stealing a private moment beneath a parasol. Wait. She'd seen the drawing before that morning. In Fiona's drawing room.

Oh God. She *was* connected to The Debutante's Revenge.

"Lily." Nash cupped her cheek in his hand. "You look dazed again. Maybe we should find a place for you to lie down."

"No, I'm—"

Drake abruptly opened the door, his expression grave. "Forgive me for interrupting."

"What's wrong?" Nash gently slid Lily off his lap and stood.

"Hopefully nothing," Drake said in a placating tone. "But one of your footmen just arrived. He said that your sister isn't at home."

Nash shrugged. "She probably went for a walk in the park."

"Maybe," Drake said. "But her maid isn't with her. She found a letter on Delilah's pillow—addressed to you."

"Holy hell," Nash muttered. He dragged a hand through his hair. "What does it say?"

"The maid didn't open it—it's still on Delilah's bed."

"*Damn* it." Nash turned to Lily, his expression grim. "I have to go."

She stood and nodded. "I'm coming with you."

Stodges met Nash and Lily at the front door. "Your Grace. I'm so sorry about all of this."

"It's not your fault." Nash was already striding toward

the staircase, his heart pounding with fear. Was Delilah so lovesick over Brondale that she'd do something stupid? "Ready the carriage," he called over his shoulder, just in case. He took the stairs two at a time and jogged down the hall toward Delilah's room with Lily on his heels.

He burst into his sister's bedchamber and quickly scanned the room. The armoire doors hung open, and a discarded gown was tossed over the back of a chair. A newspaper on top of her desk was opened to the latest column of The Debutante's Revenge.

Nash was not generally one to jump to conclusions, but a cold, insidious dread seeped into his bones. The sight of the envelope, laying near his sister's headboard, made him feel physically ill. Bracing himself, he ripped it open.

*Dearest Nash,*
*I regret leaving in this manner, but you left me little choice. I am old enough to know my own heart, and I must follow it.*
*Rest assured, I am not Emily; nor am I destined for the same fate.*
*I hope that one day you will understand.*
                                          *All my love,*
                                          *Delilah*

Shit. His head pounded with a potent mix of rage and guilt and fear. Somehow, he'd driven his sister away— and right into the arms of Brondale.

Lily rushed into the room, and he wordlessly handed her the note.

Her face fell as she read it. "Oh no. I'm sorry, Nash."

"I have to stop her." He was already stalking toward his room to stuff a bag with a few things.

Lily followed him. "Stop her from what?"

"From making the biggest mistake of her life." He yanked open a bureau drawer, grabbed some money and a leather bag, and slammed the drawer shut. "From running off with a scoundrel who only wants to win a high-stakes bet."

"Delilah doesn't think he's a scoundrel," Lily said, then stopped short. "What kind of bet?"

"The kind where you win if you steal a young woman's virginity—and provide proof."

She pressed a hand to her stomach, sickened. "That's disgusting."

"That's Brondale," he countered. Suddenly starved for air, Nash yanked at his cravat. He squeezed his eyes shut to try and stop the buzzing in his ears. His skin turned clammy. The room swirled around him. And suddenly he was eighteen again, reliving the night Emily ran away.

Holding her as the breath left her body and the light went out of her eyes.

Fuck. He dropped the bag and bent over, bracing his hands on his knees. He had to pull himself together, damn it. He needed to find Delilah before any harm came to her.

A gentle hand caressed the back of his neck and squeezed his shoulders. Caroline. No, *Lily.*

"I know this must bring back terrible memories," she said. "But Delilah is smart and resourceful. You helped raise her to be that way. She can take care of herself till we find her."

Nash stood and wiped the sweat from his brow with

his sleeve before he looked into Lily's eyes. "I'm going by myself."

She shook her head. "You shouldn't be alone right now. And I might be able to help in the search. I can place myself in Delilah's shoes easier than you can."

Nash mustered a regretful smile. "You've just regained your memory, Lily. You should go home and wait for your family." He scooped up his bag, shoved a change of clothes inside, and slung it over his shoulder. "I'm going to try and catch them before they get to Gretna Green. I'll send word when I return."

Lily grasped his forearm and forced him to meet her determined gaze. "No one is waiting for me at home. Even if they were, I'd want to be with you. Delilah may not be my sister by blood, but she *is* the sister of my heart."

Nash closed his eyes. Could feel his resolve slipping. "We'll be traveling as fast as we can. It won't always be comfortable. And I don't know how long we'll be gone."

She nodded eagerly. "I'll send word to my family that I'm all right—in case they return to town before we do."

He hesitated. "There's also the matter of your reputation. If we're seen traveling together without a chaperone . . ." He let his voice trail off and left it to her to fill in the consequences.

Namely, that she'd be forced to marry him.

If it came to that, he'd give her everything he could—safety, companionship, and pleasure. But he wasn't sure he could give her what she truly wanted or deserved—his whole heart, unguarded and exposed.

For the space of several breaths, Lily stared at him, thoughtful. "I'm willing to take my chances."

## Chapter 24

*"If he truly cares for you, he will seek and respect
your opinion. He will take note of your likes and
dislikes. He will admire you for your wit more than
for your appearance."*

—The Debutante's Revenge

Lily sat beside Nash in the coach as it rolled over the pit-
ted roads, taking them away from London. The landscape outside their windows alternated between vast,
cow-dotted fields and dense, tree-filled forests. Nash
stared at the scenery as it rushed by, but Lily doubted he
saw any of it. From the bleak expression on his face, she
suspected he was thinking of a very similar journey—
one he'd taken five years ago, when he'd chased after
Emily.

They didn't speak much for the first few hours of the
ride. Lily sensed he needed time to harness all his feelings and come up with a plan for rescuing Delilah. She
was doing the same thing—but she'd also been remembering more about her life.

Before leaving Nash's house, she'd grabbed her bag—
the one she'd had with her at the Grey Goose—and

packed a few items inside: a nightgown, underclothes, a brush, and her journal. At the last minute she'd stopped in Delilah's room, taken the latest copy of The Debutante's Revenge off her desk, and added it to her bag.

Now, she took it out, wondering if it held a clue as to Delilah's state of mind when she left that morning. Lily read the column again, and the tingling at the base of her spine returned. She recognized the sensation now. Knew that she was about to remember.

She studied Fiona's drawing in the paper—the bold strokes, the subtle shading, the raw emotion. She'd already deduced that her sister was the talented artist of the sketches in The Debutante's Revenge, but what about the column itself? The words didn't sound like Fiona or Sophie. They sounded more like . . . *her*. If she closed her eyes, she could almost see them handwritten in her own distinct script.

But that had to be her muddled mind playing tricks on her. She couldn't have written this particular column, because she'd been in Nash's house suffering from amnesia the entire week before it appeared in the paper.

Unless.

Bracing herself, Lily closed her eyes and let the memories come. Fiona and Gray's elegant yet cozy drawing room. Lily shuffling through the sketches on Fiona's desk. Fiona reading the columns Lily gave her. The ones *she'd* written and delivered before going to the tavern that night.

Sweet Jesus. Her head spinning, Lily opened her eyes and stared at the newspaper on her lap. She was more than Lily Hartley, heiress and sister to the Countess of Ravenport.

She *was* the mysterious, infamous authoress of The Debutante's Revenge.

Even as her chest swelled with pride, her head urged caution. She, Fiona, and Sophie had made a vow to protect their anonymity at all costs.

Nash glanced over at her, worry for his sister etched into his face. "We'll make a brief stop soon. There's an inn just up the road, and I want to check in there to ask if anyone has seen Delilah or Brondale."

"Good idea," Lily said. "She can't be too far ahead of us. We left London about three hours after she did."

"I'm assuming she and Brondale are together and that they're heading for Gretna Green, but I don't know anything for certain." Nash dragged a hand down his face, weary. "It's quite possible that Brondale has no intention of marrying her. He might have suggested they elope just so he can seduce her or force himself on her."

Lily's gut twisted. "Delilah's clever enough to see through such a scheme."

"She fancies herself in love with Brondale, and love . . . well, it makes people do foolish things." Nash nodded at the newspaper in Lily's lap. "Is that the column Delilah read this morning?"

"Yes," she said, her mouth suddenly dry.

"May I see it?"

"Of course." Lily handed it to him, and he read, his face impassive.

"What do you think?" she asked, holding her breath as she awaited his response.

"That it's reckless advice," he said flatly.

"*Reckless?*" she repeated, incredulous. "How so?"

"It encourages young women to ignore the counsel of people who love them."

She took the paper from him and read it again. "It doesn't say that *exactly* . . ." Though she had to admit, it was rather close.

"It advises them to base weighty decisions on feelings and intuition," he said—as if doing so was the height of idiocy.

She shook her head and impulsively reached for his hand. "I don't think that's quite what the author meant."

"She says that young women should choose a man who makes their *pulse beat faster.*" He looked at their hands, clasped on the seat between them. "But that's just a symptom of desire. Not love."

Oh God. She had to tell him the truth—that she was the authoress. After all they'd shared, she couldn't hide that part of herself from him.

"Nash," she began. "There's something important I need to tell you, and . . . well, you may not like it."

His golden eyes turned wary, and he exhaled slowly. "Can I be honest with you?"

"Always," she said sincerely.

"I'm not sure I can face any more revelations right now," he said hoarsely. "I need to reserve every ounce of my energy and attention for finding my sister."

Lily nodded and tried to keep her own emotions in check. "I understand."

"I want to hear whatever you have to say," he assured her. Outside the coach, the inn he'd mentioned came into view. "But unless it has something to do with Delilah, I'd rather wait until this ordeal is over."

The anguish on his face made her chest ache, and she would have done anything to lessen his burden. "It can wait. Let's find your sister—and we'll worry about the rest afterward."

* * *

Several hours and many miles later, the moon rose in the sky and twilight cast the countryside in a purple haze. The coach rolled up to an inn—the third Lily and Nash had stopped at that day. This one boasted vine-covered stone walls, a steeply sloped roof, and brick chimneys at either end. When a footman opened the cab door, Nash hopped out and helped Lily to the ground. "I'm going to talk to the innkeeper," he told her, "and ask if he's seen anyone matching Delilah's and Brondale's description."

"I'll stay out here and stretch my legs." She pulled her shawl over her head, mindful that the fewer people who knew they were traveling together, the better.

When he returned a short time later, his body was coiled tight with frustration. "I didn't learn anything," he said. "I don't even know if we're headed in the right direction."

"Maybe they're a little farther up the road," she said, hopeful. "We could keep going."

He shook his head. "Not tonight. The horses need to rest, and I'd rather get an early start in the morning. In the meantime, I've secured a room. Come, I'll take you there."

Lily kept her head down as she followed him past the front desk and up the narrow stairs to a long hallway with doors on either side. He walked to the far end of the corridor, unlocked the last door on the right, and ushered her in.

The room was cozy—about five paces from the door to the opposite wall. Indeed, it was so small that even if it had been completely devoid of furniture, the mattress from Nash's huge bed would not have fit inside. The furnishings were sparse and utilitarian—a narrow bed, a tiny table beside the bed with a washbowl, and one ladderback chair—but the room appeared tidy and the bed linens clean.

"The innkeeper's wife will bring you a dinner tray in a bit," Nash said. "Lock the door when she leaves and try to sleep." When he turned to go, she laid a hand on his forearm, confused.

"Where will you be?"

He shrugged, not meeting her gaze. "In the taproom for a while. I'll probably spend the night in the stables."

"Why?"

"There aren't any more rooms," he said, matter-of-fact.

"Don't you want to stay here with me?" she asked, detecting a note of hurt in her own voice.

He hesitated for several seconds as he stared at her, his eyes glowing like burnished gold. "That wouldn't be wise."

"I don't understand." Lily's own eyes stung. "We shared a bed just last night."

Nash closed the door to the room, and she sank onto the edge of the mattress. "Last night feels like a lifetime ago," he said sadly. "It's not that I don't want to stay with you tonight—I do. But now that we know who you really are, we need to be honest about what we want from each other and what we can give."

"I have been honest with you," she choked out. "I'm still *me*. Caroline, Lily, whatever name I go by, I'm the same person inside."

Nash sat in the chair across from her and looked directly into her eyes. "I know. I've tried to be honest with you too," he said, his face awash with regret. "I wanted to believe that we could go on as we were—and that it would be enough for you. But I think we both know that it's not."

She opened her mouth, wanting to deny it—but couldn't. She needed him to love her with his whole heart, freely and unreservedly. And that wouldn't be possible till he let go of the past—and his guilt.

"What we shared was special," he said earnestly. "And true. But when I read Delilah's note today, it was like a splash of cold water on my face, reminding me never to fall too hard. Never to lose my head. I came dangerously close to doing that with you."

"I would never hurt you."

"I know that," he said. "I trust you . . . but I don't trust myself. The passion I feel for you could easily overpower my good sense and make me careless in my duties—to my title *and* to my sister. I'm all the family Delilah has left. I can't risk doing something rash and destructive. I can't do to Delilah what Emily did to me."

Lily sat across from Nash, her knees a mere foot away from his. She'd tossed her shawl onto the mattress, and several thick curls dangled around her shoulders, too heavy to be confined by her hairpins. In spite of her wrinkled gown and the dark smudges beneath her eyes, she looked achingly beautiful.

"You're lucky that you were able to stop yourself from falling in love." Her green eyes flashed defiantly. "It's too late for me."

"Lily," he pleaded. "Don't do this."

"It's too late for me," she repeated, "because I already love you. With my whole heart."

He closed his eyes and gripped the edge of the chair, so he wouldn't haul her into his arms. "I can't love you back. Not like you want me to."

She continued talking as though she hadn't heard him.

"Do you remember that first night when I woke up in your house? I couldn't remember anything, and I was terrified. But then I saw your face. I heard your voice. And I knew I was safe."

"I was partly to blame for what happened," Nash reminded her. "The least I could do was take care of you. It was my duty," he added—so she wouldn't mistakenly believe he'd been bewitched by her courage and wit. Or dazzled by her smile.

She stared at him, unpersuaded. "And the night I kissed you in your study—that was my first real kiss. You were my first for . . . everything."

Nash pressed his lips into a tight line. "I know you don't want to hear this now, but you will meet someone else, Lily. Someone far better than I."

"No, I don't think so." She shook her head slowly, and a tear trickled down her cheek. "You treated me—a woman you found in a tavern dressed as a chimney sweep—with compassion and respect. And the more time I spent with you, the more I came to care for you. Even at your grumpiest, you could always make me smile, always make me feel special. And that's why I fell in love with you."

It killed Nash to see her hurting—which only proved his point. Love always led to pain. "I'm sorry," he said helplessly, handing her his handkerchief.

She dabbed at her eyes and swallowed bravely. "We've both had a long day."

"Yes," he agreed. "I'm going to go downstairs so you can rest."

"Will you return later?" she asked.

"I don't know." He stood and stepped to the door before he lost his resolve. "Try to sleep."

# Chapter 25

*"Be aware of the pressure of his hand on yours. It should be warm and firm. Easy, yet exhilarating. The mere touch of your palms should cause a flutter in your belly."*

—The Debutante's Revenge

Lily ate a few bites of the stew that Nash had sent up, then placed the tray in the hallway. Without him, the tiny room seemed so empty. Too quiet. Normally, she didn't mind solitude, but the ache in her chest wasn't from being alone . . . it was from being lonely. She was miles away from her sister and her dear friend Sophie. Worse, they had no idea of all she'd been through.

Nash was the one person who *could* know what Lily was feeling—but he refused to acknowledge it. Refused to accept what they meant to each other.

She took off her slippers and stockings, wriggled out of her gown, and hung it from a hook on the wall. After changing into her soft nightgown, she carefully removed each pin from her hair and ran her brush through her curls. And when she could think of nothing else to do, she turned down the lamp, slid beneath the bed's quilt, and stared at the ceiling, waiting, hoping, that Nash would return.

Sounds from the taproom drifted through the window and walls—boisterous conversation, drunken song, and clanking glasses. But, eventually, the noise dissipated.

The air in the room grew chilly.

A single shaft of moonlight slanted across the bed.

Lily was on the verge of succumbing to sleep when a knock sounded at the door. "Caroline." Nash's voice was muffled and filled with angst.

Heart pounding, she leaped out of bed, padded to the door, and opened it.

His cravat was askew, his hair stood on end, and he leaned against the doorjamb like it was the only thing holding his body upright.

She supposed this was Nash at his worst—and yet, his dashing good looks still had the power to take her breath away.

"Are you all right?" She reached for his arm, and though he flinched when she touched him, he didn't pull away.

He blinked and swiped a hand across his face. "You're wearing a nightgown."

She smiled in spite of herself. "That's because while you were in the taproom drinking, I was in bed. Don't stand out there. Come in."

Nash staggered into Caroline's room. That is, Lily's room. He *knew* Caroline wasn't her real name, but after a few pints of ale, his stubborn mind wanted to return to the way things were—when she was Caroline.

When she was his.

She shut the door and locked it before sitting on the

edge of the bed across from him. Her long hair hung loose around her shoulders, bare but for the lace straps of her white nightgown. The gown's neckline dipped low across the swell of her breasts, and a ruffle at its hem grazed her shapely calves. Nash's heart thudded in his chest.

Scowling at his own weakness, he slumped onto the chair and pinched the bridge of his nose.

Her brow furrowed in concern. "Does your head ache?"

"Aye."

"Don't move."

He tried not to stare at her swaying hips as she walked to the washbasin. Tried not to watch the graceful movements of her arms as she wrung water out of the cloth. And, heaven help him, he tried not to gape at the subtle bounce of her breasts as she glided back to him.

She gave him the cloth. "Hold this over your forehead and eyes."

He did as she instructed, letting the coolness numb his pain and the darkness heighten his senses.

"Lean back," she said. He did, and a moment later, her nimble fingers untied the knot of his cravat and gently removed it. "There," she murmured, caressing the side of his neck. "That's better."

He shifted in the chair and started to remove the cloth from his eyes, but she pressed a fingertip to his lips. "Stay still. Let me take care of you."

Sweet Lucifer. He felt her stand and move behind him, felt her breath near his ear. "Don't think about anything. Try to relax."

Her hands came to rest on his shoulders, kneading the tight muscles beneath his jacket and draining the pain from his body. She hummed softly, lulling him into a dreamlike state—where nothing mattered but the feel of her hands on his shoulders, arms, and neck.

She massaged his nape and gently traced the shells of his ears. She slid her hands beneath his collar and the front of his shirt, leaving his skin tingling in the wake of her touch. She speared her fingers through his hair, lightly rubbing his scalp till the pounding in his head subsided.

"Let me remove your jacket," she whispered, pushing it down his shoulders and off his arms. When it was gone, she unbuttoned his waistcoat too. Her palms skimmed over his chest and abdomen, clutching at the fabric of his shirt. "Come, lie down," she urged—and he was powerless to resist her.

He tossed the cloth on the table beside the bed and sprawled on the mattress, sighing the moment his head hit the pillow.

She pulled off one of his boots, then the other. When she was done, she perched beside him on the bed, gazing at him with shining eyes. Her hair glistened in the moonlight; her heart-shaped face shone with compassion. Between her diaphanous shift and luminous skin, she looked like an angel.

But even if she were, he was beyond saving.

She moved closer, running her fingers across his forehead, down his cheeks, and along his jaw. With every caress, she quieted the demons in his head. Healed the raw wounds on his heart.

"Close your eyes," she murmured softly. "You need to sleep."

"It's your bed. I should go."

"Do not go for my sake." She leaned over him and

pressed her lips to his cheek in a kiss that was tender and all too brief. "I will feel better if you put your arms around me and sleep more soundly if you stay."

He laced his fingers through hers, savoring the familiar, perfect fit of their hands. "One more night," he whispered, more to himself than to her.

A winsome smile lit her face as she laid beside him and nuzzled his shoulder. He pulled her close and pretended for a moment that everything was right with the world.

And maybe, for that fleeting second, it *was*.

Her lush curves pressed against his side. Her breath soft and warm on his neck. Her heart beating in time with his.

He closed his eyes and inhaled the light floral scent of her hair.

And slept peacefully until dawn.

Over the next two days, Nash and Lily stopped at every inn on the way to Gretna Green, looking for Delilah with little luck. Occasionally, a tavern owner or barkeep claimed to have seen a young woman matching her description, but it seemed Delilah was always one step ahead of Nash, just out of his reach. With every hour that passed, he grew more anxious. He told himself that as long as Delilah was safe and happy, *he* would be happy. But if Brondale had hurt her in any way . . . the bastard would pay.

Being angry at Brondale was easier than worrying about his sister.

It was also easier than thinking about his relationship with Lily.

Ever since the first night of their journey that they'd

spent together at the inn, he'd managed to keep a respectable distance. They slept in separate rooms and avoided touching each other. But it wasn't easy.

Especially when she sat across from him in the coach, as she did now, her expression full of longing and . . . something else.

He looked away so he wouldn't have to analyze it too closely. "We'll drive as long as we can—a few more hours at least—and stop at an inn tonight. We should arrive at Gretna Green by tomorrow morning."

She nodded and peered out the window at the deep orange horizon. "I can't explain why, but I feel like Delilah is close. Maybe she's looking at the sunset right now too."

"I hope you're right," he said, trying not to sound cynical. If not for Lily, he'd have spent the last three days brooding nonstop. She always managed to look at the bright side of things. Always tried to make him feel better. But today, she'd been serious and thoughtful. "Are you feeling all right?" he asked, searching her face. "You've been quieter than usual."

"I've been remembering," she said. "It turns out that losing my memory may have helped me solve a twenty-year-old mystery . . . about where I came from."

Nash leveled his golden gaze at her, curious. "What do you mean? You weren't born in London?"

Lily cleared her throat. Not many people knew the truth about how she'd come to live with the Hartleys. Just her parents, Fiona, and Sophie. "I'm not a Hartley by birth. I was left on their doorstep when I was a baby."

Nash blinked. "They adopted you?"

"Yes. I found out when I was seven." Lily could still

remember how the news had shaken her. Her stepmother unceremoniously mentioned it in the same offhand tone that she might have used to announce that they'd be having ham for dinner. "Our butler was the one who discovered me outside the door in a basket. No one saw who left me there, but two clues were nestled beneath my blankets."

Nash listened intently, and Lily could almost see his mind piecing the information together, reaching the same conclusions she had. But it still felt good to say it. To have all the facts exposed.

"The first one was a note. I still have it at home, and it says, 'Please take care of my darling Lily.'"

Nash shot her a soft smile—as if he understood what that scrap of paper meant to her. A name was *something*. It was an identity. And having lost hers for a little over a week, Lily knew just how important an identity was. How it connected you to the people and world around you. How it made you unique and human and alive.

Maybe it was naïve, but she'd always taken comfort in the knowledge that someone—probably her birth mother—had given her that name. Surely a woman who'd gone to the trouble of naming her daughter and using an endearment like "darling" had felt an inkling of motherly love. Even if she *had* left her infant in a straw basket on a stranger's doorstep in the wee hours of the morning.

Nash sat back and rubbed his chin, thoughtful. "I think I can guess the second clue."

Lily nodded, reached into her bag beneath her seat, and pulled out the baby bootie that Serena had given her. Made of cream-colored silk with light green stitching and a white ribbon lace at the instep, there was nothing terribly exceptional about the bootie—except that it was an exact match of the one she'd been wearing on the morning she'd been found. "I was only wearing one bootie when the butler picked up my basket—and it looked just like this." Lily smiled to herself, thinking of all the stories she and Fiona had spun about the missing bootie.

Fiona had said that Lily was just like Cinderella and claimed to be desperately jealous of that tiny shoe. Even if she was only saying that to be nice, it *had* made Lily feel a little better. Her favorite theory—concocted by Fiona when she was nine—was that Lily's mother was a royal princess who'd been forced to flee her kingdom and needed a safe place for her daughter to grow up. They'd imagined that one day the princess would return for Lily, the matching little shoe in hand.

The truth wasn't quite the storybook tale, but perhaps there were some parallels.

Nash sat across from her, eyes wide with a mix of wonder and disbelief. "Serena knew about your birthmark."

Lily nodded. "She said she knew me as a baby."

"And she had the matching bootie." Nash leaned forward, his gold eyes looking deep into hers. "That means Serena could be . . ."

"I think she *must* be." Lily felt a warm glow in her chest. "Serena Labelle is my birth mother."

# Chapter 26

*"Violence is rarely the answer; however, it is sometimes the only answer. Every young lady should possess some means of defending herself, and in the absence of a rapier, the pointed end of a parasol may prove quite useful."*
—*The Debutante's Revenge*

The moon had started to rise in the sky outside the coach, and bluish beams fell across Lily's face, illuminating the cautious joy in her eyes. Nash could feel both her relief and her excitement over the discovery that Serena was her birth mother.

But he knew more about Serena than Lily did—namely, that she was the madam of a brothel—and he needed to share that with Lily as directly and tactfully as he could.

"I'd begun to think that I'd never learn the truth about who left me on the Hartleys' doorstep," she said. "If I hadn't lost my memory and we hadn't placed the ad, there's a good chance I never would have." She stared at the tiny bootie in her hand. "Serena held on to this for twenty years. Surely that means something."

Nash nodded, sympathetic. "She certainly sounded eager to meet with you—but only if and when you feel ready to."

"The thought makes me anxious," Lily admitted. "But I have so many questions—and Serena's the only one who can answer them." The vulnerability in her voice made him want to pull her into his arms, but he resisted—barely.

"She seems kind," Nash said, "and concerned for your well-being. Both of those traits make me inclined to like her."

"I liked her too," Lily mused. "But I don't understand why she felt the veil was necessary—or why she didn't leave her name initially."

"I have a guess." Nash rubbed his palms on his thighs, debating how to best break the news. "Serena's name is well-known in certain circles. She's a very successful entrepreneur and has a long list of clients."

"What sort of business does she own?" Lily asked, clearly enthused.

Nash hesitated a second, then decided she'd want to hear the news in plain speech. "Serena is the proprietress of London's most famous brothel."

Lily blinked, momentarily stunned. "A brothel?"

"Yes," Nash said, giving her a moment to absorb it. "In case you were wondering, I hadn't met her before that day in Drake's office, and I've never visited her establishment. But I happen to know it's quite popular."

For a full minute, Lily sat quietly, staring out the window at the starlit sky. When she faced Nash again, her expression was sober. "Over the years, I played out so many different scenarios in my head," she said. "Stories about who my birth mother was. I thought she might be rich or poor, daring or reserved, a princess or an orange girl. I concocted all sorts of excuses for her decision—reasons that she might have had to give me up. But I never once . . . I never once thought that she might be a madam."

"It may not be the stuff of childhood fantasies," Nash said, sympathetic. "But Serena came forward when you needed her. She seems considerate and sincere."

Lily stared at the bootie she held and nodded slowly. "With the Hartleys, I had a pampered childhood, a finishing school education, and a respectable name—things she never could have given me."

"Giving you up couldn't have been easy for her," Nash said.

"No. I can't even imagine." She sniffled and swiped at her eyes.

"Are you all right?" he asked. "I have a flask of brandy under my seat if it would help."

"I don't think I want brandy," she choked out. "It might seem silly, but I feel as though what I need is a good cry."

His chest ached for her. "I don't think it's silly at all." He crossed the coach and sat beside her, offering his handkerchief. "Cry all you need to."

She erupted into sobs, leaning into his shoulder and muffling her cries in his jacket. He held her and rubbed the back of her head till, eventually, her sobs turned to hiccups. When she'd finally cried out all the shock and pain and grief, she curled up next to him, nestled her head in his lap, and fell asleep to the gentle swaying of the coach.

He pulled a wool blanket over her and listened to her even breathing, relieved that he might have said or done something right. He hadn't thought he was equipped to deal with tears and emotion, but apparently, all one needed was a clean handkerchief and a comfortable lap.

*And, maybe,* a voice inside him whispered, *it helped to have the right person.*

Nash and Lily arrived in Gretna Green the next morning. They checked at every inn, the livery, and at the blacksmith's in the center of the village but could find no sign of Delilah and Brondale. One part of Nash was relieved there was no record of their marriage, but if they hadn't made it to Gretna Green, where the hell were they?

Tired and frustrated, Lily and Nash made their way from the blacksmith's shop back to the coach. "We could stay here for another day or so," Lily suggested. "It's possible that Delilah and Brondale took a different route than we did. Maybe they're still behind us and have yet to arrive."

"Maybe," Nash said. "But a few innkeepers I checked with spotted them earlier on—before their trail went cold. I think they must have turned around before they made it here."

"Perhaps Delilah had a change of heart. She could be headed home now," Lily said hopefully. "Maybe she's already there, just waiting for us to return."

"Nothing would make me happier," Nash said. "But before we head back to London, I think we should make one detour. A tavern owner mentioned that Brondale's father has a country estate south of here. It couldn't hurt to pay a visit and see if he's been there recently."

Lily nodded her agreement. "How long will the ride take?"

"If we leave now, we should arrive before nightfall," Nash guessed.

"I'll round up some sandwiches and fruit for the ride while you speak with the driver," she offered. "I'll meet you at the coach in a quarter hour."

They arrived at Brondale's family estate early that evening. A long, twisting drive led to a stately manor house surrounded by green grass and manicured shrubs. Nash cast a sober glance across the coach at Lily. "If Brondale is here, things could get ugly," he warned.

Lily frowned. "I know you're angry at him. I am too. But violence isn't going to improve the situation."

"Maybe not." He cracked his knuckles. "But it's bound to make me feel better. If we do come to blows, I'd rather you not be in the line of fire."

"I haven't come all this way to remain in the coach," Lily said, her green eyes flashing. "Besides, if Delilah is here, she's going to need a friend."

"Fine. But promise me you won't insert yourself in any altercation," he said firmly. "You've only very recently recovered from the tavern brawl."

She raised her chin a notch. "I'm not making any promises," she said with a reluctant smile. "You might need my help."

He grinned in spite of himself. She might have a stubborn streak a mile wide, but at least she was on *his* side. Knowing he had her as an ally—not just against Brondale, but in any battle—made his chest squeeze.

A few minutes later, after a brief exchange with the butler, he and Lily were escorted into the study. Nash ignored Lily's reasonable suggestion that he sit in the leather armchair next to her, opting instead to pace the elegantly appointed room, clenching his fists.

Brondale was *here*. And if he'd harmed Delilah in any way . . . God help him.

When the marquess finally walked through the door, he drew up short and turned his head to the side. "St-Stonebridge," he stammered. "What are you doing here?"

Nash stalked toward him till they stood toe to toe. A jagged red cut with a dozen or so stitches slashed across Brondale's right cheek. Sweat beaded on his brow.

"Where's my sister?" Nash demanded.

"Not here." Brondale swallowed nervously and held up his hands. "But she's fine. I assume she's at home— or on her way. I haven't seen her in two days."

Nash leaned closer, barely resisting the urge to slam Brondale's back against the wall and throttle him. "I know you were planning to elope."

Brondale shrugged. "She changed her mind."

"You bloody bastard." Nash grabbed him by the lapels and lifted his feet off the floor. "You seduced her then cried off?"

"Nash!" Lily rushed to his side and placed a hand on his arm. "Set him down. Let's hear what he has to say."

Blood pounded in Nash's ears, but Lily was right. He needed all the facts. Slowly, he lowered Brondale and released him. "You will tell me everything that happened between you and my sister," he spat, "including how you got that nasty cut on your face. Don't even think of lying to me or you'll be staring down the end of my dueling pistol."

The marquess took a tremulous breath, stalked to his sideboard, and, hand trembling, splashed brandy into a glass. He quickly threw it back and poured himself another.

Lily narrowed her eyes at Brondale. "Put down your glass and sit," she said icily. "Then tell us everything that transpired with Delilah—from the beginning."

The marquess swiped a sleeve across his brow and slumped into a chair by the fireplace. "I asked Delilah—that is, Lady Delilah, to meet me in the park last Friday morning. You're right," he said, looking up at Nash. "We were going to Gretna Green."

"What made her change her mind?" Nash ground out.

Brondale tugged at his cravat like it choked him. "The journey started out pleasantly enough. We were getting on famously, but then . . ."

"Then *what*?" Lily demanded.

The marquess gazed at the floor. "We started arguing. She accused me of drinking too much, and that night at the inn, she told me she wanted her own room."

Nash cursed under his breath. "You bloody bastard."

"I—I didn't see the point," Brondale stammered. "We were on our way to be married. When she tried to leave the room, I blocked her way. And she was so angry that she did this," he said, pointing to the side of his face and looking pathetic. "She hit me in the head . . . with a chamber pot."

Nash's heart swelled with pride. "Good for Delilah."

"Good?" Brondale repeated, incredulous. "She could have killed me! She's fortunate I haven't reported her to the magistrate."

"*You're* fortunate to be alive." Nash loomed over him, hanging onto his control by the slightest thread. "Where is she now?" he asked slowly.

"I've already told you," Brondale said sullenly. "I don't know. I woke up the next morning in a puddle of blood and she was gone. The innkeeper at the Posh Plum sent for a doctor to stitch me up, and I came directly here."

"Let me see if I have your story straight," Nash said evenly. "You eloped with my sister, and when she realized you were a drunken blackguard who isn't nearly good enough for her, you wouldn't let her leave, insisting that she spend the night with you."

"We were *eloping*." Brondale's face flushed—almost the same angry red as the cut Delilah gave him. "We would have been wed in another day. I saw no reason to delay sharing a bed."

"You . . . bastard," Lily seethed.

Nash grabbed him by the collar again and stared him down. "You're damned lucky that Delilah didn't kill you. But if you think I'll stand for you threatening and disrespecting my sister, you're mistaken. If she were here right now, I'd let her do the honors, but since she's not—this is for her."

He let his right fist fly into Brondale's gut, making satisfying contact with a couple of ribs. The marquess grunted, dropped into a chair, and doubled over, gasping for air.

While he moaned, Nash stood over him, flexing his fingers. "I'm going to make myself perfectly clear, Brondale. You will not show your face in town for at least a year. You will not utter Delilah's name or mention this episode to anyone. If you do, you will face me at dawn—unless she catches you first. If Delilah gets her hands on you, that gash on your cheek will seem like nothing but a paper cut. If I know my sister, she will do more than maim you—she'll skewer your soul."

# Chapter 27

Lily and Nash immediately set out for the Posh Plum—
the inn where Delilah had conked Brondale on the head.
When they arrived late that night, weary and frustrated,
they spoke to the innkeeper who told them that he'd seen
Delilah leave two days earlier—on a mail coach headed
south.

The taproom was relatively quiet, so Nash suggested
they have a bite to eat before retiring to their rooms. They
slipped into a dark corner booth and sipped ale while
they waited for their steak and mushroom pie.

Nash stared into his glass, his amber eyes clouded
with worry, and Lily knew he was picturing Delilah
crammed on a mail coach, traveling through the countryside alone. "Try not to fret," she said. "Your sister has
proven she can take care of herself in the most trying

circumstances. After all, she fought off Brondale with a chamber pot."

Nash looked up and shot her a wry smile. "True."

"Maybe she's on her way home now," she said, optimistic. "Or she could be there already, sitting by the fire in the drawing room with her feet tucked under her, wondering where on earth you are."

"That's what I'm hoping for," he said. "When we first left London, I wanted to stop her from marrying Brondale. But now . . . now all I want is for her to be safe and happy."

Lily tilted her head, thoughtful. "Those are good things to wish for."

"We'll head back to town in the morning," he said. "I'm sure you're eager to go home—and to be reunited with your family and friends."

"Yes, of course." She couldn't wait to see Fiona and her parents and Sophie. Was desperate to hug them. But it wasn't quite that simple. Nash and Delilah seemed like family now too, and she'd be sad to leave them. Especially since Nash insisted on throwing up walls every time she knocked on the door of his heart.

"Have you thought any more about Serena?" he asked.

Lily nodded. For the last few days, she'd thought of little else. "I'm going to invite her to tea when we're back in London so we can talk. Our relationship is bound to be complicated, but I'm glad we'll have a chance to know each other. I think we might have more in common than either of us realizes."

"Maybe so." Nash glanced at her, uncharacteristically hesitant. "She has the same thinking face as you."

"Thinking face," Lily repeated, perplexed. "What on earth is that?"

"You're making it now," he said, his voice lilting with affection. "You frown a little, and when you do, a pair of small vertical lines appears between your eyebrows. For some reason, I find it rather enchanting," he teased.

"I had no idea you were so observant," she said, feeling touched and unexpectedly sad.

She was going to miss these exchanges with him—and so much more. Because when they reached London, she would have to go back to the life that awaited her. A good life, to be sure—but a life without him.

They left the next morning, traveling day and night, changing horses every few hours. They spoke little during the long carriage ride, but periodically, Lily would glance up at the opposite seat and catch Nash looking at her with a molten, golden gaze that made her belly somersault.

Sometimes his lips moved as though he wished to begin a conversation . . . but then he would frown and stare out the window at the passing countryside.

She longed to shake him—to make him see that in refusing to let her in, he was hurting himself. He was hurting both of them.

But now that Delilah's elopement had gone terribly wrong, he was more entrenched in his thinking than ever. In his mind, love always led to pain, devotion to disaster. And he didn't have room in his heart for those messy, unpredictable emotions. Didn't have room for her.

When Lily and Nash arrived at his town house late in the afternoon on the fifth day of their journey, a grim-faced Stodges met them in the foyer and informed them that Delilah had not returned. There was, however, a letter addressed to Nash sitting on the table near the front door.

And the handwriting on the outside looked like Delilah's.

Nash immediately tore it open and held it between him and Lily, so they could read it at the same time:

> *Dearest Nash,*
> *You were right about Lord Brondale. During the*
> *journey to Gretna Green, I discovered his true*
> *character and realized he doesn't deserve my*
> *love. Rest assured, I am no longer with him.*
> *I escaped before any harm could come to me and*
> *am now safe.*
>
> *However, I'm not ready to return to London—*
> *and I don't know if I ever will be. I'm not certain*
> *where I shall go, but I need some time to myself.*
> *The truth is that I'm not heartsick so much as*
> *humiliated. I thought I knew who Brondale*
> *was, but I was very, very wrong. And now I'm*
> *questioning lots of things.*
>
> *I may be gone for a long while, but I wanted*
> *you to know I am well. I will write again once*
> *I've determined where I'm going—both literally*
> *and figuratively. Till then, give Caroline my best,*
> *and please do not worry about me.*
>
> > *All my love,*
> > *Delilah*

"She doesn't want to come home," Nash said, his voice full of anguish.

Lily's heart broke for him. "Your sister's been through an ordeal," she said gently. "But she loves you."

The butler coughed as though his own throat was thick with emotion. "You must be weary after the journey. I'll send a tray of refreshments to the drawing room and see that a bath is prepared for each of you," he said kindly.

Lily could only imagine what a sight she was, with her wild curls and wrinkled gown. "Thank you, Mr. Stodges," she said.

Nash still gazed at the letter, his expression tormented. "She's all alone. Where the hell could she be?"

Lily slipped her hand into the crook of his arm and steered him toward the drawing room. "Come. You need to eat something." She convinced him to join her on the settee and have a few bites of a sandwich while they speculated where Delilah might have gone. He racked his brain and could think of only three locations she might be hiding out: her friend's house just outside of town, their great aunt's cottage in Surrey, and his country estate in Kent.

"After I've washed up, I'll call on her friend Miss Palmer to see if she's had any word from Delilah. If not, I'll leave at once for Stonebridge Hall. Meanwhile, I'll ask Drake to go directly to my aunt's residence and look for my sister there." He dragged his hands down his face, looking anxious and tired. "I'd give anything to know where she is. To hug her and apologize for being too protective. To tell her how much I love her."

Lily placed a hand on his shoulder. "I'm sorry she's not here, Nash. I know how much you miss her. I do too. But it sounds as though she doesn't want to be found—just yet, anyway."

He swallowed and looked at her, his golden eyes full of sadness. "I think I might have . . . driven her away. Just like my father drove Emily away. Maybe I'm no better than he was." He pressed a fist to his mouth, as though the thought made him physically ill.

Lily's eyes stung. "You're not the reason she left, and you're not the reason she's staying away. You gave her the chance to make her own decisions."

"The chance to make her own mistakes," he said, echoing the words she'd once told him.

They sat in silence for several moments. Lily wished she could erase the lines furrowing his brow with kisses, but he'd made it clear that he couldn't give her the love she wanted. And as much as it was going to hurt, the time had come to say goodbye—and they both knew it.

"There's something I need to tell you," he said soberly.

Lily's heart pounded, wondering what it could be. "Go on," she encouraged.

"If you should be with child, I will marry you—that is, if you'll have me. I will try to be the best husband and father that I can."

She swiped at the tears that came out of nowhere. "I'm not pregnant," she said confidently. Her monthly flow was just ending. "You don't need to worry about that."

"Lily, I'm sorry for everything. I wish things had turned out differently," he said, earnest. But for some reason, the platitudes stung—and only made her feel worse.

"I have something to tell you too," she choked out. After all they'd shared, he deserved to know the truth about The Debutante's Revenge. "Do you remember the day when my memory came back and I said there was something about me you should know?"

He glanced up, his expression wary. "Yes."

Her mouth turned to cotton. "The reason I was dressed as a boy on the night I hit my head was that I had just come from the offices of the *London Hearsay*."

He frowned slightly. "Why would you have needed to disguise yourself?"

"Because I'm the authoress of The Debutante's Revenge," she said, relieved to speak the words out loud. She gave him time to absorb the news before continuing. "I know that you don't hold it in very high regard, but it's important to me—and it's a big part of who I am."

"I . . . I don't know what to say to that, Lily." He stood and paced the length of the drawing room, scrubbing the back of his head.

"Maybe you could say that you respect it," she said, her voice wobbly. "Even if you disagree with some of its advice."

"I respect *you*," he said evenly. "And I respect your right to say what you believe. But this is simply more proof that we would not suit. We view the world very differently, you and I. You believe in love that's all-consuming. The kind that sweeps you off your feet and leaves you breathless and forever changed. And I . . . I don't."

Lily felt as though all the air had been sucked from her lungs. This was it, then. This was truly goodbye.

A brisk knock made her turn toward the door. A footman stood there holding her bag.

"Forgive me, Your Grace," the gangly young man said. "You left this behind in the coach."

"Thank you, Thomas." Nash took the leather sack from the footman and crossed the room to hand it to Lily—but the strap slipped through her fingers, and most of the bag's contents spilled onto the floor. A hairbrush, her journal, the bootie, and the rough sketch she'd carried in her pocket on the night she lost her memory.

Nash crouched to pick up the journal, then froze. It had

fallen open to one of her entries, and the heading, *Dear Debutantes*, was written plainly across the top. "When did you write this?" he asked, confusion clouding his eyes.

"Shortly after Delilah gave me the journal," she said. "It was just for fun. I didn't know I was the author of the column, then."

"I see." He closed the book and handed it to her. "Did you write about us?"

She felt the blood drain from her face. "Yes," she said, unable to deny it.

For several seconds he knelt there, silent, as though he was grappling with a potent mix of emotions. At last, he said, "I'm glad to know the nights we spent together won't be wasted. They should provide plenty of fodder for future columns."

Oh God. She couldn't let him believe that. "No. Our relationship was never about my column, Nash. It was about us—two souls, both a little lost, who found something incredibly special in each other."

He shrugged, clearly skeptical. "In any case, you can trust me to keep your secret. I would never expose you, if that's what you're concerned about."

Lily's heart felt as fragile as an eggshell, cracking all over. She needed Nash to understand he was much more to her than research or inspiration for her writing. And she needed him to know that, in spite of all his protests to the contrary, he *was* capable of loving deeply.

"You say it's impossible for you to love me the way I need to be loved, but I know that's not true." She leaned down to pick up the sketch of the couple and held it up to show him. "You used to look at me like this. The night we went to Vauxhall. You looked at me like I held your whole world in my hands."

He muttered a curse under his breath and walked to the window, gazing outside at the rustling leaves and sparkling sunlight. "I plan to set out again in an hour," he said. "Searching for Delilah feels a little like shooting arrows in the dark, but I have to try. What will you do?"

She swallowed the horrid knot in her throat. "I plan to go to my sister's house. I'll leave the address with Mr. Stodges in case you should need me. And if—that is, *when*—Delilah returns, I hope you'll send word."

"I'm certain she'll write to you herself."

"That would be lovely," Lily said—as if his cool, distant manner hadn't gutted her.

Nash turned to face her. "This is goodbye, then."

"Yes." Lily rose to her feet, willing her knees not to tremble. She looked into those arresting, amber eyes, searching for a hint of the tenderness that had been there before. But if it were there, it was barricaded behind a wall of pain, fear, and betrayal.

She stood on her toes and brushed a kiss across his cheek. He didn't say anything or put his arms around her, but the almost undetectable tremor that went through him gave her hope.

Hope that whatever he'd once felt for her was not entirely dead.

# Chapter 28

*"Rules dictate whom you may dance with and where you must sit and when you may pay a call. But if the number of rules begins to overwhelm you, abandon them all and remember this one thing: Be kind."*

—The Debutante's Revenge

Lily's palms were clammy as she approached her parents' house. The place where she'd skinned her knees, learned to play the piano, and shared secrets with her sister. Her *home*.

When Mr. Woodson, the Hartleys' butler, opened the door and greeted her with a spontaneous smile, her heart lurched. It was so refreshing to be recognized—and to interact with someone who'd known her since the days when she'd worn pigtails and climbed trees.

"Miss Lily, what an unexpected pleasure!" He ushered her into the house while craning his neck to look onto the street behind her. "But what are you doing here? Have you no maid with you?"

"It's a rather long story, Mr. Woodson, but no." She

smiled warmly at his wizened face and puppy-dog eyes. "How is everything here?"

"Very well, but quiet. I thought you were staying with your sister until your parents returned," he said, scratching a tuft of brown hair above one ear.

Lily opened her mouth to explain, then decided better of it. She was still reeling from saying goodbye to Nash and feared she'd turn into a watering pot. "Have you had any news from Mama and Papa?"

"We received word just this morning saying they expect to return home in three or four days. They surely miss you and your sister."

"I miss them too," she said—surprised at the pang that echoed in her chest. "If you don't mind, I think I shall go to my bedchamber to quickly fetch some items before going to Fiona and Gray's."

"Of course, Miss Lily. I'll send up one of the maids to assist."

She waved away the offer. "No need. I shall only be a few moments." Lily shot him a smile and scurried up to her room before the dear man could insist that she sit down for tea and a sandwich.

Upon entering her room, she allowed herself five seconds to soak in the sweet, familiar sight, then set about stuffing her portmanteau with gowns, undergarments, and all the other necessities she could pack in it. When she was through, she raced downstairs, bid a brief farewell to the butler, and promised she'd come home as soon as her parents returned.

She stepped out of her house into the golden, dappled afternoon light.

She'd imagined her return home would have had more

drama. That she would have had to run the gauntlet, so to speak.

But walking back into her life had been shockingly easy. So far, at least.

She still had to ease her way into her sister and brother-in-law's household, but as she strolled in the direction of their town house, she began to believe that perhaps—just maybe—she would succeed in keeping her exploits of the last fortnight a secret from the ton. She would confide in her sister and Sophie, of course, but the fewer people who knew she'd been staying with the Duke of Stonebridge, the better.

Though her heart pounded every time she encountered someone, she attempted to look assured and vaguely bored. If passersby found it odd that Lily walked through the neighborhood alone carrying a portmanteau stuffed to the gills, they said nothing. A few acquaintances nodded pleasantly, and only Lady Rufflebum—who was rather famous for her permanent scowl—looked askance. Lily called out a greeting, flashed a smile, and rushed past the matriarch.

Fiona's house was only a few blocks away from their family home, but by the time Lily arrived on the front steps, her arms ached from lugging the heavy bag. She heaved a sigh of relief as she set it down and lifted the knocker, shaped like a raven as a nod to her brother-in-law's title, Ravenport. The brass bird hit the plate on the door with a loud *clunk*, and Lily waited.

Once she walked through the door, her two-week adventure would be officially over.

And though she was undeniably glad to be home, a part of her missed being Caroline—the woman who owned a sliver of Nash's heart.

The housekeeper, Mrs. Dowding, opened the door and blinked. "Miss Lily, what a pleasant surprise! Do come in." She frowned at the portmanteau near Lily's feet and dragged it into the foyer. "Where is your footman? Or your conveyance for that matter?"

"It's a lovely day," Lily said breezily. "I walked."

The housekeeper clucked her tongue in mild disapproval. "I'm so sorry to disappoint you, miss, but I'm afraid the earl and countess haven't yet returned from their trip. I don't expect them back for at least a few days."

"I was thinking"—Lily cleared her throat—"that perhaps I'd stay here and wait for Fiona to return."

"What's this?" the housekeeper asked. "You'll have no one to entertain you."

"There's no one at home either. My parents left for Bath"—Lily neglected to mention when—"and I'll be less lonely if I have a project to keep me busy. Fiona's always saying how she wants to set up the library as her drawing studio . . . and I thought I might surprise her."

"What a lovely idea." The housekeeper beamed. "I've never met siblings who get along so well. The countess is lucky to have a sister like you."

"I'm the lucky one," Lily said softly. "I hope it won't be a burden, having me here. There's no need to prepare any special meals. I'm perfectly happy to eat with you and the rest of the staff."

Mrs. Dowding pressed a hand to her bosom. "You shall do no such thing. It's our pleasure to host you for as long as you wish. I always keep your room ready, so I'll just take up your portmanteau and open the windows to air out the bedchamber a bit. I'll send up the countess's maid to help you unpack your things. And you must let me know what we can do to help you transform the library."

"That's very kind of you," Lily replied. "I think I shall take a quick look at the room before I settle in."

"Please do—it's unlocked." The housekeeper toddled up the stairs, hefting the portmanteau behind her. Lily would have offered to carry it herself if she didn't know Mrs. Dowding would suffer an apoplexy at the very suggestion.

Besides, a large stack of mail sat on a mahogany table in the foyer, neatly placed on top of a silver salver. The moment the housekeeper was out of sight, Lily picked up the pile and quickly shuffled through it. But the letter she was looking for—the one she'd written to Fiona explaining her absence—wasn't there.

Lily went through the letters again, slower. There were notes that looked like ball invitations; a couple of missives from their friend Sophie; business correspondence for Gray. But no sign of the note she'd sent her sister. At least she'd be here when Fiona returned and could answer her questions in person.

Next, she went to the library, shut the door, and sat at the desk beneath a window. She wrote a brief note inviting Serena to tea the following day. After signing it, she realized that she couldn't very well ask one of Fiona's footmen to deliver a note to an infamous brothel without raising suspicion.

Fortunately, she still had her chimney sweep disguise—which meant she could deliver the note herself.

The next morning, Lily returned to the library. This time she took stock of the room, trying to envision it as a studio for her talented sister. She knew Fiona would love the tall windows, especially if the heavy velvet drapes were replaced with airy silk panels.

Some of the books on the two full walls of shelves could stay, but Lily planned to relocate most of them to Gray's study and the drawing room so that Fiona could fill the bookcases with her drawing supplies, framed sketches and paintings, and cherished mementos. Lily could already imagine the shelves populated with inspired collections of beach shells, dried flowers, and painted pottery.

The desk and two massive leather armchairs would need to go, but the old, comfortable sofa would provide the perfect spot for Fiona to curl up with her sketchpad—especially if Lily replaced the worn pillows with fluffy, colorful ones.

Lily also made a note to remove the rather grim oil painting of a hunter shooting pheasant. In fact, she might as well have all the artwork taken down so that Fiona's gorgeous creations could adorn the walls instead.

Only two new items would be needed for Fiona's studio—an easel and a long table where she could spread out her works in progress and stage vignettes she wished to draw. Weeks ago, Lily had commissioned an exquisite rosewood easel from a skilled carpenter in town. She'd saved up the money she'd earned from her first columns to purchase it, and it would likely be ready any day.

Lily whisked a sheet of paper onto the desk and began making a list of things she must do, grateful to have a project to distract her from thinking about Nash. She'd left him less than twenty-four hours ago, and she already missed his grumbly banter and grudging smile.

Mrs. Dowding assigned a pair of footmen to assist Lily for a couple of hours. Despite their protestations that she should merely direct them to do the work, she helped box up scores of books and dusted the empty shelves.

"Let's try moving the sofa to the opposite wall," Lily mused. "I want to save the space in front of the windows for my sister's easel." The strapping young footmen rushed to do her bidding, and—unless Lily was mistaken—flexed their arms a bit more than was necessary. She shot them a grateful smile, tilted her head, and took stock of the new arrangement.

Not bad at all. The room was starting to look less pretentious library and more . . . Fiona.

"What in heaven are you doing in here?"

Lily whirled around at a sweetly familiar voice. "Sophie!" Lily impulsively threw her arms around her dear friend. It had only been a few weeks since she'd seen her, but so much had happened. "I'm trying to turn this room into a suitable studio for Fiona."

"I'm so glad to see you," Sophie said, hugging her like they'd been apart for decades.

"You may not feel the same way after I press you into service here," Lily teased. She held Sophie at arm's length, inspecting her from head to toe. As usual, she was the picture of elegance and grace. She wore a simple morning gown of pale blue, and her golden hair was perfectly styled into a smooth twist. But the dark smudges beneath her eyes hinted something was amiss.

Lily thanked the footmen and suggested they resume their work later in the day. To Sophie, she said, "How is your family? I thought you were still out of town."

"We returned a few days ago. I came to visit, figuring I would find both you and Fiona here . . . and instead, I found *this*." She reached into the reticule dangling from her wrist and handed Lily a folded note.

A note she recognized quite well—because she'd written it to Fiona.

She swallowed. "How did you . . . ?"

"I realized that I left my journal in this room the last time the three of us were together working on The Debutante's Revenge."

"Did you find it?" Lily asked, more than a little concerned. She'd be beside herself if her own diary went missing.

"I did," Sophie replied. "It was sitting right on the desk where I'd left it. And your note was right next to it."

Lily nodded. Mrs. Dowding must have placed it there for Fiona. "You read it?"

"I did." Sophie winced. "I recognized your handwriting, of course. And I was terribly worried about you. Your note allayed some of my fears but raised others. Where on earth have you been for the last two weeks?"

Lily linked an arm through Sophie's and guided her toward the sofa. "Come sit and make yourself comfortable. It's going to take a while for me to tell the whole tale."

Lily launched into the story, sharing everything— about her injury, her recovery at Nash's town house, her birth mother, and Delilah's disappearance.

Everything except the part that was too raw and painful to put into words.

The part where she'd fallen utterly, hopelessly in love with the duke.

Serena arrived for tea that afternoon wearing another stylish hat and veil, making Lily wonder if she had an entire chest devoted to them. Her gray and lavender gown was understated but elegant, and her hair was swept away from her face in a simple chignon. She walked into the drawing room where Lily waited looking both apprehensive and hopeful.

"Please, join me." Lily smiled warmly and gestured at the chair beside her, wondering if Serena's palms were as clammy as her own. She couldn't recall ever feeling quite so anxious. She'd had plenty of occasions to be nervous before, including visits to her headmistress's office and her many escapades dressed as a boy, but this . . . this was different.

This meeting with Serena went to the very heart of who she was—and the person she wanted to be. Her relationship to her birth mother didn't define her, but the way she chose to deal with it might.

Serena sat next to Lily and gracefully lifted her veil, revealing lines of concern on her pretty face. "It was very kind of you to invite me here today," she began, "but you must know that it's not seemly for a proper young lady like you to entertain someone like me—especially in your sister's home."

Lily leaned forward and gave her hand a quick squeeze. "I am less concerned with what is proper than with what is right—and I happen to know that Fiona and Gray, my brother-in-law, feel the same way. I wanted to thank you for responding to the advertisement I placed in the *Hearsay*. The duke told me that you refused the reward."

"Learning that you were safe and well was all the reward I could have hoped for," Serena said earnestly. "I never meant to insert myself into your life. I thought it would be best for you if you didn't know me—for obvious reasons."

"Because you're the proprietress of a brothel?" Lily saw no need to dance around the issue.

Serena arched a winged brow. "Precisely. I am not ashamed of my establishment—on the contrary. But I understand the rules of polite society. You are a part of that world, and flouting its rules comes with a price."

"I appreciate your concern for me, and you're right. There are many who would judge me harshly for meeting with you. But if they do, I don't much care about their opinion," Lily said firmly.

Serena smiled, instantly transforming her face from pretty to beautiful. "That is a very sweet sentiment. But consider this. I gave you up twenty-two years ago so that you could have the education, upbringing, and respectability that I couldn't give you. If you toss it away now, that will all be for naught."

Lily hesitated, contemplating this. "I feel confident we shall be able to find some middle ground—between blindly adhering to the ton's strictures and flagrantly defying them." She cast Serena a wry smile. "You might be surprised to learn that I often skate along the edges of propriety, regularly testing the boundaries."

Serena's hazel eyes shone with affection. "Given that my blood runs through your veins, I'm not surprised at all."

They sat in companionable silence while Lily poured tea. At last, Serena said, "I'm sure you must have many questions. I will tell you anything you wish to know."

Lily took a fortifying breath. "Why the Hartleys?" she asked simply.

Serena sipped her tea, thoughtful. "One day, a month or so before you were born, I was sitting on a bench in the park. I was sixteen years of age, tired and hungry,

and my clothes were little more than rags. Mrs. Hartley—
not your stepmother, but the original Mrs. Hartley—
happened to be walking by with a basket on her arm. She
paused as she passed me and asked if she could join me
on my bench."

Just the mention of Lily's mother made her tears well.
"You met her?"

Serena nodded and briefly closed her eyes as though
she was remembering it all. "She proceeded to share everything she had in her basket—bread, fruit, cheese,
and sandwiches. She ate little herself, actually, merely
nibbling as we talked so that I wouldn't feel shy about
filling my own belly. She asked me how I was feeling and
whether I had a warm bed to sleep in. I told her I did. I
never admitted to her that I was a prostitute, but I think
she knew. Before she left, she pressed a few coins into
my hand and insisted that I keep the basket and the rest
of the food."

"That sounds just like my mother," Lily said. "She was
beautiful, inside and out."

"Indeed." Serena smiled at the memory. "The basket
she gave me had her card inside. And it was the same
basket I placed you in on the night I left you on their
doorstep," she said hoarsely. "I cried for days afterward.
For weeks I barely ate or slept. I held on to your bootie,
consoling myself with the fact that Mrs. Hartley would
be a far better mother to you than I ever could have
been."

"You were so young," Lily said, sympathetic.

Serena swallowed. "Yes. And I couldn't work, which
meant I had no money to provide for you."

"What about my father?" Lily asked.

Serena shrugged helplessly. "I don't know who he was. It could have been a number of men. I tried very hard to prevent pregnancy, but my methods were far from foolproof. And once you were born, I had no regrets about having you. I knew you were my very own miracle."

Warmth blossomed in Lily's chest. "You were very brave. I don't know what I would have done if I'd been in your shoes."

"I didn't want anyone to have to go through the same experience I did," Serena said soberly. "That's why I decided to run my own establishment. It took several years for me to make it happen, but I started small and gradually built a reputation. My girls have a clean, safe place to live and work. They keep all the money they earn. And if they find themselves in trouble, I help them. They're never alone."

"That seems like a very worthy mission to me," Lily said, smiling.

"I'd like to think so." Serena took a handkerchief from her sleeve and dabbed at the corner of her eyes. Composing herself, she asked, "What about you? Have you found your life's passion yet?"

Lily hesitated for a beat but decided that if there was anyone in the world she could trust to keep her secret, it was Serena. "I have," she admitted. "I am the authoress of The Debutante's Revenge. I try to arm other young women with information and engage in meaningful conversations about courtship and love."

Serena's eyes shone with something akin to pride and awe. "I am very familiar with your column. My girls and I anxiously await each edition and read it at breakfast every Friday."

"I'm honored," Lily said, touched.

"So, you have found a way to make a difference in the world, and that is wonderful," Serena said. "But what about your own happiness?"

Lily blinked. "What do you mean?"

"You give advice about love." Serena eyed Lily over the rim of her teacup. "Have you found it?"

"I do love someone," Lily said, gulping. "But he doesn't love me the same way."

Serena reached for a scone. "I presume we are talking about the duke?"

There was no sense denying it. "Yes."

"That day at Mr. Drake's office," Serena said slowly. "I saw the way he looked at you—with tenderness and longing. It certainly looked like love to me."

"It's quite complicated," Lily explained. "His twin sister died tragically several years ago. His other sister— who happens to be a devotee of my column—is currently missing, and he feels the column may be partly to blame. Sadly, he could be right. But the biggest obstacle is that he claims he cannot give his whole heart, and he knows I won't settle for love in half measures."

"Nor should you," Serena said, emphatic. "I don't claim to know all the particulars, but I will say this. If you're fortunate enough to find love, fight for it. Use every means at your disposal. Bring all your talents to bear. Find a way to make your duke realize that denying his feelings will do nothing but make both of you miserable."

Lily considered this, and the seed of an idea took root. "I think you could be right," she said.

But the first step to breaking down Nash's walls was figuring out how to bring Delilah home.

Lily mentally scrapped the column she'd been planning to write and deliver that evening. This week's edition was going to be different from anything she'd written before—and she prayed that it would be enough.

# *Chapter 29*

*"If a gentleman is truly smitten, you will remain
in his thoughts . . . even when you are apart."*
　　　　　　　*—The Debutante's Revenge*

Four days after saying goodbye to Lily, Nash returned
from his country house—without his sister. He'd traveled
all day, and it was well after midnight when he stumbled
into the dark foyer of his London town house. The staff
had long since retired for the night, and the thud of his
boot heels on the marble floor echoed into the soaring
entryway ceiling. The house felt appropriately empty
and cold—as did he.

He strode to the stairs, too weary to shuffle through
his mail or even shed his coat.

All he wanted was the oblivion of sleep, a brief respite
from the fear and guilt that had been gnawing away at
his insides for days.

Because of him, Delilah seemed to have vanished off
the face of the earth. And, as if that wasn't enough, he'd
driven Lily away as well.

He trudged up the stairs, wondering if he'd ever be
whole again. If he'd ever breathe easy or smile.

He reached the top landing and started to turn down the corridor to his bedchamber when he saw a soft glow from beneath a door—Delilah's door.

Heartbeat thundering in his ears, he rushed down the hall and pushed open the door.

There, sitting in her bed, reading by the light of the lamp, was Delilah.

"Nash!" she cried, her face instantly crumpling.

He stood on the threshold, momentarily frozen, trying to convince himself this wasn't a dream.

She leaped out of bed, threw herself into his arms, and hugged him fiercely.

Thank God. He squeezed her tightly to his chest and kissed the top of her head.

"I'm so sorry," she sobbed.

"You're home now," he said, his throat clogged with emotion. "That's all that matters."

But it seemed Delilah couldn't stop the tears from coming. She clutched his jacket as she cried, and he did his best to soothe her. What he'd told her was true—now that she was safe, their little family could overcome anything else fate might throw their way. As long as they stayed together.

Eventually her sobs turned to hiccups, and she peeled her blotchy face away from his waistcoat. "I owe you an explanation," she said.

He pulled a crisp handkerchief from his pocket and offered it to her. "You are my sister," he said. "And I will always want to protect you. But the last few days have made me realize something. You are capable of protecting yourself."

"Oh dear. You heard what I did to Brondale?"

"I saw your handiwork with my own eyes," he said. "I'm proud of you."

Delilah arched a brow. "What have you done with my brother?"

He chuckled at that. "You're not the only one who's growing up. But in spite of your note assuring me you were safe, I confess I've been beside myself with worry."

She blotted her face with his handkerchief, sat on the edge of the bed, and patted the mattress beside her. When he joined her, she took a deep breath. "I was scared after I hit Brondale. He was moaning, so I knew he wasn't dead, but I couldn't stay with him for another minute. So I ran."

"Where did you go?" he asked. "I looked everywhere I could think of."

She shot him an apologetic, wobbly smile. "I was staying at an inn just outside of London. I checked in under a false name and took all my meals in my room. It was as though I were paralyzed—incapable of deciding where to go and what to do. I'd risked everything for Brondale, and he made a fool of me."

"Oh, Delilah." Nash wrapped an arm around her shoulders. "I'm not very good at talking about feelings, and I'm worse at showing them. But we're family . . . and I love you, no matter what."

"I know," she said with a sniffle. "It may seem like an obvious thing, but I didn't realize the truth of it—until I read this." She handed him the folded newspaper on her bedside table and pointed to the column featured in the center of the page.

*The Debutante's Revenge (Special Edition)*
*Dear Debutantes,*
*The symptoms of romantic love are remarkably*

*similar to the effects of too much champagne:*
*a thrilling headiness, a sense of daring, and a*
*blissful disregard for what is proper. All of which*
*may lead a young woman to engage in behavior*
*that is uncharacteristically bold. And sometimes,*
*that behavior may lead to unforeseen—and*
*undesirable—consequences.*

*If a young woman should find herself in such*
*circumstances, it's natural that she might feel*
*some shame or hopelessness—but she shall*
*quickly realize that neither of those emotions is*
*particularly useful. Instead, she would do well*
*to remember one deceptively simple adage: You*
*may always go home.*

*No matter what deeds you have done, you may*
*always go home.*

*No matter what scandal you have started, you*
*may always go home.*

*No matter what your stubborn head may tell*
*you, know and believe it in your heart.*

*You may always go home.*

*Go home, literally and figuratively—to the*
*place where you're surrounded by small comforts*
*and cherished keepsakes. Return to the people*
*who raised you and have always cared about*
*you. Trust that those familial bonds will weather*
*any storm and endure any test.*

*The ones who love you are waiting with open*
*arms.*

*And all will be well.*

Nash read the column twice before he set it aside
and faced his sister. "It's true, you know. Every word."

He dragged a hand through his hair. "Damn, but I was wrong about The Debutante's Revenge."

Delilah nodded and looked at him earnestly. "There's something else I need to tell you, Nash."

Good God. He braced himself for the worst. "Go on."

"I'm almost certain that the authoress of the column is Caroline."

"Yes, she told me." He chuckled, relieved that was the extent of her news. "There's something I need to tell you too."

She swallowed soberly. "Very well."

"Caroline's real name is Lily," he said. "Her family, the Hartleys, are here in Mayfair."

"Lily," she repeated, as though testing out the name. "Mr. Stodges told me she's gone. I miss her."

"I do too," Nash confessed. "But maybe there's something we can do about that."

Her blue eyes twinkled merrily. "Do you really think so?"

He grinned at her. "As a brother-sister team, I imagine we could be extremely persuasive. Even devious, if necessary."

"Undoubtedly," Delilah agreed, rubbing her palms together. "Tell me what you have in mind, dear brother."

# Chapter 30

*"The best medicine for a bruised heart is the company of dear friends and a steaming pot of tea."*
—The Debutante's Revenge

"I know the art studio was supposed to be a surprise for your sister," Sophie said over the rim of her teacup. "But I suspect that we'll all spend many enjoyable hours in this room working on The Debutante's Revenge. The space is so lovely and inviting."

Lily looked around the nearly completed room. She'd worked from dawn to dusk the past couple of days, and the transformation was stunning. A pair of Fiona's ethereally beautiful paintings adorned the pale blue walls, and a plush gold carpet covered the waxed wood floors. Sheer silk drapes billowed in the soft breeze, while colorful pillows encouraged lounging and lively conversation.

Sophie had added her signature touches to the studio too. Fragrant greenery and wildflowers spilled out of vases she'd placed on the mantel, shelves, and table. Vines trailed over the polished surfaces, softening the room's edges and bringing it to life.

Lily sighed happily, confident her sister would adore the new studio. "It did turn out well. And the easel will be delivered tomorrow. It shall be the focal point—the piece that unites everything."

"I'm certain it will be magnificent, just like the rest of your improvements," Sophie said, thoughtful as always. "I hope you haven't overexerted yourself, rushing to ready the room. Forgive me for saying so, but you look rather weary. Almost . . . sad."

Blast. Her friend was too insightful by half.

"I'm fine," Lily fibbed. She'd barely slept since leaving Nash's house. When she wasn't worrying about Delilah, she was haunted by a pair of intense amber eyes, brimming with pain and longing. "Perhaps I am a bit tired," she admitted. "I couldn't sleep last night, so I began working on next week's column." She retrieved her journal from the table, sat on the sofa beside her friend, and handed her the paper she'd slipped inside the book's front cover. "Will you give me your honest opinion?"

Sophie acted as a curator for the letters Lily wrote and the sketches Fiona drew. She had the wonderful ability to sort through both their piles of work and select pieces from each that were perfect complements. She also had a keen sense of which topics the column's faithful readers wanted to explore each week.

"You can always count on me to be honest." Sophie eagerly took the paper and began reading aloud.

*The Debutante's Revenge*
*Dear Debutantes,*
*Love is risky. Governesses, headmistresses,*
*and matrons alike will warn you of its perils.*
*They will advise you to exercise caution and*

*guard your heart. But love does not work that*
*way.*

*To experience true love, you must give your*
*heart completely. You must disregard every urge*
*to protect yourself and jump into it with utter*
*abandon. For it is only by exposing your deepest,*
*truest self that you can allow someone else to*
*touch your soul.*

*Love is fraught with danger.*
*It is almost certain you will be hurt.*
*Even worse, you will likely hurt another.*
*Some days you will swear your heart has been*
*ripped out of your chest.*

*But you must love anyway.*


Sophie set the paper on her lap and narrowed her eyes.
"Lily," she said firmly. "Is there something you would
like to tell me?"

Lily snatched the paper back and shoved it inside her
journal. "It's horrible, isn't it?"

"Not one bit. It's beautiful . . . and gut-wrenching."

Unable to meet her friend's eyes, Lily strode across
the room, pausing in front of one of Fiona's paintings,
a lovely portrait of a young woman on a swing. "I miss
Fiona."

"Lily Hartley," Sophie scolded. "You're avoiding my
question. Do you have feelings for the duke? If you want
to talk about it, you know you may confide in me."

For a moment, Lily considered baring her soul to
her friend. But speaking the words would make her and
Nash's relationship—and its disastrous ending—all too
real. Better to let the time she'd spent with him linger in
her memory like some pleasant but fading dream.

"I can't," she said regretfully.

Sophie shot her an understanding smile. "Very well. But if you should change your mind—"

"Pardon me, Miss Hartley," Mr. Burns intoned from the studio doorway, "but you've a visitor—Lady Delilah Nash."

Lily's heart bounced with joy. "Delilah!" Lily ran to her and smothered her in a fierce embrace. "I was dreadfully worried about you. You have no idea how glad I am that you're here."

Delilah let out a muffled chuckle. "I have some idea. You're hugging me so tightly, I can scarcely breathe."

"Let me look at you," Lily said, holding her friend at arm's length. Her blond hair fell from her crown in a cascade of ringlets, and her pink cheeks glowed with happiness. "You don't appear to be any worse for the wear."

"I'll bring another place setting for tea," the butler announced smoothly.

"Yes, thank you, Mr. Burns," Lily called over her shoulder. "Delilah," she said, unceremoniously pulling her by the hand, "you must come and meet my dear friend Miss Sophie Kendall."

Sophie surreptitiously scooped up the new column and set it facedown on a table before gracefully extending a hand to Delilah. "It's a pleasure," she said, her eyes crinkling in a warm smile. "But I should leave the two of you so that you may have a proper visit."

"No!" Lily and Delilah protested in unison.

"I insist that you stay, for it is I who have barged in," Delilah said, apologetic. "And I cannot remain long in any event. Nash told me that you recovered your memory and that I might find you here. The reason for my visit is twofold. First, I wanted to apologize for giving you a fright and assure you that I am, indeed, well."

"Thank heaven." Lily waved both women back to the sofa and offered Delilah a scone, which she gratefully nibbled. Lily was desperate to ask after Nash and would have devoured even the most mundane news about him— what color waistcoat he wore or whether he'd shaved that morning—like a mongrel lunging for dinner scraps. But Sophie and Delilah were far too insightful, and Lily feared any question she posed would reveal too much. "Your brother was beside himself. He must have been so relieved to see you."

Delilah's eyes welled. "Yes. I'm terribly sorry for upsetting you both. I knew I'd made a mistake shortly after I left, but I wasn't quite ready to go home. I shall tell you all the embarrassing details another day, because I'd much rather discuss the second reason for my visit. Nash has decided to host a ball to properly launch me into society."

Lily blinked and shook her head, incredulous. "I beg your pardon. It sounded as though you said Nash—that is, the duke—is hosting a *ball*."

Delilah chuckled and nodded. "I could scarcely believe it myself—and I'm delivering the invitations before he has a chance to change his mind." She pulled an ivory notecard from her reticule and presented it to Lily. "Please say you'll come."

"I don't know," Lily said. She was imagining how painful it would be to see him, breathtakingly handsome in his dark evening jacket, dancing waltz after waltz with the most beautiful ladies in London. She wasn't sure her heart could take it. "I'm not certain that's a good idea."

"Please, Lily. It wouldn't be the same without you."

Delilah's pretty blue eyes pleaded like a puppy's. "You know that all our guests will be judging me—scrutinizing my every move. I'd feel so much more confident with you by my side."

Lily hesitated, searching her mind for some excuse. But Delilah was a true friend, and Lily couldn't leave her to face the ton alone. It would be like stranding her in a den of hungry wolves.

"Very well," Lily said, already dreading the ball. How was she supposed to greet Nash in a room full of people and pretend that they scarcely knew each other? How was she supposed to act as though she'd never kissed him or spent the night in his arms?

"I'm so glad that's settled." Delilah beamed. "Miss Kendall, I do hope you'll be able to attend as well. Your friends and families are welcome too. It's sure to be a festive event—if only because every member of polite society will wish to witness the spectacle with their own eyes: the notoriously private Duke of Stonebridge entertaining on a grand scale. If you'd told me such a thing was possible a fortnight ago, I wouldn't have believed it myself."

"I'm sure it shall be a lovely affair," Lily said with forced brightness. "And I'm very happy to hear that the duke is indulging your wish to enter the social whirl."

"He's changed recently," Delilah replied, thoughtful. "I believe you may be to thank for that." She gave Lily a saucy wink. "And now, if you'll excuse me, I should be on my way. I've a few more invitations I want to hand deliver—but yours was the first."

They stood and hugged each other tightly once more. "Everything is going to work out," Delilah whispered in her ear. "For both of us."

*  *  *

Fiona's easel arrived early the next morning, and it was as exquisite as Lily had hoped. She spent a couple of hours in the studio, rearranging items on the shelves, organizing drawing supplies, and fluffing pillows. When every last detail looked perfect, she hopped off her stepstool, set down her dust rag, and massaged her lower back.

A final gaze around the light-filled room confirmed that her efforts had been worthwhile, but she was already looking forward to a bath—and perhaps a short nap.

She returned to her bedchamber and, while the tub was readied, pulled the baby bootie Serena had given her out of her bedside table drawer. She turned the little shoe over in her hand, thinking how strange it was that she'd had to forget who she was in order to figure out where she came from. And she contemplated the words Serena had told her: *If you're fortunate enough to find love, fight for it.*

She slipped into the steaming, fragrant water and let the warmth soothe her aching muscles. When the water cooled, she climbed out of the tub and toweled off, rubbing her hair dry. And when her fluffy pillow beckoned, she slipped on her dressing gown, crawled into bed, and closed her eyes.

Lily rolled over on the mattress, hoping to block out the world a bit longer.

But the relentless tapping on her foot would not cease, no matter how many times she kicked beneath the coverlet.

"Lily," called the familiar voice. "Wake up!"

Reluctantly, she removed the pillow covering her head

and cracked her eyes open—just enough to see the silhouette of a woman sitting at the end of her bed. For a moment, Lily felt as if she were thirteen years old again, in the dormitory at Miss Haywinkle's School for Girls. Fiona was nudging her and pulling off her covers, urging her to rise before she missed breakfast entirely.

"I'm not hungry," Lily mumbled.

"No?" her sister replied, amused. "You might at least welcome your older sister home. You act as though you haven't missed me at all."

Dear Jesus. Lily bolted upright. "Fiona?"

Her sister shot her a radiant smile. Her emerald traveling gown complemented her auburn hair perfectly, and the pink glow on her cheeks was a testament to her happy marriage and devoted husband.

At the sight of her, Lily erupted into tears. The dam she'd carefully constructed to contain the torrent of emotion couldn't withstand the sudden onslaught.

"Lily!" Fiona was at her side in an instant, wrapping her in a warm embrace. "What's wrong?"

How could she tell her sister all that had transpired in the fortnight since she'd left? "I'm so glad you're home."

Fiona arched a skeptical brow. "I'm glad to see you too. But I confess I am somewhat surprised. Why aren't you home with Mama and Papa?"

"It's a long and convoluted story," Lily said, sniffling. It seemed she'd cried more in the last week than she had in her entire life.

"Might it have something to do with this?" Fiona held up the baby bootie that Lily had left on her desk.

"It might," Lily admitted. She patted the mattress beside her. "Take off your slippers and make yourself comfortable. It shall take more than a few minutes to explain what a spectacular mess I've made of my life."

Fiona listened intently as Lily told her about the tavern brawl, her memory loss, Delilah, and Serena. And Nash. As Lily recounted every incredible and sometimes painful detail, concern flicked over Fi's face, but never judgment. Clearly, all that mattered to her was that Lily was safe and sound.

When she'd reached the end of her long, pathetic tale, Fiona blinked—as if she were waiting for more. "Is that it?"

"What do you mean?" Lily asked, incredulous. "Weren't the tavern brawl, amnesia, love affair, and brothel madam enough?"

"Oh, you've been through plenty," Fiona said, slipping an arm around her shoulders. "And I didn't mean to imply otherwise. But it seems to me that your story has yet to reach its conclusion."

"You're speaking in riddles, Fi."

"While I was away, you were growing up and opening doors. You opened a door on friendship with Delilah and a door on family with Serena. You also opened a door on love with Nash—and no matter how dire things may seem, that door hasn't slammed shut yet."

Lily swallowed. "I don't know what to do. He claims he's incapable of loving me the way I need him to. Even if he could, how can I give my heart to a man who doesn't respect my life's passion?"

"I wish you could hear yourself." Fiona tickled Lily's chin with the baby bootie she still held. "You are one of the most determined, daring, and persuasive people I know. Of course, there are risks involved. There are no guarantees that all will turn out as you wish. But if anyone can turn this ship around, it's you. And if you fail . . . well, at least you'll know you tried."

Hope shimmered in Lily's chest. "I'm not at all certain I can convince Nash to open his heart to me, but I shall see him at a ball he's throwing for his sister next week."

"A ball?" Fiona grinned. "Why, all sorts of magic is bound to happen at a ball. You shall have plenty to write about in your diary, at least."

Lily moaned and covered her face with a pillow. "I'm still catching up from the events of the last two weeks."

"Well, I'm delighted to hear that we'll have no shortage of material for our column."

Lily let her pillow plop onto her lap. "That reminds me—have you been in the library since you returned home?"

"No. Why do you ask?"

She jumped out of bed, feeling lighter than she had in days. "Allow me to throw on a gown—and I'll show you."

# Chapter 31

*"A gentleman needn't be excessively dexterous or graceful to be a good dance partner. Rather, he should move with a natural confidence and hold you with care. He should look at you with something akin to wonder."*
                              —The Debutante's Revenge

Lily was aware she gripped Gray's arm a *bit* too tightly as they stood outside the richly carved doors leading to Nash's ballroom. When Fiona's dashing husband had agreed to escort both his wife and Lily to the Duke of Stonebridge's ball, he couldn't have known what an ordeal it would be.

Gray turned to his left and arched an amused brow at Lily. "I was under the impression that you wished to attend this ball."

Lily's mouth felt like it was full of sawdust. "Yes," she managed.

"Then why are your feet rooted to the marble?" he asked smoothly. "The other guests are bound to think it odd if I drag you into the ballroom."

"Give her a moment, Gray," Fiona piped up, and Lily shot her a grateful smile across Gray's chest. Fiona looked stunning in a seafoam-green gown with delicate beading adorning the sleeves and hem. She'd always been lovely, but with each day that passed, she seemed to grow more confident—and more beautiful.

"I'm in no rush." Gray looked over his shoulder at a few new arrivals. "But we're blocking the entrance."

Drat. "Very well. I'm ready." Ignoring the pounding in her chest, Lily allowed Gray to lead her into the ballroom. She held her head high, refusing to apologize for who she was.

Daughter of Serena Labelle *and* the Hartleys.

Sister to Fiona and friend to Sophie.

Alumna of Miss Haywinkle's School for Girls.

Authoress of The Debutante's Revenge.

But mostly, she was Lily, a woman who happened to love the Duke of Stonebridge.

Embellished with delicate lace and feminine ruffles, her whisper-soft, white ballgown swished around her legs and floated around her feet. If this had been any other ball, she would have looked forward to dancing the night away.

But tonight was different. Tonight, she was risking everything for a chance at love.

The last time Lily had ventured past this ballroom—while she'd been living under Nash's roof—it had seemed forlorn and empty. Dark and dusty.

But no more.

The crystal chandeliers overhead bathed the room in a twinkling glow; the honey-colored parquet floors gleamed. Lively music filled the air, causing toes to tap and bodies to sway. A rich rainbow of gowns, waistcoats, reticules, and ribbons created a festive mosaic every-where Lily looked. She could scarcely believe it was the same cold, cavernous space. And it gave her hope.

Almost immediately, Delilah greeted them. In her dusty-pink gown with wine-colored trim and petal sleeves, she resembled a perfect rose.

"You are beautiful," Lily told her earnestly. "The belle of the ball."

"Thank you. I'm so delighted you're here," Delilah said, reaching out to squeeze her hands.

As Lily made the introductions, she searched the room for Nash, hoping she wasn't terribly obvious about it. She didn't spot his broad shoulders and handsome face above the crowd, however. And she wasn't certain if she was disappointed or relieved.

"Where is Miss Kendall?" Delilah asked.

"Sophie and her mother planned to arrive separately. They may be here already," Lily replied.

"I'm so pleased to meet your friends and family," Delilah said, beaming.

"Well, you shall soon meet a few more," Fiona said sheepishly. "Our mother and father returned from Bath earlier today. I hope you don't mind, but I extended the invitation to them as well."

"How wonderful!" Delilah exclaimed.

Lily blinked, disbelieving. "Wonderful?" she repeated. "Mama and Papa will be here? Fi, you might have mentioned it before now!"

Fiona shot her an apologetic smile. "I didn't want to add to your worries."

"And yet, you *have*." Lily glared at her sister, then attempted a calming breath, which was vexingly and predictably futile. If Mama and Papa had an *inkling* of the mischief Lily had been up to, they'd ship her to the convent posthaste.

Lily cast an apologetic glance at Delilah. "Forgive us for overrunning your ball with our relatives."

"You mustn't apologize for having a large, loving family. I would give anything to have one."

The truth of Delilah's words hit Lily like a bracing slap to the cheek. "Then you shall be an honorary member of our family. We may not have an impressive lineage, but we stick together."

Delilah's nose grew suspiciously pink. "Thank you. This promises to be the best evening ever."

"Are there any gentlemen in particular you're hoping to dance with?" Lily probed.

Delilah inclined her head, thoughtful. "Perhaps. But if the last few weeks have taught me anything, it's that I shouldn't give my heart to a man simply because he possesses good looks, charming manners, and an expertly tailored jacket. I plan to enjoy the rest of my season and use the time to get to know a few gentlemen on a deeper level. Only then will I know if any of them is deserving of my affections."

"An excellent plan," Lily said approvingly.

"That does not mean, however, that I can't appreciate Lord Peckingham's broad shoulders and a boyish grin," Delilah said, focusing her gaze on the dashing earl.

"Oh?" Lily grinned. "If I'm not mistaken, he's headed this way."

Indeed, the first strains of a waltz soared through the ballroom as Lord Peckingham bowed over Delilah's hand and gallantly escorted her to the dance floor. Gray asked Fiona to dance, and when she hesitated, Lily waved her on.

"Go," she encouraged. "I'm going to fetch a glass of lemonade."

"If you're sure," Fiona said.

Lily nodded enthusiastically, trying not to envy the way Fiona and Gray fit together so perfectly—her hand tucked into the crook of his arm, his head bent to whisper in her ear.

She'd had that once.

She made a slow turn, searching the room for a head of thick, light brown hair and a knee-melting, golden gaze. She'd almost made a complete circle when she felt it. An achingly familiar pull that could only be him. Nash.

A deep voice beckoned from behind. "Miss Hartley."

Her heart fluttering like a hummingbird in her chest, she looked into his whiskey-colored eyes. Let their warmth soak into her skin. "Your Grace."

Nash couldn't believe Lily was standing there. If he didn't know better, he'd have thought she was an apparition—a vision dressed in gauzy white silk sent to torment him. To remind him of all he didn't deserve. But Delilah had assured him Lily would come, and, thank heaven, she had.

Her dark hair gleamed in the brilliant candlelight; her luminous skin glowed from within. Her light green eyes crinkled at the corners as she smiled, instantly heating his blood.

The rest of the ballroom faded away, leaving just the two of them. "I was wrong," he said.

"About what?" she asked soberly.

"Lots of things. But mostly thinking I could live without you."

She blinked and her gorgeous green eyes welled.

"Dance with me?" he asked.

Her pink lips parted in surprise before she nodded and offered him her hand.

The simple contact had his head reeling and his pulse racing. But holding her hand was more than exhilarating— it was perfectly natural. Right.

He led her to the dance floor and pulled her as close as he dared, savoring every subtle connection. Her fingers resting lightly on his collar. The wisps at her nape, brushing the back of his hand. The silk of her dress, smooth beneath his palm. Her breath, soft on his cheek.

Lily twirled in his arms, her white gown billowing behind her like she was an angel floating in the clouds. Neither of them said a word, but every look that passed between them spoke of longing, desire, and affection.

When the music began to wind down, her forehead creased. "There's something I must tell you," she said.

He leaned closer to her ear. "I'd hoped to speak to you too, in private. If you can slip away, meet me in my study at a quarter to midnight. I'll wait for you there."

Her eyes widened, and she nodded. "I'll try."

As the last note of the song echoed in the air, he squeezed her hand, reluctant to let go.

She slowly pulled away, giving him a soft smile over her shoulder. "Until later, Your Grace."

# Chapter 32

*"A gentleman's expertise on the dance floor often extends to other key areas as well."*
                    —*The Debutante's Revenge*

At precisely a quarter to twelve, Lily peeled herself away from a circle that included Mama, Papa, Sophie, and her mother, mumbling an excuse about drinking too much lemonade. She walked past the ladies' retiring room, however, and glided down the dimly lit corridor to Nash's study.

She hesitated at the threshold for a second, then turned the knob and entered.

She'd been in his study before. It was the location of their first kiss and their indoor picnic. But everything looked different tonight. Maybe because everything *was* different.

"I'm glad you came," Nash said, his relief palpable. He took a step toward her like he wanted to hold her, then drew up short, apparently as unsure as she was.

He'd lit a lamp on a small side table flanked by two leather chairs. "Please, sit," he said, gesturing toward one chair and lowering himself into the other.

She accepted his invitation, settling herself in the chair next to his. "I can't stay long," she began.

"I know."

"But there are a few things I need to say."

He propped his elbows on his knees and clasped his hands. "Please."

She tried to ignore the charming lock of hair that fell across his forehead and his shiver-inducing gaze. And she prayed for the courage to tell him everything that was in her heart.

"I've missed you, and I've missed *us*," she said, "and the way we were before my memory returned. You say you're incapable of loving me completely and unreservedly, but I know that's not the case. I've seen your heart, and it's generous and true."

"Thank you," he said, his expression serious. "I'm humbled by your faith in me."

She inclined her head, then forged ahead. "But I need you to understand something else too. The Debutante's Revenge is important to me—and to its many readers. I have no intention of giving it up."

He nodded slowly. "I don't blame you. And I'd never ask that of you."

Her eyes stung. "I'm glad you understand, but there's more to it. I can't be with someone who doesn't respect my work, because . . . because it's a part of me."

Nash looked at her, his golden gaze intense. "May I tell you something?"

"Yes." Her heart pounded wildly. She prayed he wasn't about to deliver a sentimental but nevertheless crushing send-off. A cliché along the lines of: *For as long as I live, I shall never forget you.* Or, the trite but ever-popular:

*It's not you, it's me.* No matter what, Lily silently vowed she would not cry.

He leaned forward, his handsome face heartbreakingly earnest. "I know that the column is a part of you. And the truth is . . . well, the truth is that I adore and respect *every* part of you. The part of you who dares to walk the streets dressed as a chimney sweep. The part of you who pours her heart out onto the page, empowering other young women. And I especially adore the part of you who convinced my sister to come home by writing down everything I wanted to tell her but couldn't find the words to say."

She lifted her gaze to his. "You read the special edition?"

"I did. It was beautiful and moving . . . so much so, that it brought my sister home. The next day, I asked Delilah to show me your other columns. I read them all. And I owe you an apology."

Lily swallowed, scarcely believing her ears.

He spoke slowly and clearly, his amber eyes searching her face for absolution. "I'm sorry that I denounced your column without ever properly reading it. I dismissed it out of hand, making stupid assumptions about the content and the women who read it. But I was wrong about your writing. It's entertaining and insightful. It's inspiring and enlightening. It's very much like you. And I hope you can forgive me."

Blast. She'd promised herself she wouldn't cry. "I can. I have." She swiped at her eyes and went to him, throwing her arms around his neck. "I forgive you."

He pulled her onto his lap and cradled her face in his hands. "Then you'll give me another chance?"

Her chest nearly bursting with joy, she tilted her fore-head to his. "Yes."

The word had scarcely left her lips before he slanted his mouth across hers in a deep, bone-melting kiss. She'd told him everything—and he hadn't shunned her. Hadn't run away.

He was there, holding her, and saying everything her heart wanted to hear. Almost.

Best of all, he kissed her like he'd missed her as much as she'd missed him.

When he finally stopped to look into her eyes, they were both a little breathless. "As much as I'd like to keep you to myself for the entire evening," he said, "we should not stay away from the ball too long. Your friends and family will be looking for you."

She sighed, savoring the feel of his thick, cropped hair between her fingers. "I suppose you are right."

"But before we go, I have a surprise for you."

"A surprise?"

He helped her up and tugged her by the hand. "Over here." He led her across the room to a large, flat object covered with a sheet. "I hope you like it," he said, grinning as he pulled off the cover.

There, in the center of Nash's study was the most gorgeous desk Lily had ever seen. Made of rich mahogany, with turned legs and shiny brass drawer pulls, it was fit for a king. Indeed, Shakespeare himself couldn't have wished for anything more beautiful.

"This is for me," she said, dumbfounded.

"You deserve a special place to write your column," he explained. "I chose one with plenty of compartments, and they all lock." He pulled out the center drawer and gestured toward the key tucked into the corner. "You won't have to worry about anyone reading your columns before they're published. And the top is inlaid with leather, so it will feel warm and soft beneath your hands."

"It's beautiful. I love everything about it." Her heart broke as she ran a finger over the buttery-smooth leather. "But I'm afraid I can't keep it."

His handsome face fell. "Why not?"

"It's too generous a gift. Mama would never allow me to accept something so valuable from you, a gentleman who I'm supposed to be only slightly acquainted with."

"Even if we were engaged?"

She blinked. "What did you just say?"

Nash circled his hands around her waist, lifted her so that she sat on the edge of her glorious new desk, and leveled his gaze at her, his golden eyes glowing. "I love you, Lily Hartley. Fully. Passionately. With everything I am and ever will be. From the moment I met you, you challenged me to feel more, live more . . . *be* more. I can't go back to the way I was before, and I don't want to. All I want is to spend the rest of my life with you, loving you, making you happy." He pressed a kiss to the side of her neck, sending delicious tingles drifting over her skin. "Will you marry me, Lily?"

"But . . . Serena. And the column. How would it all work?"

"We'll make it work," he said, confident. "We'll figure it out together."

Joy filled her chest, and her stubborn, cynical heart began to believe. "I love you, Nash. And knowing you feel the same . . . it's like a dream."

He swallowed and searched her face. "Is that a *yes*?"

She slid her arms around his neck and touched her

nose to his, letting their breath mingle in the space between them. "It's a yes. To marriage, to loving you always . . . to whatever adventures come our way."

He let out a low, wicked growl that made her toes curl.
"What would you say to an adventure right now? Right
here. On your new desk."

"We haven't much time, *but* . . ." She wriggled closer,
wantonly wrapping her legs around his hard, muscular
thighs. "I think we should begin as we mean to go on,
don't you?"

# Chapter 33

*"As the ball draws to a close, do not linger too long. Bidding farewell to friends can be sad, but remember: What feels like the end is often just the start of something new and wonderful."*
—*The Debutante's Revenge*

Fiona and Sophie called on Lily the next afternoon, ostensibly to take tea and exchange gossip about last night's ball.

But she knew very well what they were about. They'd seen the heated looks Nash had cast her way. They'd narrowed their eyes suspiciously each time he led her to the dance floor. They'd arched a brow at her prolonged absence from the ballroom. And now they wanted to know *precisely* what had transpired between her and the duke.

Almost as much as she wanted to tell them.

But though she longed to spill the happy news to her sister and her best friend, Lily remained deliberately vague, holding the precious secret close to her chest, basking in its glow for a little while longer.

The three sat around a cozy fire in the drawing room with their feet tucked beneath the hems of their gowns.

Fiona tossed a copper curl over her shoulder, feigning disdain. "Since Lily selfishly refuses to share any details about her handsome duke, we might as well discuss business."

"Yes, let's," Sophie said coolly.

Lily laughed. "I'm putting the finishing touches on a new column. It's about sisterhood and the importance of nurturing friendships even when one is in the midst of forming a romantic attachment to a gentleman."

"How ironic," Fiona teased. "But I shall have no difficulty drawing an accompanying sketch. I'll use you two as my subjects."

"As long as we cannot be identified," Sophie said, twisting her graceful hands. "And I do like the theme. Interestingly, I spoke with several young ladies at the ball last night about The Debutante's Revenge—all devotees of the column. They had no inkling of my connection to it, of course, but they all expressed a desire to have a safe place to gather and discuss the column with like-minded women."

"Wouldn't that be wonderful?" Lily mused.

"I think it *would* be lovely . . . to give our readers an opportunity to connect with each other," Sophie replied. "And it would give us valuable insights as to what our readers wish to know. What they would like to see in future columns."

"That's brilliant," Fiona proclaimed. "It could be quite difficult, though. For every avid reader we seem to have an equally avid detractor."

Sophie nodded her agreement. "The meetings would

have to be conducted in utmost secrecy. I'm not exactly certain how or where, but it's a project I'd like to undertake."

Lily's heart swelled. "That's very daring of you, Sophie. And if anyone can succeed, you can."

Her friend's blue eyes twinkled. "I was thinking of calling it the Debutante Underground."

"Perfection!" Fiona declared.

"I love it." Lily raised her teacup in a toast. "To sisterhood, friendship, and Sophie's deliciously scandalous new adventure: The Debutante Undergr—"

"Lily Hartley!" Mama burst into the drawing room, her cheeks flushed and her palm pressed to her chest.

Lily jumped up, sloshing her tea. "What is it, Mama? Is everything all right?"

Her stepmother collapsed on the settee, then artfully arranged an arm across her forehead. "You tell me, missy. *The Duke of Stonebridge* has come to call."

"He's here?" Pulse racing, Lily straightened her bodice and smoothed her hair.

"Yes," Mama breathed, with a bit more drama than was strictly necessary. "To be more specific, the duke is in the study because he requested an *audience with your father.*"

Fiona gleefully glided to the settee, picked up a silk pillow, and began fanning Mama with it. To Lily, she said, "Does this mean what I think it means?"

"You might have given me some warning, Lily," Mama interjected. "I shall never forgive you for this."

Sophie hid a smile as she joined the little gathering near the settee. "Shall I fetch you a glass of water, Mrs. Hartley?"

"You'd better make it something stronger, dear," she

said with a moan. "It's not every day that one's daughter is courted by a . . . by a . . ."

"There's brandy on the sideboard," Lily said, shooting Sophie a grateful smile.

All four women decided a bit of fortification was in order, and all were quite composed by the time the gentlemen joined them.

Papa strode through the drawing room door first, chest puffed out, proud as a peacock. Nash followed, meeting Lily's gaze with a smile that was just for her. Good heavens. She suspected that even if she lived to be one hundred, his wicked grin would still have the uncanny power to melt her insides.

"Good afternoon, Mrs. Hartley, ladies," Nash said, bowing gallantly.

Mama whimpered, then recovered her manners. "What an unexpected pleasure, Your Grace."

"I wondered if I might have a word with Miss Hartley."

Lily decided not to torment Mama further. "Actually, Your Grace, we may speak freely here."

He arched a brow, clearly amused. "Excellent. Would you care to do the honors, or shall I?"

Mama's eyes turned to saucers. "*Someone* enlighten me."

Lily squeezed Mama's hand. "Nash—that is, the duke—and I . . . have decided to marry."

Fiona and Sophie hugged each other, squealing with delight.

"I love your daughter to distraction, Mrs. Hartley," Nash said earnestly. "And I promise to spend the rest of my days caring for her, trying to make her as happy as she's made me."

"My daughter . . . a duchess?" Mama said, clearly stunned.

Sophie fetched the decanter of brandy again.

Fiona beamed. "A whirlwind courtship," she said knowingly. "I look forward to hearing all the romantic details, someday."

"Perhaps." Lily linked her arm through Nash's leaning into his broad, hard shoulder. "Someday."

That night, shortly after sunset, Nash sat at his desk, alternately poring over ledgers and contracts in a futile attempt to keep his mind off Lily. Damn the reading of the banns and a respectable engagement period.

He missed her. Needed her now.

And if it wouldn't have been the height of hypocrisy, he'd have begged her to run away to Gretna Green.

An odd tap at the window of his study made him snap his gaze away from his work.

He stood and peered through the pane at the dusky purple sky suspended above the verdant garden and shrugged. Probably just an insect that had flown into the glass.

But as he turned back toward his desk, two more taps sounded behind him.

Exasperated, he threw open the sash and stuck his head outside. "Is that you, Drake?"

"It's me," the sweetly familiar voice answered in a stage whisper. "Are you trying to alert the entire household?"

*Lily.* His blood heated as he searched the shadows, finally spotting her beneath the garden trellis. She stood there in a shaft of moonlight, wearing delightfully snug trousers and sheepishly waving her cap at him.

"Don't move," he said. "I'll be right down."

A moment later, she was in his arms, pressing her lithe body against his.

"What are you doing here? Not that I object, you understand," he added quickly. "In fact, it's the best possible surprise."

"I just delivered my column." She ran a wicked finger across his lower lip. "Surely, you did not expect your fiancée to retire her chimney sweep disguise?"

"On the contrary. I'm delighted to discover that you have not."

She purred, rocking her hips against his. "I decided to make a stop on my way back from the newspaper offices."

"Did you pop into the Grey Goose?" he teased.

"You mock me, but if I hadn't ventured into that tavern, we would never have met."

Growling, he slid a hand beneath the hem of her shirt and tugged on the binding beneath. "I would never have met the chimney sweep, or Caroline, or Lily. Which, I freely admit, would have been a tragedy."

"You'd still be a grumpy, semi-reclusive bachelor," she mused, tracing the shell of his ear with her tongue.

"I grow less grumpy by the second." He deftly loosened the linen strip beneath her shirt, let it fall to the ground, and skimmed his palm over her tantalizingly lush curves.

Her eyes fluttered shut, and a blissful sigh escaped her lips. "You've changed me too. I've figured out what the debutante's best revenge truly is."

"What is that?" he murmured.

"It's freedom . . . and pleasure . . . and happiness. But most of all, it's love."

"You have my heart, Lily. Now and always."

"You have mine as well." She cradled his face in her hands and gazed at him, her heavy-lidded, green eyes glowing. "Take me to your bed, Nash. Love me till"—she shot him a wicked grin—"till I cannot recall my own name."

Chuckling, he swept her into his arms, cradled her body against his chest, and carried her directly to his bed-chamber, where he proceeded to do *just* as she'd asked.

Don't miss these other charming titles
by **Anna Bennett**


## The Debutante Diaries

### FIRST EARL I SEE TONIGHT


## The Wayward Wallflowers

### THE ROGUE IS BACK IN TOWN
### I DARED A DUKE
### MY BROWN-EYED EARL


And don't miss the next sensational novel in
the *Debutante Diaries* coming Summer 2020